This Lie Will Kill You

THIS
LIE
WILL
KILL
YOU

CHELSEA PITCHER

Margaret K. McElderry Books

New York London Toronto Sydney New Delhi

MARGARET K. McELDERRY BOOKS
An imprint of Simon & Schuster Children's Publishing Division
1230 Avenue of the Americas, New York, New York 10020
For information about special discounts for bulk purchases, please contact Simon &
Schuster Special Sales at 1-866-506-1949 or business@simonandschuster.com.
The Simon & Schuster Speakers Bureau can bring authors to your live event.
For more information or to book an event, contact the Simon & Schuster Speakers Bureau
at 1-866-248-3049 or visit our website at www.simonspeakers.com.
Interior design by Mike Rosamilia
Jacket design by Dan Potash
The text for this book was set in Iowan Old Style.
Manufactured in the United States of America
First Edition
2 4 6 8 10 9 7 5 3 1
Library of Congress Cataloging-in-Publication Data
Names: Pitcher, Chelsea, author.
Title: This lie will kill you / Chelsea Pitcher.
Description: First edition. | New York : Margaret K. McElderry Books, [2018] |
Summary: Five teens who were partly responsible for a death a year earlier are lured by
the promise of a $50,000 prize to an isolated mansion by someone bent on revenge.
Identifiers: LCCN 2018037604 (print) | ISBN 9781534443242 (hardback) |
ISBN 9781534443266 (eBook)
Subjects: | CYAC: Secrets—Fiction. | Murder—Fiction. | Friendship—Fiction. |
Family problems—Fiction. | Mystery and detective stories.
Classification: LCC PZ7.P6428 Thi 2018 (print) | DDC [Fic]—dc23
LC record available at https://lccn.loc.gov/2018037604

For Sunny
Thank you for your proud, wild heart

This Lie Will Kill You

ONE YEAR AGO...

The forest was on fire. Flames licked at the darkness, stripping bark from the trees and turning the leaves to ash. Inside the great, glimmering inferno was a car, the front hood dented and the windows cracked.

Inside the car was a boy.

They didn't know, at the time. The firefighters were just arriving on the scene, and the police were keeping onlookers from getting too close. From their vantage point, they could see only red, ominous light pulsating from the forest.

Then everything went white. Smoke curled over the world, settling into their lungs and forcing their eyes to close. Ash covered whatever it could touch, and soon, outlines formed in the dark woods.

That was when they saw the vehicle. Paint flaked away by the heat. Leather seats sunken and distorted. They prayed aloud that no one was inside, but deep down, in the marrow of their bones, they must've known they would find someone. Cars didn't drive themselves down long, twisting roads. They didn't slam into trees, flip several times, and explode.

Not on their own. But when cars made friends with mortals, they could do all these things and more. They could transform a beautiful forest into a wasteland. They could transform a beautiful face, with moon-pale skin and startling blue eyes, into a candle of wax, dripping and contorting until none of the loveliness remained.

The fire had stripped away almost everything. Where there had once been long, lithe fingers, now there was bone. Smoke billowed off of him, as if his soul was slipping into the sky. People whispered that they would need dental records to identify the remains.

But that would come later. For now, the authorities made their little calculations, focusing on the things they could control. How would they wrench the door open? How would they get the body out?

Farther back, in the darkest part of the forest, a girl made calculations too, counting off suspects on a gloved hand.

One, two, three . . .

Four? The specifics were fuzzy, but time would reveal everything. Time, and a carefully crafted plan. Until then, the girl would put on a mask and sit like a doll on a shelf, waiting patiently. It was the only way to survive. That smoldering skeleton had once been a boy, and that boy had been loved.

Held.

Kissed.

Not anymore. The fire had transformed him into a creature of ashes and bone, and the sight made the girl tremble, tears sliding down her cheeks. She needed to be strong. No, she needed to be *cold*, like an unfeeling doll. Porcelain limbs couldn't tremble, and a heart made of plastic couldn't ache this terribly. It couldn't break. It couldn't bleed.

But glass eyes could watch everything. And now, as the girl turned away from the wreckage, new images unfolded behind those eyes. There was a beautiful mansion, high up on a hill, and a very exclusive guest list. A gloved hand striking a match. And maybe, if everything went exactly as planned, her porcelain limbs would turn back into flesh and her heart would soften to red.

But first, there would be fire.

1.

CLASS ACT

Juniper Torres woke with a smile. Today was the day. She knew it, though there was no particular reason to think today would be different. The sun wasn't shining. The sun was barely even up, but it didn't matter much. The universe was speaking to Juniper directly, lighting a fire in her veins and making her heartbeat thrum. It whispered to her in a soft, lilting voice:

Today is the day your life is going to change.

She sat up in bed. Kicking away her tangled sheets (and running a hand through her equally tangled hair), she crawled to the window, looking down. And there she was. The blond, bedraggled mailwoman was leaning over the mailbox, stuffing a host of envelopes inside. Juniper couldn't tell for certain, but she had a sneaking suspicion the envelope was among them.

She raced from her room. Down the hallway she went, past her baby sister's nursery, and the bedroom where her parents slept, their limbs entwined like the branches of neighboring trees. Soon the family would wake, and she wouldn't be able to scour the mailbox in secret. But if she was very quiet (avoiding this floorboard, and that creaky step), she could slip outside without anyone noticing.

So she did. Out of the olive Victorian she went, into the white, winter world. Overnight, the yard had been transformed. Icicles dangled from the oaks, threatening to impale Juniper as she passed beneath them. And at the end of the yard, the snow-frosted mailbox stood out like a sore thumb.

Juniper yanked it open. Her fingers danced over advertisements, brushing the edges of a coupon packet, and then she was pulling the envelope out of the darkness. She knew it was the envelope she'd been waiting for, even before she saw it. It was big, and it was fat, and the writing was . . .

Blood red? The envelope leapt from her hand. It fluttered slowly, like the snowflakes falling around her, and by the time it hit the ground, she'd registered two things: This was not the letter she'd been waiting for. It was an invitation.

She scooped it out of the snow. Someone had written, *You are cordially invited to a night of murder and mayhem!* on the back of the ebony envelope, and Juniper turned it over, confirming that it was addressed to her. It was. *Thanks but no thanks,* she thought, ripping it in half. She had zero interest in getting wasted with her classmates, and even less interest in pretending death was hilarious. The only reason she was stalking her mailbox was because she was expecting an acceptance letter from Columbia University. Their online system was down, which meant she'd be getting her news the old-fashioned way.

And so it went. Juniper raced to the mailbox on Monday morning, then Tuesday. By Wednesday, her confidence had started to ebb. Why was she so convinced she'd be getting an acceptance letter? Yes, her grades were mostly stellar, but last winter, after that party up in the hills . . .

Juniper shook herself. She'd only fallen off track for a month, and most of her teachers had let her make up the work. Even if she didn't get into the college of her choice, she had a couple of safety schools that would take her far away from this town. She'd still go to med school. Cure people. Save lives. Everything would go according to plan.

She was about to return to the house when a black envelope caught her eye, way back in the corner of the mailbox. A shiver skittered up her spine. She already knew what the envelope was. An invitation to "a night of murder and mayhem!"

They'd probably mailed two by mistake, she thought, rolling her eyes. But as she drew the envelope from the darkness, an undertow of guilt started tugging at her limbs. This was how it always happened. She'd be going about her day, not even thinking about Dahlia Kane's Christmas party, and out of nowhere, her limbs would get heavy. She'd feel herself sinking, the way a body sinks to the bottom of a swimming pool, while people stand by, laughing—

"Junebug!" Mrs. Torres appeared in the doorway, her face flushed from standing over the stove. "Breakfast, mi amor. What is that?"

Crap. Juniper's reflexes were dulled this early in the morning. Two hours (and three cups of coffee) from now, she'd never have let her mother see this envelope. But now she was trapped, and she couldn't very well shred the thing in front of her mom. She'd have to play this just right.

Forcing a smile, she jogged up to the doorway. "Just some dork's idea of a good time," she said, holding up the invitation. She wasn't offering it to her mother; she had a very good grip on the envelope. But Mrs. Torres must've seen *a night of murder and mayhem!* scrawled across the back, because she snatched it out of her daughter's hand.

"Ooh, a party. You should go."

"What? No." Juniper scrunched up her face. "It's probably on Saturday. I'm watching *Rudolph* with Olive." Olive was her baby sister, and now that the kid could walk, Juniper was pretty much on permanent call. She chose to think of it as practice for when she was actually on call at the hospital of her choice. Better get used to functioning on two hours of sleep, right?

"Junebug, she's my kid." Her mother disappeared into the hallway, and Juniper followed close behind, plotting to retrieve the invitation. "Believe it or not, I like spending time with my kids."

"And yet, you're forcing me out of the house."

"I'm just making a suggestion." Her mother pulled out a chair at the kitchen table. Olive was in her high chair, giggling and dancing in that I-can-see-invisible-fairies way that babies had. "Don't you want to have fun with your friends?"

"They aren't my friends. They probably sent one to every senior at school."

"All the more reason to go," her mother said, swooping in with the old, chipped coffeepot. "Just think about it, okay? It wouldn't kill you to go to a party."

It might, Juniper thought, her hands starting to shake. She took a gulp of coffee, hoping her mother wouldn't notice her jumpiness. Luckily, Mrs. Torres was busy fussing with the tostadas on the stove. But somebody did notice, and when coffee sloshed over Juniper's fingers, her baby sister frowned, reaching for their mother's purse. Two years old, and she'd already decided makeup was the cure for sadness. Juniper wasn't sure where she'd learned it. This wasn't exactly a beauty pageant house. But wherever the lesson had come from, Juniper didn't mind being her sister's living dolly. Olive's eyes got so bright and her mouth got so smiley.

"Tip-sick!" the baby announced, pulling out a vibrant burgundy gloss that would make Juniper look like she'd been eating berries. Or drinking wine. It was kind of pretty, and Juniper was okay with looking kind of pretty, as long as it didn't eclipse her other accomplishments. She felt a pang as Olive dabbed the gloss on her lips, wishing she could stay in town and teach her sister about making people better, rather than beautiful. But she couldn't stay after everything that had happened—she couldn't—and besides, nothing she could say to Olive would be as influential as becoming the doctor she'd always wanted to be. She'd do everything she'd set out to do, and one day, she'd whisk her family out of this creepy little town, away from all of its secrets.

Its ghosts.

After the lip gloss was on, Olive clapped her hands, squealing, "Pretty!" and Juniper felt the cracks in her heart close.

"You are, baby girl," she said, as tiny fingers encircled one of her own. Meanwhile, their mother had gone completely silent by the stove. Juniper turned, goose bumps rising on her arms, to find Mrs. Torres leaning against the counter, staring at a single page.

"What? Mama, what?"

Her mother didn't answer, so Juniper snatched up the invitation. She made no attempt to be sly about it. One second the paper was fluttering in her mother's fingers, and then it wasn't. One second the breath was filling Juniper's lungs, and then it was gone.

Dear Miss Torres,

Due to your achievements in ACADEMIC EXCELLENCE, you are cordially invited to a murder

mystery dinner! Prepare to be challenged as you,
and five of your esteemed classmates, fight to unravel
the mystery and apprehend a killer!

The world will become a stage!

A friend will become a foe!

Costumes will arrive later this week!

And, of course, the winner will take home the
coveted $50,000 Burning Embers Scholarship, to be
used at the school of his or her choice.

Your humble benefactor,
The Ringmaster

"It's a scam." The words were out of Juniper's mouth before she could stop them, and even after she'd spoken them, she felt no desire to take them back. Even after her mother sank into a chair, studying the invitation in shock.

"You were right, it is on Saturday," Mrs. Torres said. Her voice was breathy, and Juniper hated the thought of disappointing her. "They must've had a last-minute opening—"

"Mom, it's a scam. Real scholarship offers don't sound like this." She'd never even heard of the Burning Embers Scholarship. She'd never heard of it, and she didn't like the sound of it.

"It isn't an offer," her mother said calmly. "It's a contest."

"Real scholarships don't make you compete," Juniper insisted. "Not like this. Not at a *murder mystery dinner*."

"Misery dinner!" Olive shouted, and Juniper cringed. She did not want her sister repeating that.

"Calm down, baby girl. Eat your Cheerios."

But it was an exercise in futility. Juniper's own breakfast sat, forgotten, on the stove. Even her coffee cup couldn't entice her now. "Look, I'll do some research," she said, plucking her mother's phone from the table, "but I'm pretty sure scholarship foundations don't sign their letters 'The Ringmaster.'"

"They're trying to make it fun."

"They're trying to make money off me." She typed *Burning Embers Scholarship* into the search engine, waiting for zero hits to come up. "Just wait. The day before the contest, I'll get a second letter, asking for an entry fee. If there isn't a website . . ."

Juniper trailed off, clicking the first of several links. Not only did the Burning Embers Foundation have a website, it looked legit. There was an "About" page that highlighted the project's aims (*finding unique and exciting ways to reward students who excel in academics, fine arts, and athletics*) and a "Contact" page with a phone number, an email address, and a physical location. Juniper made a vow to contact them in every way possible before Saturday's event, to prove that real people worked at the foundation.

Or rather, to prove that they didn't.

She wasn't certain why she was being contrary at this point. A fifty-thousand-dollar scholarship would change her life. Hadn't she spent the past six months applying to every scholarship she could find, hoping for one-fifth of that amount?

"I never applied for this," she mumbled, her last-ditch effort at logic. "I would've remembered—"

"Sometimes teachers submit you. Guidance counselors. You're such a good student, and you were going to be valedictorian."

Yes, I was going to be valedictorian. Then I went to a party, last December . . .

"Wait, let me see that." She smoothed out the invitation on the table. It didn't take long to locate the date of the event: December 21. One year *exactly* since Dahlia Kane's Christmas party.

"Mom—"

"This money would be a big deal for us," her mother broke in softly. "Your father could use the good news."

"I know." Juniper glanced at his empty chair. After fifteen years of teaching music at Fallen Oaks Elementary, a recent round of budget cuts had left Mr. Torres jobless. Now Juniper could hear him milling around upstairs, choosing the perfect tie for another set of dehumanizing interviews.

"Are you going to tell him you're passing up fifty thousand dollars?" Her mother fixed her with a stare. "After everything he's been through?"

"Of course not." Juniper swallowed, her chest tightening. "I just don't understand who would submit me for this sort of thing. I'm the world's worst actress."

"Maybe Ruby did it."

Juniper blinked. She could see her mother staring at her, could see her baby sister bouncing in the periphery, but she felt completely displaced. Like she was floating outside of space and time.

"I'm just saying, she has quite the flair for the dramatic. This sort of thing is right up her alley," Mrs. Torres explained. "Why don't you give her a call and ask about it?" Then, almost too quietly for Juniper to hear, she added, "I miss that girl."

I miss her too. Juniper's vision blurred as she thought of Ruby's smile, Ruby's laugh, Ruby's touch. She pushed off from the table, her chair screeching behind her. *Too bad she doesn't miss me.*

+ + +

Juniper slammed her bedroom door, leaning against it. She knew she was overreacting, but she didn't know how to stop it. It was like being in one of those dreams where you *are* yourself, and *see* yourself from outside your body. Like being God and Jesus at the same time.

She shook her head, crossing the room. If she was any kind of religious, it was casually Catholic with atheistic leanings. She just wasn't sure she believed in anything anymore. Still, she'd always been fascinated with the idea of being God and Jesus at the same time. Of being inside your body and watching from high above. Maybe that was what it meant to have a body and a soul, to be at one single point, and everywhere, all at once.

Juniper dug her phone out of her purse. She told herself these thoughts were random, the musings of a girl who still desperately needed her morning caffeine, but deep down, she knew the truth. After everything she'd done to Ruby, she wanted to believe in the possibility of redemption.

She wanted to believe she had a soul.

With trembling hands, she typed out the message, **Did you submit me for the Burning Embers Scholarship?** Ruby's number was still in her phone. She couldn't bring herself to erase it, which was definitely ironic, considering the thing she'd erased from Ruby's life.

The person.

She hit send, then dropped the phone onto her bed. She absolutely would not wait by the phone like a sad little girl on prom night, hoping and hoping while her heart sank to her knees. But maybe *Ruby* had been waiting for *her*. The phone pinged almost instantly, and she found herself scrabbling to pluck it from the bed, her eyes scanning the message frantically: **No.**

Juniper started to laugh. It was the cold, brittle kind of laughter, like twigs snapping underfoot. Of course Ruby hadn't submitted her for the scholarship. Of course Ruby wasn't looking out for her from behind the scenes. Their friendship was over. It had been over for a long time.

She sank down to her bed. When her phone lit up again, she was surprised to feel her heart leap. How could she still have hope after everything that had happened? Her heart was a bruised and bludgeoned thing. A Pandora's box filled with grief and regret. But somewhere, hidden in the darkness, hope was glittering. It caused her breath to falter as she read Ruby's text.

I didn't submit you, Ruby wrote, **but I'm going to the party. Maybe we can solve the mystery together?**

Juniper didn't trust herself with words, so she sent back a smile.

2.

DRAMA QUEEN

Ruby Valentine was a lit firecracker ready to pop. Her skin crackled and her fingertips buzzed. Ever since she'd received the invitation from the Burning Embers Foundation, she'd been bouncing from foot to foot, brimming with excitement. What a fabulous opportunity! Strange, yes, but strange things were always happening in Fallen Oaks. People appeared out of nowhere and disappeared just as quickly. Pretty girls fell head over heels for monsters. Boys were transformed into fire, into pure, glittering light.

A town of freaks wearing beautiful masks, Ruby thought, looking away from her reflection. She knew a thing or two about putting on a show. And now, before she could leave for the party of the century, she'd have to perform for her mother. Wrapping a robe around her red sequined party dress, she dusted some blush over her nose.

A ruddy complexion would help sell the story.

Out of her room she raced, like a princess fleeing a beast. Someone else would've tripped. But unlike Juniper Torres, who couldn't balance on one foot for more than ten seconds, Ruby had been born with a ballerina's grace, and when she was determined, her limbs filled with light. She floated. Slipping into the living room, she knelt at the back of the ratty old sofa and whispered in her mother's ear. "Mom? I can't sleep."

Her mother turned. So did Scarlet, Charlotte, and May. Four pretty red heads turning. Four sets of eyes trained on her. "What time is it?" Mrs. Valentine asked with a yawn. Her ginger hair was pulled back in a messy ponytail, and her floral nightgown had seen better days.

"After nine," Ruby said, glancing at her phone. The party started at ten. "You girls should get to bed."

Her sisters started to fuss, and Ruby's mother sighed, already sinking under the weight of responsibility. Once upon a time, Mrs. Valentine had had a husband, and that husband had helped put these little girls to bed. He'd helped get them up in the morning too, and helped make their lunches. Now he was gone, and Ruby's mother had four girls to raise on her own. Most nights Ruby shouldered the burden, but she couldn't tonight. She had to imitate going to bed so she could sneak out of her window. But first, she needed access to the safe in the basement.

Mrs. Valentine studied her daughter. They had the same pale blue eyes, the same freckles along the bridge of their noses. The same terrible taste in men. "Five more minutes, girls," she said after a moment. "Charlotte, you're sleeping in my room tonight, so you don't bother your sister."

"She doesn't bother me," Ruby said. "My *brain* bothers me. When I can't sleep, I—"

"Are you having the dream again?"

Ruby froze. She honestly hadn't thought her mother would bring up the nightmare. When they'd first discussed it, Mrs. Valentine had gone completely white. Considering all the girls in the family had milky-pale skin, it was a sight to behold.

Ruby had watched her mother transform into a ghost, and it scared her more than she would ever admit. Ruby wasn't scared of life, and she wasn't scared of death, but she was scared of ghosts.

She had good reason to be scared.

"I was just lying there, trying to fall asleep," she began. "But I kept thinking about the dream, and trying not to think about it, and that only made it worse." Ruby lowered her head. If she came on too strong, she'd have to go back to that psychiatrist. But if she didn't come on strong enough, her mother wouldn't let her into the safe.

"I only need one pill," she promised. "I can bring up the bottle, and you can count—"

"Don't bring it," her mother said. "I have to trust you with it. That's the point."

Ruby nodded. *Now give me the code,* she thought, sniffling softly. Reminding her mother that she was a young, innocent girl. Not a survivor, oh no. Just a child who needed her mom.

Mrs. Valentine smiled, lifting a hand to Ruby's cheek. "Three-eleven-nineteen," she said, and Ruby exhaled, replying, "Thank you. Last one." She rose to her feet. It took all the restraint in her body to keep her movements fluid and slow. She wanted to flee. To get the hell out of there before her mother changed her mind and ruined everything.

Twenty seconds later, she stood before the basement door. It opened with a twist of the knob, unleashing a torrent of dust onto her head. The basement was off-limits to the younger girls, who could trip and crack their heads open on the stairs. They could get lost in the labyrinth of boxes or get nibbled by mice. It really wasn't worth it for them to come down here. But Ruby liked being in the one place in the entire house where nobody would follow her, tug on her sleeve, or fill up the silence. Even cold, even dark, it was pleasant.

It was her sanctuary.

Then, with the simple pulling of a string, the light came on and the room became what it really was: a basement. A wasteland of discarded clothes and decapitated toys and small puddles of water that no one could trace to a source. On the far wall, there was a bookshelf her father had built, which had once held the family photo albums, but now the shelves stood empty.

Ruby tore her eyes away from it, blinking back tears.

She would not cry for real. Tears were for the stage, and for her mother, in times of desperation. Tonight, she *desperately* needed to get into the safe. As she neared the small, black rectangle, chills raced through her body.

She knelt and turned the dial. Three. Eleven. Nineteen. The little safe clicked, and Ruby yanked open the door, pulling an object out of the darkness. It was heavier than she expected, and cold.

After Ruby's father had disappeared, Mrs. Valentine had invested in two items: a bottle of sleeping pills and a revolver she'd found in the back room of an antique shop. But while the pills were a prescription for Ruby (and thus, had spent their first few months on her bedside table), the revolver had taken up residence in the basement safe. Several refills later, Mrs. Valentine had locked the pills away as well, insisting on monitoring her daughter's drug intake.

Now, two years after their family had been fractured, Ruby had almost forgotten about the pills. She hadn't forgotten about the revolver. She traced her finger along the curve of the weapon, keeping the barrel pointed away from her. She knew how dangerous it was. She'd taken a class on gun safety after her father disappeared and her mother got paranoid about men kidnapping her daughters. According to Mrs. Valentine, men could kidnap you at any moment. Walking to school in the sun. Sleeping in your bed at night. And while Ruby knew these things happened, she was much more frightened of her sisters stumbling onto the revolver and thinking it was a toy. She'd convinced her mother to purchase the safe that week, to keep the weapon locked away in a place they could reach if they needed to without risking the safety of her sisters. And so the gun had rested, hidden in the darkness and collecting dust, more a symbol than a weapon.

Until now.

The safety was on. Ruby made sure of it, before she slipped the gun beneath the folds of her robe. Closing the safe with a clang, she spun the dial. She knew her mother wouldn't come down the stairs that night. She wouldn't check the bottle of pills to make sure her daughter hadn't taken too many. Over the past year, Ruby had earned back her trust. And now, with the revolver pressed against her hip, Ruby would cash in on that trust.

No one would suspect a thing.

She climbed the stairs on soft feet, stopping behind the couch to kiss her mother's cheek. Then she kissed each of her sisters, one by one, before hurrying down the hall. Once she'd closed the door to her bedroom, she slid the weapon into her red sequined purse.

It was part of her costume. The purse had arrived in the mail yesterday, along with the dress, the gloves, and the shoes. Everything matched. Even her lipstick would match, once she had a minute to put it on. But first, she threw off her robe and tucked it under the comforter, making it look like a body was sleeping there. It was an amateur illusion, and it wouldn't fool most parents, but Mrs. Valentine lived in a kind of blur. She'd lost herself, completely faded into nothing when Ruby's father had disappeared, and while she'd been getting herself back day by day, she was a long way from solid.

Ruby was banking on that. She was also banking on the fact that nobody would disturb her if they thought she was sleeping. Charlotte had learned her lesson two years earlier, when she'd gone racing across the room at the sound of Ruby's screams. She'd tried to wake her sister, and Ruby had thrashed about so terribly, poor Charlotte had been hurled to the floor.

Ruby felt guilty about it, even now. After their father had disappeared, the bruised arms and legs were supposed to go away. Those little girls were never supposed to worry about being tossed aside, so carelessly, like they weighed nothing at all. Ruby had asked for the sleeping pills that night, hoping they would make her limbs so heavy, she couldn't hurt anyone again.

It hadn't really been about eliminating the nightmare.

The nightmare was vivid. It always started the same, with Ruby sitting up in bed. She'd think she was coming awake, and then the humming would start. Soft and low, the pretty tremble of a baritone.

"Daddy?" Ruby would whisper.

First came the fingers, curling around the slightly open door. Then a face would appear, framed in shaggy ginger hair. Soft brown eyes. Smiling eyes.

"Daddy?" Ruby would ask again.

It was a foolish question. Of course it was him. Even with maggots falling from his eye sockets. Even with skin so pale, it was impossible to believe he was alive. And yet, he pushed the door open farther, stumbling on limbs that were starting to decay. Sometimes a bone snapped and he fell to his knees. But still, he would get to her.

Walk, stumble, or crawl.

"I didn't do anything!" she'd tell him. It was what she'd always told him before, when those bright, twinkling eyes became hooded in shadow.

"You're a liar," he would say. "You know what happens to liars."

Ruby did. She had known since she was a little girl and could still hide inside crawl spaces and under beds. She had known later on, when she'd taught her sisters the same tricks. And when she was fully grown and fully incapable of escaping him, he'd loom over her, and his hand would lash out. Grip her collar or her face. In the dream, his fingernails would dig into her cheeks, threatening to tear her apart. She'd look down and see dirt covering the floor. She'd look up and see trees surrounding her bed. And she'd realize this wasn't her room anymore.

It was her grave.

The scream would tear out of her, a wild and anguished thing. But nobody would come to her aid. Nobody could hear her, until that one night, when Charlotte came racing across the room, shaking Ruby awake. Charlotte had saved her from him, and Charlotte had paid the price.

Then Ruby got ahold of the sleeping pills, and the nightmare softened around the edges. Now, two years after the fact, it had almost faded away. But as Ruby stared at herself in the mirror, her skin drained of all color, she had the most terrible premonition of standing at her own funeral, trying to convince people she wasn't dead.

"He isn't dead," her mother had promised, the one time Ruby had divulged the contents of her dream. "He left us, Ruby. He didn't die."

Ruby had nodded, keeping her thoughts to herself. Alive, her father could return to the family. Turn over a new leaf, or lose it completely. Ruby was ready to be done. Done with missing him, and with hating him.

And maybe she could be. Maybe tonight was the beginning of the end. She would go to the party, solve the mystery, and leave everything behind. This town. Its dirty little secrets.

All the memories of terror and elation.

A clean slate, Ruby thought, tucking her phone into her purse. The screen was lighting up, informing her that her ride was here. She couldn't exactly drive off in her own car. Her mother would notice that.

And so, she rolled back her shoulders, telling herself it was only a short drive. She didn't even have to speak to the driver. Ruby flicked off the light. Pulling on her shoes, gloves, and purse, she climbed out her first-story window and disappeared into the night.

3.

GOLDEN BOY

Parker Addison could not believe his good luck. Ruby Valentine was climbing into his car. *His* Ruby, the girl he'd lost his virginity to. The girl who owned his heart. One year ago, she'd slipped out of his grasp.

Tonight he was going to win her back.

Parker shifted the rearview mirror, checking his reflection for the fiftieth time. His suit was a deep forest green that made his emerald eyes *pop*, and his blond hair was perfectly tousled. Touchable. Just the way Ruby liked it. But he didn't try to kiss her, not yet. Didn't put a hand on her knee. He would play this right, and she would fall back into his arms.

Beside him, Ruby sighed.

"What's wrong, babe?" The word slipped out of his mouth. No other name would've felt quite right. Still, to remedy the mistake, he added, "You look hot, by the way."

Ruby snorted, looking out the window. "Just drive."

Parker's skin flushed as he pulled onto the road. "Damn it, Ruby, why won't you give me a chance?"

"To do what? Go back in time? Become a different person?" She wouldn't even look at him, and that was worse than the snarling. Worse than the laughter. If she'd *look* at him, she'd remember why she loved him, and all of this would be different. They could stop pretending they weren't meant for each other.

As Parker sped down the street, his eye caught on every restaurant they'd gone to, every movie theater they'd made out in. But Fallen Oaks was filled with generic chain restaurants stuffed between mini malls. He couldn't exactly point to the Dairy Queen and conjure up some romantic memory.

Still, a memory came to mind as they passed the parking lot of a run-down thrift shop, and Parker tapped the window, drawing Ruby's attention. "Remember that Halloween, sophomore year? You were heading into the shop with Juniper Torres—"

"I remember," Ruby said softly. She wasn't smiling, but she wasn't scowling, either. It was a start.

"You were the most beautiful girl I'd ever seen."

"You'd seen me before."

"I know," Parker said. "But every time was like the first."

Ruby looked down. He wanted to crawl into her mind and read her thoughts. He almost reached for her hand. Instead he peered out the window, thinking back to that night.

It had been after sunset. Parker had been waiting for a while. He'd heard the girls talking at school, plotting to meet at the thrift shop after dinner, so he'd driven over to the strip mall around five thirty and waited in his car. When the girls finally arrived (almost an hour after he did) he was psyching himself up, listening to 102.5 The Rock at full blast, practicing what he was going to say.

I love you was far too much.

I want you would never go over well with a girl like Ruby.

I need you would make him sound clingy, and Ruby would laugh.

But he did need her. He wanted her desperately. And he'd loved her for longer than he could remember.

Parker climbed out of the car. The girls were crossing the parking lot, chattering as they neared the thrift store. He knew, based on snippets of their conversation at lunch, that they were going as zombie versions of Romeo and Juliet for Halloween. Beyond that, Parker didn't really care. It was enough to know that every douchebag in town wouldn't be catching flashes of Ruby's behind. Her pale, curvaceous thighs. The breasts that kept bouncing, even when she stopped.

Parker was halfway across the parking lot when he heard the voice. High and nasally, it hit him at his back, and his entire body tensed. "Yeah, she has great tits, but her family's trash."

Parker turned, his hands balled into fists. There, hovering by some garbage cans, was a group of scrawny freshmen with vampire-pale skin. The one in the center was leering at Ruby.

Parker didn't even think. He just stalked over to the kid and picked him up by the collar. Tossed him into the row of trash cans like he weighed nothing. The rest of the assholes scattered, and Parker wiped his hands on his pants. When he walked over to Ruby, she was staring at him like he was the sun and she'd been living in darkness. She lifted his hand and placed it on her chest.

"Do you feel that?" she asked, her heart beating into his skin. Racing, like she'd run a marathon. "It's beating for you."

That was it. He was hers and she was *his*. Now, as the parking lot disappeared in the distance, Parker asked her if she remembered how she'd felt that day. The heat between them.

"It was warm for October," she said, and his guts clenched.

But after a minute, she added, "It was like something out of a story. You came for me, and you fought for me. Nobody'd ever fought for me before."

Parker nodded, feeling like something had shifted between them. "It's definitely not anything your shithead father would've done," he said, reminding her that he wasn't like the rest. Reminding her that he was better.

"No, he would've been more likely to fight *with* me." Ruby cringed. "The man loved to argue."

Parker frowned. He shouldn't have brought up her dad. The topic made Ruby sad. Even before her father left town, it'd made Ruby sad. "I always wanted to protect you," he admitted.

"I wanted you to protect me," Ruby said, startling him with the sound of her voice. "I thought I needed protection, back then. Now I think you're like the gun my mother bought after my father disappeared. A powerful symbol, but meaningless. What's the point of a gun if you don't shoot it?"

"So shoot it, Ruby. Take out the gun and—"

"That's the other problem, isn't it? If I pull out the gun, what happens if you turn it on me? Who's going to protect me then?"

"Shane Ferrick?" he spat, and he wasn't even sorry. He hated Shane Ferrick. Even now, he hated him. Maybe more, because Ruby hadn't had the chance to get tired of the guy. To toss him aside, like she had with Parker.

"Don't you *ever*—" she began, her face as red as it had been that day in the parking lot. Flushed with fury this time, rather than excitement. Her hand twitched, and she clutched her purse to her chest.

"I'm sorry, Rubes," Parker said. "I didn't mean it. Just . . . seeing you again—"

"You see me every day at school," she spat, still clutching her purse. Holding it close, like she loved it.

Parker wanted to rip it from her hands. "I see you, and you look through me."

"I do," she agreed. "I see through you now. I see through the illusion."

"What does that mean?" Parker slammed on the brakes as a yellow Jaguar zipped past them, almost sideswiping the car. They both jumped, then shook their heads. They knew who the driver was.

"Do you think he's going where we're going?" Parker asked, watching the car weave between lanes. The Jaguar, which had been a gift from Parker, was covered in dents and dings.

Ruby shrugged. "It makes sense. Brett had a boxing scholarship. Brett quit boxing—"

"And lost his scholarship. He has to get out of here somehow."

"What about you?" She leveled a gaze at him. "Can't your daddy pay for school? How many families did Jericho Addison's big-box chain put out of business this year? Surely some of that money has trickled down to you."

Parker didn't even flinch. He was used to people being jealous of his family's success. "You don't get rich by turning down free money, Rubes. A fifty-thousand-dollar scholarship is a big deal."

"You don't even need it!"

"You do. Hey, I have an idea. If I win, I'll tell the foundation I want to split the money with you."

"You'll split the scholarship?" she asked, casting him a sidelong glance.

A shiver danced up his spine. He knew she was setting him

up for something, but he didn't know what. "Of course I will, Rubes. You know I—"

"Who are you trying to fool?" Ruby flashed a wicked grin. "Parker Addison doesn't share."

They spent the rest of the drive in silence. Parker was fuming, gripping the steering wheel the way he wanted to be gripping Ruby. He wanted to be holding her, kissing her, making her remember how it felt to be completely connected.

Ruby stared out the window, saying nothing.

As they neared the long, twisting driveway that led to the Cherry Street Mansion, Parker's gaze drifted to the bag in the back of the car. His invitation had asked him to bring a rope to the party. And if *anyone* tried to stop him from winning back the love of his life, Parker would take that rope and get creative.

4.

MEAT HEAD

Brett Carmichael hated his life. He knew it, with startling clarity, as he neared the Cherry Street Mansion. The estate was guarded by a pair of wrought-iron gates, and when they swung open, Brett envisioned one of the spires sliding into his stomach. Ending it all. Over the past year he'd had thoughts like this quite often, and while he wouldn't call them fantasies, there was always a moment of pleasure, followed by a moment of panic. Harsh and hot, like flames licking his body. And in that moment of panic, he knew he wouldn't be climbing the gate and impaling himself.

He wanted the darkness to come, but he wouldn't be the one to beckon it.

It wasn't fear, exactly, that was holding him back. It was that tiny, shriveled person that still lived inside of him, and it wanted to survive. It screamed, voice muffled under layers of sadness, layers of guilt, to *fight, fight, fight*. But Break-Your-Neck Brett had been fighting his entire life, attacking guys in the boxing ring and playing bodyguard to Parker Addison. Fighting had gotten him into this mess.

It couldn't break him out. Brett knew that now, as the wrought-iron gates closed behind him. There was no way out; only further *in*. And so he drove, past the garden of topiary creatures, the scent of chlorine tingeing the air. The smell made Brett's stomach turn. In the back of his mind, he envisioned a boy sinking to the bottom of a swimming pool, his face purpling as his hands scrabbled for purchase. It must have been terrifying to barely escape the depths only to be taken by the flames.

Brett put the car in park. Climbed out. Took a deep breath. He just had to get through this party, win fifty large, and get the hell out of this suffocating town. Sure, he'd been offered a boxing scholarship last year, but after that party up in the hills, he couldn't turn people into pulp anymore. Couldn't mash up a boy's face with a smile on his own. Unfortunately, with boxing off the table, paying for school was damn near impossible. Brett was a straight-C student, and that was thanks to the pity of his more understanding teachers. He'd honed no other talents, learned no other skills. Destruction was his only ability.

That's why he was going to win *this* scholarship, he thought, hurrying up the path. He'd go to any school that would take him, as long as it was far away from here. And yeah, even in his desperation, Brett knew the arrangement was odd and the Ringmaster was playing a tricky game. Why else would his costume require brass knuckles?

This murder mystery dinner had a jagged edge.

The house came into view, and it was jagged as well. Brett tilted his head back to take in the sight. The structure was pale stone with black roofing on the turrets. A black arching door. Back in the 1920s, the mansion had been the site of many a lavish party, but as the era of Gatsby bled into the Great Depression, the house had fallen into ruin. Since then, the mansion had changed hands several times, finally landing in the clutches of a wealthy philanthropist who owned more houses than fingers. Mr. Covington Saint James rented the mansion out for a number of events, determined to reclaim its former glory.

But some things couldn't be reclaimed. Yes, the mansion was breathtaking, but it was also crumbling in more places than it was whole. The ebony door desperately needed a new coat of paint. From Brett's vantage point, it looked like every room was lit by chandelier, but that light only served to illuminate the house's flaws.

That was something Brett could understand. From a distance, his face looked cherubic, with rosy cheeks that could rival a porcelain doll's. He kept his hair shaved, for practical reasons, but that only added to the baby-doll aesthetic. Still, the closer people got to him, the better they could see his flaws. The tooth that had been chipped during his first boxing match. The scar on his stomach. His bright hazel eyes had a feral look to them, as if Brett were a wolf who'd realized his leg was in a trap. Should he gnaw it off or wait for the hunter to find him?

Brett always felt this way, trapped between giving up entirely and destroying a piece of himself to survive. He'd felt it before Dahlia Kane's Christmas party, even before he'd taken up boxing. But if he could get away from this town, maybe he could get away from that feeling and start fresh.

Now the doorway loomed over him. Brett felt small, like a boy approaching the house of a fabled giant. He'd expected a heavy door knocker, maybe a lion's head made of polished brass, and the sound of his knuckles against the wood seemed insignificant. He was about to ring the bell when a voice called out to him. Brett spun around, his heart springing to life. There, striding up the walkway, was the only person in Fallen Oaks who made him feel alive.

"I hoped you'd be here," Parker Addison said.

5.

LONE WOLF

Gavin Moon watched from a distance. He felt more comfortable there. Back in his younger days, he'd wanted to step out into the open, to walk beside the rulers of Fallen Oaks High. It wasn't some generic cheerleader-jock brigade. Parker Addison would never get down in the dirt (that was what Brett was for), and Ruby Valentine couldn't shake a pom-pom without knocking herself out with her own boobs. No, the Fallen Oaks hierarchy was ruled by the best and brightest in all categories. That was what made Gavin so mad. Not only was he a prolific writer, his guitar solos could give you an out-of-body experience. In spite of all this, Gavin had never been welcomed into the fold, and so he got used to living on the outside.

He used to hate it, but now he understood that distance could give you a broader perspective. As he ambled up the walkway, he could see the makeup Ruby used to hide the dark circles under her eyes, and the way Parker's fists tightened in her presence. Meanwhile, Brett kept *his* fists tucked into his pockets, probably to hide the feeling of blood on his hands. Juniper Torres was the only clean person among them, and even she had a secret.

All of them did.

Maybe that was why she was fretting about the scholarship. "Did you guys apply for this? Like, did you actually fill out paperwork?" She glanced from person to person, brow furrowing.

"I did," Parker said before anyone else could speak. "Well, the guidance counselor submitted me, but that's kind of her job. I even suggested some names to her when she told me the scholarship was open to everyone."

"You did?" Ruby looked at him, biting her lip. "Who did you suggest? All of us?"

Parker shook his head. "Just you and Brett. But I saw the list of names she was considering, and I'm pretty sure Juniper's was on it. Hers, and that kid who's always hanging around—"

"Hey, guys," Gavin called, cutting Parker off. He jogged up the porch steps, giving Juniper a casual, confident nod. Super cool. Totally suave. At least, that was how he hoped it looked, but the second his eyes met Parker's, his jaw tightened. "Are we doing this or what?"

"Nobody's answering," Ruby said, toying with her hair. Something about that crimson dye job made her look alien, her blue eyes peering out of an eerily pale face. "Maybe there's a back door?"

Gavin smiled, tilting his head. "Maybe there's a back door? To a house? Good work, Veronica Mars."

Ruby gave him a withering stare. "You know what I meant. Maybe the back door's *open*. I'll go check."

"I'll go with you," Parker said, offering his arm. He had a duffel bag slung over his shoulder, and Gavin couldn't help but wonder what was inside it.

"I'm going alone," Ruby snapped. Then she was gone. She seemed unusually bold, Gavin thought, as she clutched her purse and looped around the stranger's mansion. But maybe she'd just do anything to get away from Parker. He couldn't exactly blame her for that. Nowadays, he thought Ruby Valentine was the only person in the world who hated Parker as much as he did.

Of course, Gavin hadn't had to date the guy to learn the truth.

Ruby wasn't gone long. Five minutes after she'd left, she returned, her purse swinging at her side. "Back door's open. You're welcome," she added for Gavin's sake, flashing a haughty little smirk that made his blood boil.

The group traveled around the house. Ruby went first, then Parker and Brett, with Gavin and Juniper bringing up the rear. It was obvious that Juniper wasn't used to walking in heels, and when her shoe skidded across the icy ground, Gavin offered his arm.

"Here. Let me . . ."

"Be my escort?" Juniper suggested, sliding her arm through his. "I swear to God, I'm taking these off as soon as I can."

"You should. I'd hate for you to go plummeting down the stairs. Then we'd have two murders to solve."

She laughed, but it sounded forced. "I like your costume," she said after a minute, shifting the focus from herself. Typical Juniper.

"Oh, this? I had this in my closet," Gavin quipped. The three-piece suit was a ridiculous getup, but fitting. Gavin was a reporter in real life. Or rather, he was going to be, after he graduated. For now, he worked on the school's newspaper and ran his own blog.

"Yeah, well, it suits you." Juniper set his hat at a slant. The fedora was mustard brown, just like his suit, with a little PRESS card poking out of the side.

"The suit suits me," he said, playing with a Brooklyn accent. "You got a way with words, you know that, doll face?"

Juniper grinned. It was a gesture that was fleeting with her, these days. Here one moment, gone the next. He wanted to keep her smiling, so he said, "And you, well. Look at you, kid. Mermaid-chic is the next big thing."

"I doubt that," she replied, shuffling along in her blue sequined dress. Or maybe it was aqua? Gavin couldn't get a read on the color in the near darkness, until they reached the mansion's back patio and came across an Olympic-size swimming pool.

Ruby noticed it too. "You match," she said, gesturing to the water, which matched Juniper's dress. Like, *perfectly* matched. In response, Juniper hugged the edge of the mansion, staying away from the pool.

"You're all right." Gavin guided her around a potted plant. The gnarled, thorny branches held no blossoms, but one of them must've snagged Ruby when she'd come around before. A single red sequin sparkled in the dirt. "Nobody's going swimming tonight," he promised.

Juniper nodded, leaning into him. Her wavy, shoulder-length hair tickled his neck, and her skin was warm against his. For the first time in a long time, Gavin was happy.

Then he wasn't. The group had arrived at the back of the mansion, and Gavin sucked in a breath. There was nothing particularly foreboding about the sight. If anything, it was inviting, the glass double doors leading into an elaborate dining room. The walls were a deep ebony wood, and the furniture was too, but all of the accents were gold. Gold pillows on the high-backed chairs, gilded mirrors on the walls. A chandelier so large, the room sparkled with light.

"It's like a Golden Age starlet got her hands on a castle," Ruby gushed, reaching for the doors. They opened with little resistance, and the group stepped inside.

"This place is dope," Parker agreed, sliding his fingers over the dark, polished wood of the table. No dust clung to his fingertips. Gavin was surprised. He'd half expected the house to be covered in cobwebs, it felt so . . . abandoned. Like a palace preserved by a spell. Still, someone living must've come through in the recent past, because a black candelabra sat in the center of the table, holding freshly lit candles. The gold tapers were dripping only the slightest bit of wax.

There were six place settings at the table—six, Gavin noted, not five—and at each setting was a wineglass and a folded card. Parker immediately opened the bottle of sparkling cider on the table, and with the help of Brett's pocket flask, he doctored up his drink. Ruby stood by, amused. Meanwhile, Juniper untangled her hand from Gavin's and sat down in a chair. But she must not have been paying attention, because she sat at the head of the table, in front of the card labeled *Ruby Valentine*.

"I think you're supposed to be here," Gavin said, pointing to her spot.

Juniper nodded but didn't rise from her chair. She looked dazed, like she'd walked into a fun house only to realize she was being chased by murderous clowns. After a minute of staring, she shook herself, saying, "Where's the Ringmaster?"

"What?" Parker's head snapped toward her.

"Our guide for the party. Didn't you get instructions?" She opened her peacock-blue purse and unfolded a sheet of paper. "Mine came with my costume."

"Mine, too," Ruby said, reading over Juniper's shoulder.

"For the duration of the murder mystery dinner, you will play the characters, accompanied by your guide, the Ringmaster. With his help, you will discover the victim, uncover the clues, and solve the mystery."

"Right. So, where is he?" Juniper pressed.

"Maybe he's hiding?" Ruby's eyes lit up. "Oh! Maybe he's the victim. That'd be a good twist."

Juniper hunched over the table, reading the instructions again. At least, that was what Gavin thought she was doing, until he realized she was *texting* under the table. When his phone vibrated, he slid into his chair, reading her message: **I'm right, aren't I? We shouldn't be here alone.**

Definitely, he wrote, keeping his gaze above the table. **Maybe Parker's pulling a prank on us? He's got the money, and he's making a freaking cocktail while we figure things out.**

Juniper snorted, glancing at Parker. He was swirling his drink around, taking little swigs, as she sent her next message. **I doubt it. I've been researching this scholarship for days, and I didn't find anything shady. I emailed the foundation and got back a pretty quick response. I even found blog posts from previous winners!**

Not a Parker prank, then, Gavin wrote. **Unless he really–**

A voice, female and vaguely robotic, drifted through the air. Gavin stopped typing in mid-message. Scanning the dining room, he located a pair of speakers above the patio doors.

"Please hand over your cell phones," the voice intoned.

"Uh. What the hell?" Parker spoke first, because that was Parker's job. To speak before thinking. "Hand them over where?"

"It's not a person," Gavin said, using the slow, patient voice of a kindergarten teacher. "It's a recording, probably set to a timer."

Parker flipped him off. Behind them, Brett was searching the room, happy to solve Parker's problem and get a doggy treat. God, Gavin despised them. And he realized that the sooner he gave up his lifeline to the outside world, the sooner the competition would begin.

He rose from his chair. There were two entryways in the room, one leading to a dark hall, the other leading to a kitchen. Gavin headed toward the latter, glimpsing something on the tiled floor. "Here. Guys?"

Everyone turned. Even Juniper, who was being coaxed by Ruby out of her chair, turned to see what Gavin had found on the floor of the kitchen. A doll. It was one of those jiggling, wiggling baby dolls that children loved to cradle, and there was a tray in front of it, with a card that read *Electronics*.

Gavin hesitated. There was something about the doll's coloring that gave him pause. That tuft of ebony hair, and those piercing blue eyes . . . they reminded him of someone. He thought Ruby might freak out if she saw it, so he scooted the doll to the left, out of the entryway. Juniper was already on edge because of the pool. He didn't want some small thing to set off Ruby as well.

He delivered his phone to the tray. Brett delivered his next, along with Parker's, because Parker couldn't be bothered to leave the table and do it himself. The girls ambled over last, and as Juniper drew near, Gavin saw that she was clutching her phone like a raft.

"It's just a stupid rule," he told her, holding out a hand. "The Ringmaster probably thinks we'll use our phones to cheat."

"How?" Juniper glanced from him to Ruby.

"Murder mystery dinners tend to follow a certain formula," Ruby said, handing Gavin her phone. "There might be clues about our characters online. Obviously, *we* wouldn't play that way, but not everyone here is so ethical."

Ruby wiggled her eyebrows, not even deigning to look at Parker, and Juniper relinquished her phone.

Gavin delivered their cell phones to the little tray, nudging it, and the baby doll, farther away. Into the lighted kitchen with the white marble island. A wooden knife block sat in the middle of the island, but all the slots were empty. *At least we won't be stabbing each other in the back,* he thought with a laugh. Then he glanced at the doll and his pulse quickened.

Hurrying back to the table, Gavin took his seat as the intercom screeched to life. "Welcome to the fifth annual Burning Embers Foundation murder mystery dinner! Please make yourselves at home, have a drink, and introduce your characters."

Gavin lifted his card from the table. On the outside, it simply said *Gavin Moon,* but inside, there was information. A character name, a love interest, a weapon, and a secret. He closed his card as quickly as he'd opened it.

All around him, he saw more of the same: people opening, scanning, and then closing their cards. Brett was blushing. Ruby was scowling. Parker stuffed his card into his pocket. Only Juniper seemed to be taking in the information before reacting, but her gaze kept flicking to the patio. Gavin wished he could pull heavy curtains over the back doors, hiding the pool from her sight. But that was the thing about demons: they could follow you through curtains, follow you through glass. Gavin's demons were listed inside his card:

1. My name is THE INVISIBLE MAN.
2. I am secretly in love with THE UNDERWATER ACROBAT.
3. My weapon is a CAMERA because I WILL EXPOSE EACH ONE OF YOU.

4. My greatest secret is I WOULD KILL TO BE POPULAR.

Gavin snorted, shaking his head. He wouldn't kill to be popular. Popularity could kiss his ass. Still, there was a grain of truth to each piece of information, and he had the strangest feeling the character was an exaggerated version of himself. At least, he *hoped* it was an exaggerated version. Yes, he'd brought a camera, as he'd been instructed to do, but he wasn't planning on "exposing" anyone tonight.

Well, maybe Parker, if the guy wouldn't shut up.

"Wait." Gavin pushed out of his seat, hurrying around the table. He wanted to get to the sixth card before Parker could snatch it up. Unlike the other cards, which had been folded to stand on their own, this one had fallen flat on the table. That was why no one had reached for it yet. *Well, that and the fact that we're total narcissists,* Gavin thought, *myself included.* Everyone wanted to study their own characters before thinking about anyone else.

He lifted the card, goose bumps rippling over his skin. *One of these things is not like the others,* he thought. For one thing, the card didn't have a full name on the outside. Just scattered letters:

a n e r i k

And on the inside, the list was different too. Gavin read it aloud to the group:

"1. My name is DOLL FACE.
3. My weapon is THE ELEMENT OF SURPRISE because NO ONE WILL SEE IT COMING.
4. My greatest secret is I AM ALREADY HERE."

"There's no number two," Ruby said, coming up beside Gavin. Parker snorted, no doubt amused by her wording.

I hope he dies first, Gavin thought, then swallowed, unsure of where the thought had come from. Sure, they were at a murder mystery dinner, but they weren't going to be the victims. He'd been certain of that, going in.

Hadn't he?

Parker snatched the card from Gavin's hand, ripping him out of his thoughts. "Maybe Doll Face doesn't love anyone," Parker suggested, giving away more than he'd intended. Before now, Gavin hadn't been certain everyone's card was like his own. Now he was confident in assuming each card listed the same set of information, except this one.

Ruby tilted her head. "But why leave the number out? Why not number them one, two, and three?"

"Because the absence is significant," Parker answered, glancing at the candelabra. He eyed the burning candles the way Juniper had eyed the swimming pool. All of them had a weakness.

"Oh," Gavin said, realizing the answer. "Doll Face has no weakness."

"You think love is a weakness?" Juniper frowned at him, and he flushed, looking away.

"Love is definitely a weakness." Ruby glanced at Parker in his crisp green suit. "But then, some people think they're in love, when they're really just insecure."

Brett rounded on her. "Why don't you keep your insults to your—"

"Whoa, whoa," Gavin said, stepping in. If people were going to tear each other apart, they could do it after they'd solved this mystery. "I'm not saying love is a weakness. I'm saying people can use it against you."

Juniper nodded. "Like the way superheroes always try to stay single, because they know the villain will go after the person they love."

"Okay, show of hands," Ruby said, lifting her own. She was wearing scarlet elbow-length gloves, the exact same color as her hair. "Whose card lists a love interest?"

Everyone raised their hand except for Brett. Juniper scooted closer to him. "It's just a game," she said. "Characters. Come on, Brett."

Gavin was surprised at how softly she was speaking to him, like he was a puppy who needed love, and not the henchman to a monster. But Juniper had known Brett before he got twisted up in Parker's web, and she must've been thinking of that sweet-faced little boy. Gavin didn't have the luxury of remembering Brett fondly.

He just wanted to forget.

After all, the two used to be friends. It seemed impossible now, but back in grade school, Brett and Gavin had been inseparable. They used to meet in the forest behind their houses and go on adventures. They'd pluck branches from the ground and brandish them like swords. They'd search for treasure. Once, they'd found a bird's nest that had fallen from a tree, and six-year-old Brett had burst into tears, worried the babies wouldn't make it.

Now it looked like he might cry again. Gavin felt the strangest urge to reach out to him. But he knew *exactly* how that would end, knew how it always ended, since Parker had come into the picture.

Slowly Brett lifted his hand, saying, "My character has a love interest."

"So everyone has a weakness," Gavin said, "except for Doll

Face. What about these letters?" He gestured to the front of the card.

"Maybe it's an anagram?" Parker suggested.

"With six letters? Everyone else has their full name on their card. Wait . . ." Gavin studied the card again, fingers tracing the letters. "Everyone's initials are capitalized. Right?" He held up his card, so they could see the name *Gavin Moon* printed across the front in calligraphy.

Everyone nodded, even Brett.

"Okay, well, these letters are all lowercase," he said, pointing to Doll Face's card. "So maybe instead of an anagram, some letters are *missing* and we have to fill them in. We can assume two of the missing letters are this person's initials."

The intercom scratched to life, and Gavin half expected the voice to award him points for his discovery. Instead it said, "Please make yourselves at home, have a drink, and introduce your characters."

Juniper shivered, and Gavin slid off his jacket, laying it over her shoulders. "Thank you," she said, clutching the edges. "You still think it's a timed recording?"

"I'm less confident than I was a minute ago. But hey, I'll go first." In a booming voice, Gavin announced, "I am the Invisible Man."

"The Human Torch," Parker said, not to be upstaged. "Which makes no sense, by the way, because I'm wearing green."

Everyone eyed his forest-green suit. It was Ruby who made the connection. "Oh! You're the hottest part of the flame," she surmised, at which Parker grinned.

"I'm the Underwater Acrobat," Juniper murmured.

"The Iron Stomach." That was Brett, and Gavin hadn't heard him speak so softly in years. He wondered if Brett was actually shaken. In the light of the chandelier, his deep purple suit made him look like a bruise.

"And I'm the Disappearing Act," Ruby said with flair. Gavin waited for her to curtsy, but she didn't.

After a minute, the intercom spoke again: "Please make yourselves at home, have a drink, and introduce your characters."

"We just did!" Parker barked, engaging with the intercom the way he engaged with the drive-through window. Gavin knew this for a fact. Once, when he was a sophomore, Brett had thrown him into Parker's trunk, and together, the boys had taken a joyride around the town, getting food, then shoulder-tapping at the local market, and finally hitting on girls outside some sleazy club.

"Please make yourselves at home, have a drink, and introduce your characters. Please make yourselves at home, have a drink, and introduce your characters. Please—"

"We introduced ourselves! We had a drink! We—" Parker froze, his gaze settling on Gavin. "It's you."

"What? I introduced myself first."

"Look at your wineglass." Parker snorted, glancing at Brett. Both of the boys had polished off their drinks already. Ruby's glass was only half-full. Even Juniper had taken a sip or two.

That left Gavin and Gavin alone, and Parker would never let him forget it. "This infant is afraid of apple cider."

"I'm not afraid," Gavin snarled. He hated how easy it was for Parker to get under his skin. "I'm just not drinking anything *you* poured. You probably spiked—"

Parker cut him off with a laugh. "Feel free to check it. Not that you'd know what whiskey smells like—"

"Oh, for God's sake." Gavin snatched up his glass, inhaling

deeply. When the smell hit his nostrils, he jerked back, eyes swimming with tears. There was something *off* about the cider. He wanted to check the others' glasses to see if their drinks smelled the same, but he didn't know how to do it without incurring Parker's wrath.

Gavin inhaled again, but his coordination was off. His vision blurred and his nasal passages felt like they were on fire. Something pungent had been dumped into his glass. Something you'd smell in a chemistry lab, or . . .

"Gavin?" Juniper's voice sounded faint, like she was calling to him from a tunnel.

"I . . ." He set the wineglass on the table, leaning away from it, but his movements were jerkier than he'd expected. As he jolted backward, the chair jolted with him. Together, they tipped. Together, they toppled. Gavin threw out his arms to protect his head. The last thing he saw was Parker staring down at him, green eyes glittering like emeralds in the light of the chandelier.

Then his eyelids fluttered closed, and he saw nothing.

6.

PUNCH DRUNK

When Gavin hit the ground, Brett leapt out of his chair. His heart was hammering. Had someone spiked Gavin's drink? Or was this all part of the game? It was funny, how easy it was to forget you were at a murder mystery dinner when a classmate passed out on the hardwood, but Brett wasn't the only one who was confused.

Everyone was hurrying to Gavin's side.

Parker got there first. He held a hand to Gavin's mouth, to make sure he was breathing, while Juniper checked for a pulse. Brett couldn't remember a time when Juniper wasn't playing doctor (and not the fun kind). Meanwhile, Ruby hovered over the body, looking particularly pale. Then again, it was hard to tell with Ruby; she was so ghostly pale to begin with. In fact, she'd always struck Brett as someone who would fade out of existence if she didn't feed off the energy of boys like Parker Addison. Everyone she touched ended up broken or dead.

"His vitals are okay," Juniper said from her place on the ground. "But I think we should call an ambulance, in case—"

"Too bad, so sad," the intercom broke in. "The Invisible Man knew too much. But who in this group wanted to silence him?"

Brett's breathing quickened. He was afraid to say what he

was thinking: that he knew exactly who wanted to silence Gavin. His gaze flicked involuntarily to the left, to the guy who was reaching for Gavin's wineglass.

"It's all part of the game," Parker said, swirling the contents of the glass. But there must've been cider on the outside, because the glass slid out of his fingertips.

Onto the ground.

"Shit!" He leapt back, as the glass shattered. "That wasn't my fault," he said quickly.

Juniper fixed him with a glare. Together, the two huddled around the fallen wineglass, searching for signs of contamination. There was nothing. Nothing on the glass, and nothing in the amber liquid spreading across the floor. Still, some things didn't leave a residue, and Parker must've known it, because he lifted a shard to his nose.

"Don't," Brett ordered. "You'll cut yourself."

Damn it. He shouldn't have said that. He had been good, so good this past year. He'd distanced himself from Parker. He'd stopped pulverizing people, in and out of the ring. And even though keeping out of trouble could never be mistaken for atonement, he kept hoping he'd *eventually* get to a point where his past would slip away from him, and he would be clean.

Then Parker walked into the periphery and everything went to hell.

Luckily, he was walking *out* of the periphery now, to wash his hands in the kitchen. Juniper exhaled, saying, "That was a good call, Brett. If he'd sliced his hand, any drugs would've gone right into his bloodstream."

"Juniper, it's a game." Ruby rolled her eyes. "See how Gavin's arm is draped over his face? That's so he can hide his smile. He didn't even take a drink!"

"I know," Juniper said, visibly shaken. "But I want to be cert—"

"Look." Ruby knelt down, tickling Gavin in the ribs. He sighed, twitching a little, as if he wanted to curl into himself. "See? He's trying not to laugh. He's really good—"

"Uh, guys," Parker said, returning from the kitchen. "I think we're supposed to be playing along."

"Oh, my stars," Ruby gushed in the most ridiculous southern accent. "Our dear friend Gavin has departed . . . Let's read his card," she added, flashing a mischievous grin.

As quickly as she'd fallen into character, she'd fallen out of it. Of course, it would've been easier to play along if there were hired actors here. You couldn't throw five classmates into a room together and expect them to stay in character every second. Especially since they'd just been given their character details. But even that was suspect, Brett thought, as Juniper lifted Gavin's card from the ground. If Gavin was the murder victim, he must've known about his part before he got here. And if the intercom's story was to be believed, one of the people here was the killer. Brett certainly hadn't been given any indication of his character's guilt when he'd received his invitation, but he wanted to be prepared for the possibility.

He wanted to win.

By now, Juniper had unfolded Gavin's card and was reading aloud to the group: *"My name is the Invisible Man. I am secretly in love with the Underwater Acrobat. My weapon is a camera because I will expose each one of you. My greatest secret is I would kill to be popular."*

"Kill to be popular. Cute." Ruby snorted, and Brett couldn't help but wonder if she was trying to distract the group from Juniper's reaction. At the mention of "the Underwater Acrobat," her face had gone beet red. Gavin's card was a little too accurate. Quietly Brett scanned the group, imagining what each card would say if it told the truth.

His name is the Human Torch, he thought, glancing at Parker, *and he's in love with the Disappearing Act.*

That one was easy. Juniper, too, was simple enough to assess. She was the Underwater Acrobat, and if rumors at school were to be believed, she was in love with the girl sitting next to her. Still, Brett had never really gotten the impression that Juniper wanted to push Ruby up against a wall and kiss her. Juniper was obsessed with Ruby in the way that little girls are obsessed with each other before they even know boys exist, as if she'd honestly believed the two would grow up, get married, have children, and still love each other more than anyone.

Unfortunately, things hadn't played out the way Juniper wanted. Ruby had ruined it all by falling too deeply in love. First with Parker and then . . . Well, Brett still didn't know the truth about Ruby and Shane.

Even after seeing the video.

"First things first," he said, looking down at the boy on the floor. Gavin's shirtsleeves were rolled up to his elbows, and his vest was askew. "Why is Gavin the Invisible Man? He's dressed like a reporter."

"He's the observer," Juniper said instantly. "He watches everyone. No one watches him."

Brett nodded in agreement. After all, Gavin never would've pulled off what he had at that party last year if people had been watching him. "Okay, it makes sense that he'd be the person to die, then, if he had the power to see everything without being seen. But why come to the party at all?"

"Maybe the foundation paid him?" Juniper suggested. "It

would've been much less than fifty thousand—that's what you all got offered, right?"

"A fifty-thousand-dollar *scholarship*," Ruby said instantly.

But Parker pushed out the word, "Yup," almost as if it had stuck in his throat. Brett knew this old trick; as smooth as Parker was, a part of him always wanted people to know when he was lying. Maybe he wanted to get caught, or maybe he wanted to prove he could drop hints and *still* get away with whatever he wanted. Either way, Brett's eyes drifted to the duffel bag slung over Parker's shoulder, wondering what he was keeping from them.

"Let me ask you guys something," Juniper said after a minute. "Did anyone think it was weird? I mean, does anyone think this whole thing is weird?"

Brett swallowed, his stomach twisting at the words. "Sure, it's a little weird. But what choice did we have?"

A quiet settled over the group as they each thought about what they wanted, and how desperate they were to get it. One year ago Brett was a rising star in the ring. Juniper was on track to become valedictorian. Ruby was preparing her Juilliard audition, while Gavin and Parker visited the Ivy Leagues.

Then, in one horrible night, everything had changed.

"I'm doing okay," Juniper said, talking to her hands. "If I ace all my finals, and do extra credit work, I'll be fine," she went on, and nobody corrected her. She'd be fine, meaning she'd get to *attend* the school of her choice. But bye-bye valedictorian. Bye-bye free ride. That was what happened when you lost a month of school.

Of course, none of their grades had been particularly stellar in the weeks following the accident. Any academic scholarships had drifted away with the smoke. And for someone like Brett, whose grades were mediocre to begin with, quitting boxing meant losing everything.

He needed this money more than anyone.

"So we have the basics," he said. "But if Gavin's the victim, does that mean there are clues . . . *on* him? Oh! Juniper, check the jacket."

"What?" Juniper narrowed her eyes. Clearly, she'd forgotten that Gavin had draped his jacket over her shoulders moments earlier. Now she shrugged the jacket off, turning the pockets inside out. "Nothing," she said.

"Hold on." Parker crouched down, sliding a hand into Gavin's pants pocket. It was awkward to watch, but seconds later, he pulled out a crumpled piece of paper. "Booyah," he crooned, smoothing the note. *"Wait until a quarter after . . . Appear reluctant to take a drink . . . Barely touch the cider to your lips, then take a tumble.* Oh, crap. These are just his instructions."

Juniper snatched the note, reading in silence. "Oh, thank God. I thought he was—" She broke off, shaking her head. "You really scared me, you jerk," she told Gavin, who sighed in response.

"Told you he was acting," Ruby said with a smirk. "Now, to find his killer. But where—"

As if in answer, music drifted in from the hallway. Carnival music, which matched the theme of their characters perfectly. Everyone in the group turned to look at each other—well, everyone but Gavin.

Then they bolted from the room.

They came to a stop at the base of a grand, wrought-iron staircase, which spiraled to the second floor. The music was coming from upstairs. Still, not everyone was mesmerized by the staircase and all the secrets that lay beyond. Ruby had turned and was looking behind them.

"Holy passage to Narnia," Brett said, following her gaze. There, pressed against the front entrance of the house, was a wardrobe. Brett strode over to it. He'd seen enough movies to know that killers had a penchant for hiding in ridiculous places, and even though the intercom had hinted that one of *them* wanted to silence Gavin, Brett wouldn't have been the least bit surprised to find another killer lurking nearby. After all, the table had been set for six, and Doll Face's card said, *I am already here.*

Maybe the trick was to find her.

Unfortunately, the wardrobe was empty. It wasn't even housing winter coats. And as much as Brett had loved the idea of slipping into another world when he was a kid, he'd long since given up on finding magical solutions to his problems. "Why is this here?" he asked, trying to nudge the wardrobe away from the door. It didn't budge. At all. "Is the Ringmaster trying to keep us in the house?"

Parker shook his head. "I think it means the front door is off-limits. Like we have to stick—"

"To certain areas of the house," Brett said, and immediately cringed. Why had he said that? Why did he finish Parker's sentences like they were *bonded*? But Parker just nodded, smiling in that bright, easy way of his. Parker's smile was like the sun. It warmed Brett to his core.

"That would explain why the back door isn't blocked," Ruby reasoned. "We're supposed to investigate the patio."

"The pool," Juniper said, hugging herself. Ruby wrapped an arm around her shoulders. It was sweet and comforting and entirely un-Ruby-like. But then, Ruby hadn't always been the unfeeling statue that she was now.

Last year had changed all of them.

"So, we make our way upstairs then," Ruby said, letting her

arm slide away. But she stayed next to Juniper, and Parker followed close behind. Brett was at the front of the pack, taking the stairs two at a time.

"What do you think we'll find?" he asked, tossing the words behind him.

Nobody answered, but all of them were racing up the steps. Getting into the investigation. Brett started to feel like a kid again, racing through the forest in the middle of the night. One summer, when he was six, he'd snuck out *every night* to meet Gavin in the woods, and together, they'd fed a couple of baby birds with an eyedropper. The birds had fallen from their nest during a storm, and Brett had refused to let them die.

Now, bounding to the top of the stairs, he told himself he could save another life. His own. He just had to solve the mystery before anyone else. A dark, wood-paneled hallway spread out in front of him, leading to five doors, and he stepped up to the first door on the left. Someone had painted a drop of water there. It was a crude, elementary drawing, like something a child would scribble when his parents weren't looking.

"The Underwater Acrobat," Brett said. When Juniper tensed, he added, "I'm guessing."

But he knew he was right. Even before he found his own door, with a little sword drawn on it, he knew he was right. Parker's door had a flame on it. Ruby's had a ghost. As the group made their way to the door at the end of the hallway, Brett noticed the painting hanging from the wall. A black-haired family stared back at him, two parents and two children. A girl and a boy.

"What the hell?" Parker muttered.

Brett's head snapped to the side. "What?" he asked, his mouth going dry. The sight of those children was unsettling.

"There's nothing here," Parker said, pointing at the fifth door. "Maybe Gavin doesn't get a bedroom. He is dead, after all." He made big air quotes around the word "dead," as if to assure them he was joking.

Still, Brett's stomach clenched.

"We should look inside," Ruby said, reaching for the doorknob, and the pain in Brett's stomach worsened. He was pretty sure the music had been coming from inside that room.

He held his breath as Ruby twisted the knob.

"It's locked," she said, pulling back her hand like it'd been burned. Without speaking, the four of them returned to their respective doors. Brett and Parker jiggled their own knobs to see if they were unlocked.

They were.

"I think it's pretty obvious what we have to do," Brett said. All of them looked a little smaller than they had a minute before. Rule number one for avoiding a killer was: *Don't split up.*

And yet, none of them was going to back out first. Their mysterious benefactor had put together the perfect group. Each of them had a secret. Each of them had an obsession. Each of them had a weapon, probably, considering the way Brett's card had been laid out. If the Ringmaster played his cards right, he'd never have to reveal himself tonight. The players would take care of the competition. Screw each other over. Stab each other in the back.

Together, they opened their doors and slipped into their rooms.

7.

CHILDHOOD ILLUSIONS

Juniper stepped into the first bedroom on the left, closing the door behind her. For a minute, she considered blocking the door with some furniture, but there was no point in keeping her classmates out. She was just playing a game.

So she kept telling herself, but when she turned around, taking in the contents of the room, her breath caught in her throat. The place was set up like a college dorm. There was a twin bed on either side of the room, one with a scarlet comforter, and one with practical white. Juniper knew immediately which one was hers. But it didn't really matter, she thought, as she crossed the hardwood floor. Both sides of the room were decorated the same way: the walls were covered with photographs of two smiling girls, one with golden-brown skin and dark hair, the other a pale-skinned redhead. Juniper and Ruby dressed as an angel and a devil for Halloween. Juniper and Ruby riding miniature ponies at the fair. Juniper and Ruby taking swimming lessons together.

She swallowed, leaning against the wall. The feeling of vertigo was overwhelming, like she was being torn in two. The Ringmaster had created the unique effect of tossing her into the past and the future at the same time. The walls were a

testament to all that had been, but the rest of the room was a shrine to what could never be.

The beds were the tip of the iceberg. On Juniper's bedside table—the table beside the bright white bed—sat a copy of *Gray's Anatomy*, a framed medical license, and dozens of hand-made greeting cards. Opening the one on top, Juniper read the crude black writing that danced across purple construction paper:

> *Dear Dr. Torres,*
> *Thank you for saving my mommy's life! She's much*
> *better now.*
> *Your friend,*
> *Quinn P.*

Juniper shuddered, closing the card. The name Quinn P. was meaningless, but the Ringmaster's intent was clear. This room was a representation of everything Juniper wanted: the dorm room, the medical degree, the letters from children of patients she'd saved. Honestly, the level of detail was astounding. It was like someone had reached into her chest and taken hold of her heart. Every wish, every desire, was laid out before her. If she'd kept a diary, she would have sworn someone had stolen it.

But that was the thing: Juniper didn't keep a diary. She didn't even keep an anonymous blog. There was *no way* the Ringmaster could know this much about her, unless he'd been watching her for a very long time.

Or he'd broken into her actual bedroom.

Juniper's legs wobbled, and she perched on the edge of the bed, taking slow, measured breaths. There had to be a logical

explanation for this. Half the kids in her grade knew that she wanted to be a doctor, and anyone with access to her Facebook page could've printed these photos.

She wasn't being stalked.

She'd almost steadied her heartbeat when she noticed the photograph on the dresser. Unlike the rest of the pictures, which had been plastered across the walls, this one sat alone in a mahogany frame. Blood rushed through Juniper's ears as she strode over to it. This picture was *not* in any of her Facebook albums.

This picture, she'd deleted. It had been taken on Christmas Eve, eight years earlier. Juniper and Ruby (of course) were sitting beside a sparkling tree, holding up two unwrapped presents.

Porcelain dolls.

Beautiful or terrifying? Juniper thought with the ghost of a smile. Back when the girls were young, they'd believed the dolls to be beautiful, but as they'd gotten older, their perception had shifted. The dolls had become terrifying, their eerie glass eyes watching the girls as they huddled in bed. Those perfect bow lips, when spied in a certain light, looked like they were curling into a smile. Eventually, the girls had gathered up all their toys and divided them into two sections: "beautiful" or "terrifying." Anything that fell into the terrifying category was torched in a bonfire.

Now, disturbed by those perfect porcelain faces, Juniper set the photograph, facedown, on the dresser. That was when she noticed the present behind it. The box was small and black, wrapped in a pretty red ribbon. She knew she should leave it *exactly* where it was and get the hell out of this room.

But she didn't. If the room contained her deepest desires, that box could contain her darkest secret. She needed to know

what the Ringmaster knew, and besides, opening the present would take seconds. Look, the ribbon was already off! Soon Juniper was lifting the lid. Inside, she found a folded sheet of paper, and beneath it, the box was molded so that she could stick an object inside. She reached into her purse. There, she pulled out the object the Ringmaster had asked her to bring to the murder mystery dinner.

The "weapon."

Some weapon, she thought, sliding it into place. The bright red marker fit perfectly, as if the box had been made for it. But then, it probably had, she thought, unfolding the sheet of paper with trembling hands. It was a photocopy of two plane tickets. Both to Cuba, leaving June 13, the day after graduation. Underneath the tickets, someone had scribbled: *Hand over your weapon, and I'll make all your dreams come true.*

Tremors raced up Juniper's arms, causing her to sway. The room had been disturbing enough. But this was too real. Two tickets to Cuba, the exact place Ruby and Juniper had wanted to go, on the exact day they'd planned to leave. This was *vicious.*

"She'll never go with me," Juniper said, blinking back tears. She was speaking to an empty room. To the Ringmaster. To herself. Even as she said it, her mind swam with possibilities. If she could convince Ruby to get on the plane, they'd have one week away from this place. One week away from the memories. The mistakes. She could apologize for the pain she'd caused, the two could make peace . . .

No, Juniper thought. *This is ridiculous. Like, full-blown nonsense.* She needed to grab Ruby and get out of this mansion. They could carry Gavin between them, if he wasn't pretending to be asleep. Parker and Brett could follow. Or they could kill each other to win a prize.

A chill unfurled in Juniper's stomach, and she went to pull the marker back out of the box. But as her fingers brushed the tip, she heard a scream from the room next door. Then a crashing sound, like a body hitting the wall.

Ruby.

8.

DADDY'S GIRL

Ruby took slow, measured breaths. She steadied her hands. But she couldn't steady her heart. Every time she looked around at the eerily arranged bedroom, her stomach tightened and her heartbeat spiked.

She was standing in a room that had been plucked from her dreams. There was a red velvet bedspread, so old that the red was fading to pink, and a vanity covered with antique jewelry. Ruby adored old things, unloved things, forgotten things. None of her stuffed animals had their original eyes. And that, too, was reflected here. Half a dozen teddy bears were strewn across the bed, each with glowing beads for eyes.

Red, of course. Ruby's favorite color.

She stepped up to the bed and cradled a teddy bear to her chest. It was comforting, even in this curious situation. Climbing onto the velvet bedspread, she lay back on the bed, hoping to calm her erratic heartbeat.

It took her a moment to notice the man. He was staring at her from the ceiling, his ginger hair messy. His brown eyes bright. Here, he was smiling. Here, he was pensive. Here, he was holding a redheaded baby in his arms, looking down at the child with so much love, tears filled Ruby's eyes.

She sat bolt upright, but she couldn't escape him. There was a framed photograph on the bedside table, which had been taken at a picnic, and it contained the whole Valentine family. Mother and father and kids. It was the last photograph they'd taken together, before her father disappeared.

Ruby screamed, hurling the photograph against the wall.

Glass shattered. For an instant, she felt better, vindication surging in her chest. Then she dissolved into tears. Her vision was swimming when Juniper burst into the room, a blur of blue sequins and black hair.

"What happened?" Juniper asked, hurrying to her side. "Was someone in here? Did they hurt you?"

Ruby lifted a finger and pointed. There, on the floor, lay the shattered remains of the photograph. Juniper crept over to it, lifting the wooden frame. "Who threw this?"

This time Ruby actually laughed, before her smile slipped away. "I did."

Juniper's eyes narrowed. "You threw . . . Oh." Understanding dawned on her face as she studied the collage above the bed. That thing was like a shrine to Ruby's father. There were giant poster-size photos. Itty-bitty wallet-size prints.

"Okay, I have to ask you something," Juniper said.

Ruby stared at the ground. Even now, two years later, the sight of her father's smile left her doubled over, gasping for breath. No matter how much time went by, the pain remained fresh. "Ask."

"Where did these pictures come from? I thought your mom tore up everything after he left."

Ruby nodded slowly. "She did," she said after a minute, unsure of how much she should say. "But she never cracked the password to his Facebook page. For a while, she kept checking it for updates, every hour on the hour, obsessing over it. Searching for a sign that he was out there. After a year of nothing, we ended up blocking him, because we couldn't . . ." She trailed off, dropping her head into her hands.

"I'm sorry," Juniper whispered, and Ruby knew what was coming. Even before the words passed Juniper's lips, she knew it. "I'm sorry for what's happening now, and for what I—"

"Don't." Ruby pushed off the bed, crossing the room. "I don't want to talk about it. I want to get out of here."

"We will," Juniper said at her back. "But I need you to hear this, one time. If I had any idea that he would *leave* because—"

"What did you think was going to happen?" Ruby spun around. "You called the cops on him."

"Ruby."

"The *cops*. Do you have any idea what it's like to have total strangers come into your house and ask you the most personal, humiliating questions? Questions about your father touching you, and 'can you show me where?' And 'can you tell me how many times?' My God, it wasn't even like that!"

"No, it wasn't like that." There was an edge to Juniper's voice. "It was only bruises in the crook of your arm. Little half-moon imprints on your neck. And then there was the day you came to school covered in bruises, and you told us that story about falling out of the tree in your yard. You said—"

"I must've hit every branch on the way down."

"And people believed you, because hey, Ruby Valentine was always a little bit reckless. Always a little bit feral. It was easy to imagine you, dangling from the topmost branches, trying to brush the moon with your fingertips. When you came to class in sunglasses, and told us you were playing 'Hollywood starlet,' it made perfect sense. But my favorite lie"—Juniper huffed, shaking her head—"was when you said you were being intentionally clumsy, so Edward Cullen would swoop in and save you from your own awkwardness."

Ruby chuckled, her cheeks flushing with heat. She was actually kind of proud of that one. It took a certain flair to keep people distracted, to keep them looking left, so they didn't realize what was happening right in front of them. It took sparkle and it took sleight of hand, and by the time she was in middle school, Ruby had become a master of illusion, at school and at home. She'd had to, in order to protect her sisters. Her mother. Herself. Every time her father's gaze had darkened, Ruby had leapt into action, putting on a show. She knew exactly what it took to make him laugh, to make him forget how angry he was.

Most of the time, she was successful.

But once in a while Ruby wasn't fast enough, and those were the nights she spent cradled in her father's arms while he sobbed into her hair. He told her that he loved her, and that he was sorry, and that he'd do whatever it took to get help. Because that was what he needed. Help. A loving support system. Not a slew of judgmental strangers interrogating his daughters in separate bedrooms while their mother sobbed in the kitchen.

"Everyone lied to protect him. But after the officers left, he looked so broken. So hurt. We'd spent so much time figuring out how to help him, and it all went out the window, didn't it? Because the next morning, he was gone, and there was no trace of him. His car was there, but he'd disappeared."

A soft sound escaped Juniper's lips. She sounded like someone had taken a bat to her stomach. Reaching into her little sequined purse, she pulled out her character card and handed it to Ruby.

Ruby read it aloud. *"My name is the Underwater Acrobat. I'm secretly in love with the Disappearing Act. My weapon is a marker because I ruin lives with labels. My greatest secret is—"*

"I wanted him to disappear," Juniper finished for her. "I thought it was part of the game, you know? Because we were at a murder mystery dinner."

"But we aren't, are we?" Ruby's gaze traveled to the ceiling. To the man so familiar, she still dreamt of him almost every night. "What is the point of this? Why taunt me with the one thing I can't have?"

"I don't think that's what's happening." Juniper glanced around the room. "Did you get a present?"

"What?"

"I got a gift. Like a Christmas present, except, you know, from a really twisted Santa Claus." She circled the bed, tossing stuffed animals aside. Behind the largest one, she discovered a black box with red ribbon.

Ruby's jaw dropped. "How the flying—"

"Everything is personal," Juniper said, returning to her side. "And nothing is here by coincidence. Remember when we used to play Bear Hospital?"

"Yeah, because my sisters always destroyed my babies." Ruby glanced at the bears on the bed. No matter how hard she'd tried to keep a couple of toys for herself, the girls had always managed to find them. And hug them. And pretty much love them to death. "But who would know that? You're the only person—"

"I don't know." Juniper tore at the ribbon. "I don't know, and it's freaking me the hell out. We played that game *years* ago."

Ruby swallowed as Juniper opened the box. Inside was a

single sheet of paper, and Ruby snatched it up, reading over the contents. "No, this is impossible."

"What is it?"

Ruby held out the paper with a shaking hand. The name JAMES VALENTINE was typed across the top, and below that, there was a list of information. Aliases, last known locations. According to the printout, Ruby's father had recently been spotted one county over, but all the crucial information had been blacked out. At the bottom of the page, someone had written, *Hand over your weapon, and I'll make all your dreams come true.*

Ruby turned to the box. There was nothing inside. Less than nothing, actually, because the box had been hollowed out in a very specific shape.

The shape of a revolver.

"Ruby?" Juniper whispered, scanning the room. Her gaze landed at the foot of the bed, where Ruby had dropped her purse. "What did the Ringmaster ask you to bring to the party?"

"I think you know." Ruby inched toward the foot of the bed.

Juniper followed. "And you brought a toy, right? Tell me you brought a toy."

"I . . ." Ruby dove for the purse. Juniper did, too, but Ruby got there first. "I wanted it to be realistic. The letter said authenticity was import—"

"Ruby!"

"I thought we were going to a party! A murder mystery dinner. And God, Juniper, it's not like I'd bring a *loaded* gun into a party with Parker Addison. What if he got his hands on it?"

"I don't even want to think about that. I just want to grab Gavin and get out of here. Do you think he's really passed out?"

"Passed out from what? He didn't drink anything! He lifted his glass to his lips, and then took a tumble." Ruby shook her head, hugging her purse to her chest. "He's probably sitting downstairs, wondering what the hell's taking us so long."

"Let's check on him, and then we'll come back for the guys."

"The guys are right next door! And if we brought weapons, I think it's safe to assume—"

"They brought weapons too." Juniper's gaze drifted to the door. "They could arm this stalker with a knife or—"

"A rope," Ruby said, slinging her purse over her shoulder. "But we have a revolver, and as far as anyone knows . . ." She paused, lips twisting into a grin. "This baby is loaded."

9.

HOPELESS ROMANTIC

Parker coiled the rope around his hand and tucked it neatly into the box. *Perfect fit,* he thought, before yanking the rope back out. Now, where to hide it? He shoved it under the mattress of the four-poster bed. Throwing himself onto the black satin sheets, he rolled around on his back, trying to feel for the rope. He could distinctly feel a lump under his right hip.

Nope, that wouldn't do. Parker lifted the mattress and pulled out the rope. Carefully, he scanned the room. A gilded mirror hung opposite the bed, something an evil queen might look into and proclaim herself the fairest of them all. But he couldn't secure the rope behind the mirror without risk of it falling down. There were no dressers in this room, no shelves. It was perfectly, elegantly simple. A bed with a mahogany frame. A little bedside table, with a bouquet of roses—

The bedside table, of course! Parker slid the rope into the tiny drawer, tucking it way up in the back. Then he fussed in front of the mirror for a minute, messing up his hair. His heart was racing. It had been a long time since he'd been alone in a bedroom with the love of his life. When the knock came at the door, he was sitting on the bed, toying with a rose.

"Parker? Park?" The voice was soft and sweet. Ruby Valentine. *My Ruby,* he thought, clearing his throat.

"Come in."

"No, you need to come out." This time, the voice was harsh and grating. Juniper Torres. *Of course.* Parker had left those girls alone for ten minutes, and already they were teaming up. Conspiring to keep Ruby away from him. He rose from the bed. He had to be delicate here. One wrong move, and Juniper would poison Ruby against him for good.

Opening the door a crack, he stuck his head outside. "Rubes," he said in a tentative voice. "I need to tell you something."

Ruby leaned in close, just like he knew she would. And before she could change her mind, Parker grabbed her arm and pulled her into the room. Closing the door, he turned the lock, keeping Juniper out.

"What the hell?" Ruby demanded, while Juniper pounded on the door. "You think you can grab me and—"

"Ruby, there's something weird going on here." Parker leaned against the door, letting his hair fall into his eyes. He knew how much Ruby loved it when his hair was a little messy. She used to trail her fingers along the edge of his face, tucking strands behind his ear.

Now she just stared at it, making no move to touch him. "I *know* something is wrong," she said, glancing at the door. "That's why we wanted to talk to you. This Ringmaster person is—"

"A stalker! You wouldn't believe what he tried to pull with me. He actually thought I would *trade* . . ." Parker shook his head, lifting several sheets of paper from the bed.

Ruby took the pages, scanning them in silence. "How the hell did you get these?"

"The Ringmaster gave them to me. I found them in a box."

"Parker, this is *everything* I've done in the past three months. My acceptance letter from Juilliard, the apartment I tracked down in the city. The lead on a job in a bookstore. Only the addresses are blacked out." Her hands shook as she read over the pages again. "Why do you have this?"

"So I can follow you."

Ruby's head snapped up, her eyes narrowed in fury. "Excuse me?"

"No, you don't understand." He reached for her arm, but she pulled away. "I would never do that. I'm not going to stalk you. That's just what the Ringmaster thinks I want."

"Why?" She sat down on the bed, wiggling a little in her sparkly red dress. Parker was glad he hadn't hidden the rope under the mattress.

"Because I love you," he said, kneeling in front of her. "You're the only person I've ever wanted, and when I lost you, it made me crazy."

Ruby snorted. "No shit, Park."

"I . . ." He swallowed, lowering his head. This time, when his hair fell into his eyes, he saw her fingers twitch. "I know I made mistakes. Big ones. But this . . ." He gestured to the pages still clutched in her hand. "I would never resort to this. Following you to New York? Staking out your apartment? Hell no."

Ruby watched him carefully, her breath coming out sharp and fast. "You want to know what's messed up? I don't even know if I believe you. Part of me thinks you would follow me to New York, stake out my favorite café, and pretend to run into me. You haven't exactly given me cause to believe otherwise."

"I know, but look." Parker plucked a box from the mess of pillows on his bed. "I was supposed to leave a weapon in this box in exchange for the information that's blacked out. A rope."

"And you didn't do it?" Ruby asked, picking up the box and searching it herself. "You're keeping the rope?"

"I left it in my car." Parker reached for his duffel bag, opening it to show there was nothing inside. "I was going to bring it in, but at the last minute, I got the creepiest feeling, like I shouldn't."

"Then why bring the bag?"

"To create the illusion that I was playing along. Plus . . ." He lifted a pair of jeans and a T-shirt from the bed. "I brought a change of clothes. You know I hate these things." He tugged at his collar, loosened his tie. He could see his reflection in the mirror, and in the dimness of the chandelier, the dark green suit looked black. "I look like a corpse."

Ruby laughed, and Parker saw a hint of her former sweetness. That girl was still in there; he just had to draw her out. "You do kind of look like you're dressed for your own funeral." She frowned, and her eyes clouded over. "That's why we need to get out of here. Everything about this is creepy, and now that we know we're being messed with—"

"We can't leave! We need to track this stalker down and kick some ass."

Ruby tilted her head. "Kick the ass of a stalker? That's brilliant. Did Brett come up with that?"

Parker scowled, glancing at the wall next to him. For the bulk of their conversation, Brett's room had been quiet, but now it sounded like somebody was moving furniture in there. "I don't think we're dealing with a stranger," he said. "I think someone from school is messing with us. Honestly, if Gavin wasn't playing dead downstairs, I'd say it was him."

Ruby bit her lip, looking toward Parker's door and the hall-way beyond. "We should check on him."

"Yeah, to make sure he's not laughing behind our backs."

"Parker," she started, but didn't finish. Something about his suggestion seemed to bother her. "You know, it is a common trick in horror movies to have the killer pretend to be dead."

"We'll check on him together," Parker said, leading her across the room. When he reached the door, he turned to face her. Their bodies were practically touching. "Rubes, I want you to know something. If this party turns out to be more than some twisted game . . . if it turns dangerous, I will do everything in my power to protect you. I'll throw myself in front of a bullet to keep you safe."

Ruby looked up, her eyes bright with the spark of tears. He knew, in that moment, that she was his. As she brushed the hair from his eyes, she smiled softly, as if remembering how good it felt to be close to him. "I really hope you mean that," she said.

10.

MOMMY DEAREST

Brett couldn't stop shaking. Sitting on the edge of the bed, head between his knees, he took great, heaving breaths, trying to calm himself. But the pictures on the wall taunted him.

You can have everything you want, they whispered. *You just have to play the game.*

Problem was, Brett didn't know what game they were playing. He'd suspected, in the depths of his subconscious, that the scholarship offer had been too good to be true. But like the rest of his classmates, he'd been desperate enough to attend the party anyway.

What did he have to lose?

Now, tearing a photograph from the wall, he knew the answer to that question. The image was bittersweet, enchanting and taunting at the same time. He wanted to cradle it. He wanted to rip it to shreds. In the end, he let it flutter from his hands, the way everything did.

Happiness. Power. His mother.

Brett looked up. Where had the thought come from? He hadn't thought of his mother in a very long time. But here, in this slate-gray room, with bars on the windows and the harbinger of death lingering at his back, he found himself struggling to remember the last time he'd actually been happy.

And there she was. Bright-eyed and beautiful and wearing a string of pearls. Taking her baby's face in her hands. Fawn Carmichael was the most affectionate person Brett had ever known, the exact opposite of his father.

No wonder she'd had to go.

Brett had been seven years old when it happened, and he remembered every detail of the dinner party. His father was a heavyweight champion. Or rather, he *used* to be a heavyweight champion, but after a series of wins in his youth, he'd gone on to suffer loss after humiliating loss. Now he was close to declaring bankruptcy. But if he could gain the sponsorship of one of the local business chains, he could make a dazzling comeback, and he wouldn't have to retire in shame.

And so, he threw a party. He decked out the Carmichael estate (which the bank was close to repossessing), and invited two dozen businessmen to spend an evening with his family. All Brett had to do was play the part of the perfect son. The fierce little boy who would follow in his father's footsteps.

A fighter, just like his daddy.

Getting ready in his parents' bedroom, Brett was trembling with nerves. "What if they don't like me?" he asked as his mother straightened his tie.

"Are you kidding?" She brushed the curls from his eyes. Those curls were chestnut brown, like hers before she dyed them. Everything about her was a little enhanced, but no matter how much work was done, her eyes remained as bright as a deer's. She was a domesticated animal, and that was something Brett understood, even at seven years old.

They were one and the same.

"They're going to love you," she promised, holding out her hand. "And it's only a couple of hours. We'll do our little dance for daddy's friends, and then we can dance for real when they're gone. All right?"

Brett took his mother's hand.

After that, they were partners in crime, putting on a show for the masses. Brett traded jabs with his father, ducking at all the right moments. Meanwhile, his mother stood perfectly still, like the statuary in the entryway to the house. Silent and poised.

Practically porcelain.

All she wanted to do was go out to the balcony and dance. Brett knew it. She used to be a ballerina, a real-life replica of the girl in her music box. Later that night, after everyone had gone home, she would lead Brett back to the second floor dining hall, pull him through a pair of french doors, and twirl with him on the balcony. Their house had been built onto a hill. With the city spread out beneath them, and the stars twinkling above, Mrs. Carmichael wouldn't seem like a caged animal anymore.

She'd be free.

She'd be *happy*, instead of a frozen, fairy-tale statue of herself. A nodding, doting wife. Two hours into the party, Brett knew her limbs were itching to move. She kept shifting from foot to foot, her ballerina's feet stuffed into high-heeled shoes.

And suddenly, the balcony was empty.

Mr. Carmichael was putting on a show for his guests, reenacting his first victory in the ring. The performance was elaborate. It required a volunteer from the crowd. If Brett and his mother were very stealthy, they could slip off to the balcony before the final punch.

So they did.

Like spies on a mission, they kept to the back walls, stifling their giggles. Mrs. Carmichael was tipsy on wine. She always drank a little too much at parties, to calm her nerves, and Brett took her hand as they neared the balcony. He wouldn't let anything happen to her. He would protect her from the wrought-iron railing, and the drop-off below.

They started off slowly, doing a little waltz in a little square. But over time, the dance grew more frantic. The louder the crowd became inside the house, the wilder Brett's mother became outside. Soon, she was spinning him in circles, and his feet were lifting off the ground. Brett shrieked in delight. His curls fell into his eyes, the world becoming a blur of laughter and light.

He didn't realize it, at first, when his mother's grip loosened. Everything was moving too fast. The feeling didn't register. It wasn't until he caught sight of his father, glaring at him through the balcony doors, that he felt himself slip out of his mother's hands.

For a second, he wanted to go over the edge of the balcony.

It was a desperate thought. He knew, in the depths of his bones, that his punishment was going to be fierce for ruining his father's performance. They could lose the house because of him. They could lose everything. But if he went careening over the railing and landed on the rocks below, his father would be too worried to be furious.

Brett didn't go over the edge. Instead he slammed into the wrought-iron railing, and one of the spires slid into his stomach. His vision blurred. His mouth tasted like copper. Then Mr. Carmichael was swooping in, lifting Brett into his arms. He was oddly gentle, and as Brett looked into his father's eyes, he honestly believed everything was going to be all right.

He wouldn't think that for long.

He was coming back from the hospital when the screaming started. He'd spent two hours in the emergency room, gotten twenty-three stitches, and had been in too much pain to ask where his mother was.

Now he felt a little drugged. He felt a little delirious as his father led him up to the house. When the front door burst open, and Brett heard his mother screaming, he thought he must be asleep. He must be having a nightmare. Then two men in white were dragging his mother out of the house, and she was sobbing that Brett was *her* baby and nobody could take her away from him. At that moment, a cold dread settled over Brett's skin. He wrestled out of his father's grip, scrambling toward the door. If he could reach his mother in time, her arms would encircle him and she'd tell him that everything was fine. She wasn't going away. She was always going to be in his life.

Brett never reached his mother's side, because his father wrapped him up in a bear hug. "You'll hurt yourself. Stay still." Brett didn't listen. The men in white were guiding his mother into a car, and Brett was screaming and clawing, just like she had. And, just like she had, he failed to break free from the arms that held him, and eventually, his snarling gave way to exhausted sobs.

His father carried him into the house.

All through the night, he listened for the click of the front door opening, and the sound of his mother's voice. The soft hands and the bright eyes. But she didn't come for him. Instead his father swept into his bedroom at the first light of dawn, kneeling before his son's bed. "Your mother is sick."

"No, she isn't."

Mr. Carmichael rubbed his eyes. "You must've seen the signs. The woman is determined to disappear into nothing, and the alcohol doesn't help. If I hadn't installed cameras on the balcony, I never would've been able to prove—"

"Cameras?" Heat flooded Brett's cheeks, fierce and hot. "You were watching us?"

"I needed to prove how dangerous she was," his father said gently. "To herself. To you. Now she can get the help she needs."

"Help?" Brett whispered, trying to make sense of his father's words. Yes, his mother was constantly restricting her diet, and yes, she drank a lot at parties, but Brett would've done the same if he were a grown-up. Those parties were horrible. And Mrs. Carmichael was bored. Unfulfilled. A ballerina trapped in a snow globe, trying to make the best of the situation.

He opened his mouth to defend her. But his father cut him off, wrapping an arm around his shoulders. Brett couldn't remember the last time they'd touched when there weren't people around. "If your mother's going to get stronger, you need to get stronger too. All this giggling and dancing together . . . it was cute when you were a baby. But it's not healthy for a boy of your age."

Brett narrowed his eyes. Never, in a million years, had he suspected that he'd been *hurting* himself by dancing with his mother. Their time spent together was the only thing that made his home life bearable. But now, with his father peering down at him, his stomach twisted and his chest felt tight. "I can be stronger," he promised. "I can be the strongest, and then she'll come back."

"You can try," his father said, brushing the curls from his eyes. "Maybe we can train together. I can teach you to fight, and when she sees how hard you're trying, she'll want to try hard too."

"And then she'll come home," Brett said, already planning how to get big and strong, like his father wanted. Like his mother needed. He would be unstoppable, and his mother would come back.

Now, sitting on a bed in the Cherry Street Mansion, he thought of all the sacrifices he'd made to bring his mother home. He'd given up dancing. He'd given up joy. He'd weeded out all the sweet, elegant parts of himself, and still, she hadn't come home.

Even after she got better. Even after she left the facility. Instead she met another man and started another family. She moved on.

And now, it seemed that Parker had moved on too. Brett could hear him, one wall away, murmuring to the only person he'd ever cared about. Ruby Valentine. For a minute, he just sat there, listening to their voices. When silence fell, Brett didn't have to search his imagination to know what was happening. Would they tear off each other's clothes right there and devour each other on Parker's bed? Would Brett have to listen to it?

A pang shot through his stomach, and he lifted a box from the floor. A single sheet of paper sat inside of it, and he pulled it out, reading with resignation.

It would be quick. Painless. Exactly how you want it.

Brett took the pair of brass knuckles from his pocket, passing them from hand to hand. Left to right. Right to left. Was he really doing this? He could hear Parker murmuring again, could hear Ruby's voice softening, and he came to a decision.

The brass knuckles slid out of his hands, and his heartbeat calmed. He returned the lid to the box. The sheet of paper was still lying on the bed, and he left it there as he pushed the box under the mattress, where his classmates wouldn't find it.

Then he set to work destroying the evidence.

11.

PICTURE PERFECT

The way Juniper saw it, she had two options. She could pound on Parker's door until her hands went numb or she could get help. Brett Carmichael was the only other person in the world who knew how dangerous the Ruby/Parker partnership could be. Those two were either all over each other, drooling and pawing and letting the rest of their lives fall to ruin, or Parker was chasing after Ruby like a stalker.

Like, seriously. Multiple times, Juniper had seen him stationed outside of Ruby's car, making sure she went straight home after school. Once, he'd snuck into the auditorium during play practice, only to start a fight when Ruby's scene partner got "too handsy."

The dude was unstable.

Juniper kicked his door. But she wasn't used to wearing heels, and she ended up hopping backward on one foot, knocking into a portrait on the opposite wall. Funny, she hadn't really examined it before.

But she did now.

It featured a family of four, all with black hair and blue eyes. Startling blue eyes, the kind that people called "magical" if they liked you and "creepy" if they saw you as a threat. One year ago, a boy with eyes like that had walked the halls of Fallen Oaks High, and Parker Addison had seen him as a threat.

Three weeks later, that boy was dead.

Juniper turned away from the painting, telling herself she was making an unfair connection. Tons of families had a little girl and a little boy with piercing blue eyes. Dark, disheveled hair. Things may have been getting weird in this mansion, but she wasn't ready to go *there* yet.

She'd rather go out the front door. But she couldn't leave without Ruby, so she picked up her feet and walked toward Brett's room. Just as her knuckles hit the wood, the door flung open and Brett pushed past her. In that moment, Juniper's mind went to the worst possible place. Brett was being attacked.

They were all going to be captured, toyed with, and killed.

One glance into Brett's room confirmed that she was being irrational. No other person was in there. No discernible *thing* was in there, except a bed with messy gray sheets and a floor that was covered—literally covered—with some kind of confetti.

"You okay?" Juniper asked, studying Brett's face. His cheeks were a dangerous magenta, as if he'd exerted himself almost to the point of passing out. That was saying something, for someone in Brett's physical condition.

"I'm fine," he said, leaning against a wall. His teeth were clenched. Still, his face had an incongruous sweetness to it, and Juniper found herself thinking of the boy he'd been before his life had fallen apart. First his mother had been taken from him. Then he'd lost his family home. For the past ten years, he and his father had been crammed into a one-bedroom apartment in the worst part of town.

What would he give to change all of that?

"Can I?" she asked, gesturing to his bedroom. The door was wide open. When he nodded, practically dismissing her with a wave of his hand, she stepped into the room and realized why. Much like the previous two bedrooms, this room had been covered with photographs. And Brett had torn every single one of them to shreds.

"Clearly, the Ringmaster offered you something," she said, and Brett's breathing quickened. "Don't worry, I'm not going to ask you what it was. I only care about what he wanted—"

Brett started to move. Right in the middle of her sentence, he turned away from her. Normally, this wouldn't have been surprising—they weren't exactly friends—but the movement had been deliberate. He'd seen something, and he was following it.

Juniper stepped out of his room. Her eyes were drawn, inevitably, to the family portrait. But Brett hadn't turned to face the wall. He was staring, completely frozen, at the door at the end of the hallway.

The door that was open.

"What the hell?" She was certain the door had been closed when she'd entered Brett's bedroom. "Did you . . ."

"What, with my wizard magic? You've seen me standing here this entire time."

She swallowed. "Maybe Gavin, then? Could he have snuck up here while we were in our bedrooms?"

"It wouldn't have mattered. The room was locked." Brett brushed past her, toward the open door. "Whoever's in there has probably been there the entire time. Stay here while I find out—"

"No, you . . . you can't go alone," Juniper managed, creeping after him. From Parker's bedroom, she could hear snippets of hushed conversation. No crying. No screams. She reminded herself to remember the actual threat while she was investigating the invisible one.

She *knew* Parker was dangerous.

As she neared the open doorway, she noticed the portraits on the wall were changing. Not that the portraits were different, exactly. The *same* portrait had been hung over and over again, with changes made to each one. The first, which Juniper had already seen, contained four people: a mother, a father, a son, and a daughter. In the second portrait, on the opposite wall, the mother was missing. Like, photoshopped out. Except these weren't photos, and the eeriness of her absence reminded Juniper of dead things, of ghosts. The mother had *vanished* from a *painting*.

"How the . . . ?" she whispered.

Just ahead of her, Brett looked back. "What?"

"Eyes on the road," she said, fists tightening. If she was going to be studying every detail of the house, she needed him to pay attention to the task at hand. The mysterious door that had opened of its own accord. Juniper wouldn't entertain the possibility that the house was haunted, but she was starting to wonder if her theory about the portraits was correct. She was starting to wonder, while at the same time bending over backwards to convince herself it was impossible. *Ruby didn't go to the party last year,* she reminded herself. *Gavin went, but he didn't hurt anyone.*

Then she saw the third portrait. There, an arm's length from the open doorway, which now seemed to be emitting the faintest of music. It was soft and tinkling, like something you'd hear when you opened a music box. Juniper tried to envision a ballerina dancing on one foot. She tried to envision a pretty porcelain unicorn. Anything, really, to distract from the reality of what was in front of her.

In the third portrait, the little boy was missing.

"Hey." A voice called from inside the room. Brett's voice, but Juniper could barely see him. She reached for a light switch before entering. Her fingers flipped the switch, but nothing happened.

"I'm right here," Juniper said, placing a hand on his back.

Brett jumped. The ass-kicking, unstoppable force of nature leapt at the feel of her. Wheeled around. For a minute, they stared at each other, eyes wide. Then Brett muttered, "Prepare yourself."

Juniper couldn't. She was already freaked out. But as she peered around him, she told herself to take in the room in little pieces, analyzing everything. She told herself, and immediately forgot.

"It's a playroom," she said. A playroom fit for a giant. A ridiculously large train set looped in circles in a corner. Stuffed animals the size of lions littered the floor. French doors were opened on the opposite side of the room, leading to an empty balcony, and moonlight filtered in, revealing glimpses of a table.

That table was huge, of course. Not quite as long as the one in the dining room, but large enough to seat eight, and positioned in the center of what was obviously the master bedroom. Oversize teddy bears were stuffed into chairs, and on the table was the most elaborate tea set Juniper had ever seen. *Something Ruby would kill for,* she thought, and felt a pang as she looked in the direction of Parker's room. She needed to get Ruby out of there. Brett could break down the door if he needed to. Then they'd escape from this weird, creepy tea party where animals drank from little cups and humans weren't invited.

Oh wait, there they were, down at the far end of the table. Two dolls, the size of people, sitting side-by-side. A boy and a girl. His hair was dark as midnight, and hers was a startling white. Juniper couldn't make out the color of their eyes. In fact, their eyes seemed to be closed, and she took a step closer, wondering if she could get them to open.

Plenty of dolls could open and close their eyes.

She wasn't sure why she was fixated on that now. The girl at the end of the table didn't have black hair. That threw off her entire theory, but she wanted to know. She needed to know. She stepped closer.

"What are you doing?" Brett asked.

This time, Juniper jumped. His voice seemed to shake her out of a spell. *The house isn't haunted. This party isn't about revenge. Get a grip.*

"I just need to check something," she said, glancing around the room. There was a door to the left, likely leading to a bathroom, but someone had pulled a bookshelf in front of it, and the closet to the right stood empty and open. Juniper and Brett were the only ones in here, except for the toys.

They were safe.

And so, she crept up to the life-size doll on the right. The girl. The boy's face was shadowed by a large top hat, but the girl's was perfectly visible. Juniper saw white skin, cheeks dusted with rouge, and a mouth that looked . . . strange. Almost like darker lipstick had been drawn over the painted doll's mouth, to give the impression of a stain. Juniper half expected her to smile. It would start out slowly, with the tiniest twitch in the corner of her mouth, and then bleed across her face like blood in the snow.

Juniper swallowed, listening for the sound of Brett's breathing. He was behind her. She could hear him. Reaching out a hand, like Sleeping Beauty drawn in by a spindle, she touched the pale shoulder. The doll was wearing a white lace dress, and Juniper was heartened by the fact that she hadn't touched its skin. She'd never seen a porcelain doll of this size before, and the sight was unnerving. She gave it a shake and leapt back.

Nothing happened.

She pushed out a laugh, turning to Brett. But Brett wasn't laughing. He was staring behind her back, his arm rising, as if pulled by a string. Right back at the doll, he pointed.

Right back at the doll, Juniper looked.

Suddenly she was falling into cerulean pools. The doll's eyes were a startling blue, made out of realistic glass. Juniper's heart started to pound, and she took a step back. She should've looked away. But every time the shadows shifted, she thought she caught sight of the girl's lips moving. A trick of the eye, she knew, but she couldn't turn around.

The scream hit her back. It was raw and jagged, like the knife a killer would use to carve out a doll's mouth on a person.

It was also familiar.

"Ruby." Juniper spun around. Then she was bolting across the room, but her leg caught on a chair and she stumbled. She envisioned herself hitting the floor. Envisioned that girl rising from the chair, slowly, like a reanimated corpse. Her hand would lift, and there would be a knife clutched in her fingers, and then—

"I got you," Brett said, grabbing hold of her before she hit the floor. With little effort at all, he pulled her toward the door. Just as she reached the threshold, Juniper heard a creak behind them, and she burst forward, passing through the doorway.

Together, they raced down the hall. Parker's door was open, and it took only a glance to see that nobody was inside. Then they were thundering down the staircase, chasing the ghost of a scream that had trailed off moments ago.

They found the body at the foot of the stairs. Someone had dragged him out of the dining room, the better to wrap him up in pretty red ribbons. Except . . . the ribbons weren't literal ribbons, and Juniper slapped a hand over her mouth as she realized what had been done. Bright red slashes covered Gavin's face, his forearms, his neck. But this was no arbitrary hack job, oh no. On every inch of exposed skin, *words* had been carved into him.

"Oh God." Juniper swayed on the bottom step. Someone must've brought a knife to the party, but who? Parker, with his wicked sense of justice? Brett, with his fists so powerful, he didn't need to hold anything in them to get the job done? Juniper knew for a fact that Ruby had brought a revolver, and she'd brought a simple marker—

"Wait," she said, as the others crowded around her. Ruby and Parker were there, dancing in her periphery like ghosts. But she couldn't take her eyes off Gavin; she couldn't breathe until her suspicions were confirmed. Kneeling beside him, she slid a finger across his wrist. Her finger came away clean. Gavin hadn't been carved into with the sharp edge of a knife. He'd been *written* on in red marker.

Juniper actually smiled.

Then her gaze trailed up the stairway, toward the room where the permanent marker should've been hiding. She couldn't see it from her vantage point at the base of the stairs. All she could see was the edge of that first creepy portrait, the one that reminded her of two very specific people. A girl and a boy.

"You guys," she started, still looking up. Before she could give voice to her fears, Ruby cut her off.

"Shithead," she whispered, and Juniper's head snapped to the left.

"What?"

"Loser. Tool."

"What the hell, Rubes?" Parker broke in, his laughter entirely inappropriate in that moment. "Do we need to hire an exorcist?"

"Screw off," Ruby snarled, which didn't exactly discredit his theory. But one glance at Gavin's arm showed Juniper what she'd missed before. Ruby wasn't spouting off nonsense. She was *reading*.

"Who would write this?" Juniper asked, studying Gavin's skin. She was heartened by the fact that his chest was moving, up and down, like it had been when she'd checked his vitals in the dining room. Still, they should get him off the floor. They should get him out of this house, away from all the creepiness.

The danger.

And yet, there was a part of Juniper that wanted to understand, here and now. Maybe it was a design flaw, the part of the human brain that got pretty girls killed in horror movies. *Things can't possibly be as bad as you think*, the brain reasoned, and sometimes it was a good thing. It kept you calm in dangerous situations. Allowed you to plot your next move. Other times, it rooted you to the spot just long enough for the killer to sneak up behind you, and the second you turned around, a dagger slid into your chest.

In that moment, a single phrase kept Juniper rooted to the spot, her eyes narrowing and narrowing but never focusing on the words. "White trash?" she said, turning Gavin's arm as if it were a hologram. As if, when turned two clicks to the left, those words would transform into something that made sense.

Behind her, Parker snorted. "How can he be white trash? The dude's Asian."

"Gold star, Parker," Ruby muttered, shaking her head. "You come up with that all on your own?" Still, her eyes were narrowed, just like Juniper's, staring at those words as if there was a code inside them. Now that "white trash" had been discovered, the girls found more words that called the vandal's rationality into question. "Deviant" was curled into the crook of Gavin's elbow in grand, swooping letters. Juniper couldn't make sense of it. It wasn't until she looked up at Brett that her heart really started to pound. Sure, it had practically stopped beating when she thought Gavin had been carved up like a Thanksgiving turkey, and had sprung back to life when she realized he hadn't. But now, looking at the *understanding* in Brett's eyes, she felt all the blood in her body rushing to her heart.

"What?" she asked, holding Brett's eye.

"I . . . I've seen this," he said, backing away. For a minute, she thought he might back out of the house that way, never turning around. She shuddered to think of what would happen if someone came up behind him before he made it to his car. Someone who decided a marker wasn't powerful enough. "Last year," Brett told her, "at Dahlia Kane's Christmas party, I found that boy passed out by the pool with writing all over him."

That boy, Juniper thought, as if Brett could ever forget his name. As if it wasn't etched into each of their memories. Carved, the way she'd thought Gavin's skin had been carved.

"Somebody wrote 'white trash' on him?" Juniper asked, her gaze returning to Gavin. Out of the corner of her eye, she spied Brett glancing at Parker. Parker nodded, the tiniest bit.

"Yeah," Brett said, and then, still looking at Parker, added, "Gavin wrote it."

Juniper's head snapped up. "What? No, he didn't."

Brett and Parker nodded.

"No, Gavin wouldn't do that. You're setting him up." Still, even as she said it, she realized how illogical it sounded. As illogical as someone writing *white trash* on Gavin. As illogical as being haunted. "Can everyone back up? I need to check his vitals—"

"*No,*" Ruby shouted, and her voice startled all of them. "Don't you know what's happening? He's coming for us."

"Who?" Brett asked, daring her to speak the boy's name. But Ruby was too afraid to utter it, too afraid to dig up the secret they'd buried with a body so badly burned, he'd had to be identified by his teeth.

Parker wasn't afraid. Maybe he simply refused to admit the possibility that the boy had come back for them. Or maybe he'd gone his entire life without suffering repercussions for anything, so he couldn't see what was coming. Either way, Juniper saw Ruby close her eyes as the name passed through his lips. It should've been whispered like a secret, but Parker spat it like a curse. "Shane Ferrick."

12.

FERAL CHILD

The morning of their arrival, Fallen Oaks was hit with a storm. The doors of the high school rattled and an oak branch crashed through a window during AP Bio. Then the fog parted to reveal two strangers. Skinny legs and tattered clothes. Pale skin and ebony hair.

At ten o'clock on December 3, they pushed through the great crimson doors of the school, bringing with them the rain. Everyone turned to stare. You couldn't blame them, really; the Ferricks were mesmerizing. The kind of people who might've been ghosts slipping onto the mortal plane for a time, and then vapor.

And then wind.

Ruby Valentine was pulling a chemistry book from her locker when it happened. Later she would attribute meaning to this, as if the universe were some great, conspiring witch and everything she did, she did with a wink and a smile, giving you flashes of her grand design. *Chemistry, indeed,* Ruby would think, heat flooding her chest. But at the time, she wasn't looking at the title of the book. She knew it by its cover, and besides, her focus was entirely elsewhere. She was looking inward, lost in some daydream or another, when Shane Ferrick walked by.

His twin sister must've been with him. They were always together, back then. But Ruby remembered Brianna's presence the way she remembered the book: important in retrospect, but irrelevant at the time. A whisper in a storm. What mattered was that the chemistry book went flying out of Ruby's hands the minute she met Shane Ferrick's eye. All around her, boys looked on, perfectly capable of picking up that book, of doing the gentlemanly thing. But none of them moved, and whether it was because Ruby was *Parker's*, or because they wanted to see cleavage when she bent over, Ruby wasn't sure. In the end, it didn't matter, because Shane waved his sister along, dropped to one knee, and picked up her book.

Ruby froze. She'd dated Parker long enough to know the kinds of games boys played, and she squared her shoulders, preparing to fight Shane for the book. First he'd tuck it under his arm and rise to his feet. Then he'd take a step back, holding it over his head. Before long, she'd be standing on her tiptoes, bouncing and reaching and making a fool of herself.

Down on the floor, Shane looked up. Ruby shivered, wrapping her arms around herself. She was wearing a pale pink cardigan with little strawberries all over it, and a short, kind of swishy pink skirt. She knew she looked adorable. But Shane wasn't looking at her like she was *cute*, or even like she was beautiful. He was looking at her like he could see right into the core of her being and was awed by what he found there.

Humbled.

"You dropped this," he said, holding out the book. Ruby took it before he could change his mind. Still, he knelt there, staring up at her, and she wasn't chilled anymore. A warmth was spreading from her head to her toes. She curled the latter, wanting to dance. To spin. To twirl.

Just that moment, someone's phone started to ring. It could've made Ruby jump, could've broken the spell she had over Shane, but it didn't. A smile curved over his face. Everything about him was celestial—moon-pale skin, a smile as bright as the glittering stars, and those twilight-blue eyes—and Ruby felt she'd do anything to step into his universe, for even a second.

As the sappy, poppy love song blared from the nearby phone, he held out his hand. "May I have this dance?"

Ruby didn't think. She didn't breathe. Instead, she slipped the book into her backpack, then pulled the boy to his feet. Her arms went around his neck, his hands slid onto her hips, and for the briefest of moments, they danced.

What Ruby would remember, later on, was that his eyes never left her face. She could feel a blush creeping over her cheeks. But when she tried to duck away from him, resting her head on his shoulder, he whispered, "You don't have to do that with me."

"Do what?" She looked up.

"You don't have to hide."

Tears sparked in Ruby's eyes. She'd been hiding for a very long time. Ever since her father disappeared, and people started looking at her with pity, she'd boarded up the windows to her soul and kept a mask on at all times.

No one could get inside.

Now this stranger was looking at her, and the sadness in his eyes mirrored her own. Did he understand what she'd been through? Had he been through it too? Ruby was desperate to know more about him, and she opened her mouth to ask his name.

When the bell rang, it nearly jolted her out of her skin. The boy stepped back, bowing deeply, like this was some grand masquerade ball and she'd picked him to be her partner. Like he'd been honored by her choosing him. And she felt, as he looked up at her, that they were both wearing masks, and no one could see her true face except for him. No one could look into his eyes and recognize his soul the way that she could.

She stepped away, shaken. The bell had stopped ringing, but she could hear the echo of it, and it was so much less pleasant than even a cheesy pop song could be. Ruby was cringing at the thought of saying goodbye. She hadn't noticed the boy's clothing before, but now she could see that his jeans were faded and his T-shirt had a couple of holes. He was a feral child, dropped into the land of domesticated, obedient humans, and Ruby wanted to run away with him to the forest.

She wanted to keep dancing.

He rose from his bow, his cheeks pink and his hair falling into his eyes. "Until next time, Strawberry."

She frowned. "Strawberry?"

He nodded to her top. The silly pink cardigan covered in berries. Suddenly she felt like a child, dressed that way. But he leaned in, as if to brush her cheek with his lips, and whispered, "They're my absolute favorite. How did you know?"

"The universe told me," she replied, not wanting to play the baffled, blushing girl anymore. That wasn't her. Not really. "But she looked like a wrinkled wicked witch, and she promised if I wore this today, my life would change."

His eyebrows shot up. They were dark and expressive, and Ruby wanted to trace her fingers along them, feeling him lean into her touch. "Was she right?" he asked.

Ruby shrugged, growing aware of the people gathering around them. "We'll see," she said, disappearing into the crowd.

+ + +

By fourth-period lunch, everyone was talking about the exchange in the junior hallway. Ruby knew she'd made a mistake. When Parker tracked her down in the courtyard, he sat next to her so hard, the bench shuddered under his weight. And he looked at her, with this searing gaze that seemed to say, *Do you have anything to say for yourself?*

Ruby didn't. The high school rumor mill was just that, and if she didn't cave under the pressure of Parker's stare, he'd never know the truth. Not for sure. Still, later on she would think, *Maybe that was all it took*. One dance in the hallway, and Parker would start plotting his revenge. Ruby was, after all, his girl, and everyone in Fallen Oaks knew it.

Shane Ferrick would know it soon enough.

13.

POKER FACE

"He's coming for us," Ruby said, backing away from the staircase. Away from Gavin, and the ugly red words written on his skin. "We have to go *now*."

Parker hurried to her side. He could not let her leave this house. If she left, he'd never be able to win her back. And so he looped an arm around her waist, led her right to the patio doors . . . and stopped.

"Park?" She looked up at him. "What is it?"

Parker paused, inhaling sharply. His eyes were narrowed as he stared at the patio, and the sparkling pool beyond. "It's nothing," he murmured, reaching for the doors.

Just like he knew she would, Ruby stopped him. "Tell me," she said, peering into his eyes.

"Shane can't be coming for us. You know he can't."

"I know," Ruby said softly. Then, even more quietly, she added, "I know, and I don't."

"Look, I get where your mind is going. We're all thinking it: dental records can be switched. What if he pulled off some grand illusion last year and is coming back to—"

"I wasn't even at the party," Ruby interjected.

"I know." Parker sighed, brushing the crimson hair out of

her face. "And you don't deserve any of this. You don't deserve to be messed with. But we *are* being messed with, Ruby. Some punk saw too much at that party last year and wants to screw with our heads. Shane Ferrick is exactly where he was the last time we saw him. At the Fallen Oaks Cem—"

"Please." She twisted out of his grip. "I can't talk about him. I just want to go home."

"We will." Again, Parker paused, looking out into the darkness. "But really think about that night, Ruby. Think about how it ended. If someone isn't messing with us . . . If they're actually trying to hurt us, then what happened to Gavin is just the beginning. The first in a long series of attacks. And it all comes to an end—"

"In a car," Ruby whispered, pressing gloved fingers to the glass. Brett and Juniper had followed them into the dining room, and Gavin was dangling from Brett's arms.

"Look, it's probably some jackass playing a prank," Parker said, guiding Ruby away from the glass.

"And if it isn't?" she asked. "If this person is trying to hurt us?"

Parker caught her gaze and held it. "Then getting into a car is the most dangerous thing we can do."

Ruby sucked in a breath. She looked small and helpless, staring up at Parker with her big blue eyes. He wanted to pull her into his arms. Instead he ushered her out of the dining room. He was the leader now, the protector, and he was going to lead this ragtag crew to salvation.

He waved them down the hall.

"Wait! Where are you going?" Juniper demanded, tossing glances back the way they'd come. Out of everyone, Parker pitied her the most. Gavin's punishment had been fairly tame.

But Juniper, well. Parker still didn't understand why she'd lashed out at Shane Ferrick the way she had. Even if it had been a desperate attempt to get into Ruby's pants, it wouldn't have made sense. Juniper was the save-the-world-or-die-trying type.

Girls like that didn't try to drown people.

"Living room," Parker called behind his back, leading the group past the stairs. He could feel Ruby tensing the farther they got from the exit. Leaning in, he whispered, "We need to keep Juniper away from the pool."

She nodded, pressing into him.

They came to a set of double doors, so dark they were almost black, and Parker pushed them open with absolutely no fear. Inside, black velvet sofas lounged about like lazy panthers. Someone had lit a fire in the fireplace. The others fussed over this, feeling their tormentor's presence behind every closed door, but Parker appreciated the warmth. Between the soft sofas and the flickering light, he'd have Ruby cuddled up in his arms in no time. But first, the investigation. Every mystery had a detective running the show, and Parker was happy to slip into that role. After Brett laid Gavin down on a sofa, Parker enlisted his help in blocking the doors. There was no lock to keep people out, but the glass coffee table was sturdy enough to keep someone from entering the room silently, yet light enough to toss aside if they needed to escape.

He gestured to the doors. "I want everyone on alert. Until we know what we're dealing with, it's best to assume the worst."

"I thought you said some punk was messing with us," Ruby said, perched on the edge of a sofa. No one had really gotten comfortable yet, in spite of the room's warmth.

"I did," Parker told her, keeping his distance. Now that he'd led her here, he wasn't going to crowd her. "But until we have proof, you'd better believe I'm going to do everything I can to keep you safe."

Ruby's eyes softened, and inside, Parker cheered. Outside, his face was dead serious, his jaw set in a firm line.

"No, I don't like this." Juniper was hovering by the doors. "We can't just hide in here all night."

"Why not?" Ruby pulled tweezers out of her purse, along with her keys. "In the morning, we'll be able to search our cars for anything suspicious. But right now, it's pitch black out there, and the yard is filled with hedges carved into monsters. There are dozens of places to hide, and if this person is dangerous—"

"This person is dangerous! They knocked Gavin out! We can carry him between us—"

"What if we get attacked? We can't defend ourselves if we're carrying a person, and if we set him down, we'll be leaving *him* defenseless." Ruby looked mournfully at Gavin. "I'm sorry, Junebug, but this is the right choice."

Parker's chest swelled. This, more than anything, was what he loved about Ruby Valentine. She was a queen. And as long as she stayed in her castle, Juniper would stay to protect her.

Just like Brett would stay to protect him.

"See, this is why you're my defense team," he said to the girls. "You're always thinking of ways to defend the group."

"Defense team?" Ruby's brow furrowed. "And what does that make you, exactly? Offense?"

"Yep." Parker lifted a poker from a stand by the fireplace. "I figure a two-pronged approach is best. Brett and I will track this asshole down while you girls stay here, keeping Gavin safe." He smiled, like he was so damn proud to see Ruby sitting there, clutching her tweezers like a weapon. "Honestly, I feel bad for the idiot who tries to take you on."

Ruby swallowed, taking her lip between her teeth, and it was all Parker could do not to push her against the wall. Lift her up, and feel her legs wrap around him. There was a bedroom *right upstairs* with their name on it, a fantasy palace with satin sheets and a four-poster bed. But Parker told himself to wait. By the time the third victim got hit, Ruby would be begging him to lock her up in that room.

And then . . . bliss.

Still, he told himself it would be okay to take one little taste, and he sidled up to her. "If I don't make it back—"

"Stop." Her voice was cold, but she was leaning into him. This rudeness was just a game she played, that hard-to-get fuckery that made him want her more. "You're coming back. You told me it wasn't dangerous."

"I did," he agreed. "But I've been wrong before." It was the first time he'd admitted it. The first time those words had *ever* come out of his mouth. "And I want you to know, I would die a thousand times for you."

"That's easy to say—"

"Well." He backed away, looking wounded. "Maybe if you're lucky, you'll get your way and I'll prove it."

"Park."

He turned, stalking to the doors before she could stop him. He'd thought it would be good to leave on a sappy note, but honestly, this was so much better. Now she'd spend the entire time feeling guilty. She'd spend the entire time thinking about how horrible it would be if he died before she could take back her words. By the time he returned, she'd be desperate for him.

With Brett's help, he inched the coffee table away from the doors and peered into the hall. Finding the coast clear (surprise, surprise), he slipped outside, letting Brett follow him. Then he closed the doors with a click.

14.

KARMA POLICE

When Parker closed the doors behind them, Brett stared straight ahead. He was shaken, more shaken than he'd been in a long time, and the words on Gavin's skin were only the tip of the iceberg. As Parker turned to him, a concerned look in his eye, Brett realized this partnership had nothing to do with Parker wanting his company. Clearly, he could see Brett coming undone at the seams and wanted to do damage control.

"Relax," Parker said, so easily. As if panicking was only a choice, and not the result of a lifetime of suffering. A lifetime of guilt. Parker's voice was powerful, and Brett could feel warm honey sliding over him, soothing the broken parts. He had this beautiful moment where he thought that everything was going to be okay, no matter what they'd done or what had been done to them. Then a flash of movement caught his eye, and fear slammed into him at full force, stealing his breath. He lifted a hand, pointing toward the entryway to the kitchen.

"I saw something," he said.

Parker didn't question him. That was the beauty of their relationship, the thing that always kept Brett coming back. He could say anything, literally any ridiculous thing, and Parker would accept it. It was the exact opposite of his life at home, where everything he said was wrong. Or nonexistent. He couldn't count the times his words had been entirely ignored, as if, the moment he walked through the door of his father's apartment, he lost the ability to make noise. His dad looked right through him, but his friend simply nodded.

"Let's do this, then," Parker said, clutching the poker he'd stolen from the living room.

Together, they hurried to the kitchen. The white marble island was deceptively cheery, the appliances glistening as if they'd been recently polished. Everything about the room was exactly as they'd left it, with two exceptions: their cell phones were gone from the tray, and a freestanding chalkboard, the kind restaurants used to list their daily specials, had been set up against the far wall.

Parker reached the chalkboard first, muttering, "Was this here before?"

"If it was, I didn't notice it. But either way, someone's been in here since we left." It was obvious now. Brett couldn't blame the flash of white on a trick of the eyes. Someone had been in here *seconds* before them, writing each of their names on the little specials board. Each of their character names. And now, the Invisible Man had been crossed out.

"It's true, then," Brett murmured. "Someone's coming for each of us. It couldn't be Shane, but what if—"

"Oh my God, Brett." Parker was smiling, like, actually *grinning* while Brett's heart thrashed about in his chest. Slamming and slamming against him. "Haven't you figured it out yet?"

"Figured out what?" Heart pounding. Hands shaking. God, where was his flask? Even as he thought it, he knew he couldn't succumb to the craving. After what he'd done in his bedroom, he needed to keep his wits about him.

He leaned into the counter, facing away from the specials board. He was not some delicacy to be sliced up. He was not the Iron Stomach. He was a boy. A boy who'd gotten mixed up in some very, very dark shit last year and had been paying for it ever since.

"Come on." Parker jogged into the dining room. The sixth character card was sitting at the end of the table, and he snatched it up. "We'll need this, if we're going to fill in the blanks. Got a pen on you?"

"You're still playing the game? After everything that's happened?" Brett stepped closer, softening his voice. "After everything we did?"

"*I* didn't do anything," Parker snapped. "All I did was hold the guy while you . . ." He shook his head, leaning in. "You're going to be fine. I'd never let anything happen to you, all right?"

Brett nodded, that honey-gold voice washing over him. All of his muscles relaxed. At first he didn't react to the sight of the girl standing on the other side of the glass, so ghostly pale she could've been an apparition. Lips so dark, they looked like a gash. Like someone had slid a knife across her face and made her mouth out of blood and scars.

She lifted an object in her hands.

"The rope," Brett said, pointing to the glass.

Parker spun around. But as suddenly as she'd appeared, the girl was gone.

Brett blinked, rushing to the patio doors. No trace. No glimpse of white. Just cold, cold darkness. "She was holding a rope."

"Who was holding a rope?"

"It was . . ." He couldn't even put it into words. That girl, well, she'd looked familiar. He'd seen her upstairs. Except the girl upstairs had been made out of porcelain, and this one was made out of flesh and bones.

"Brett." Parker broke into his thoughts. "You see something?"

"I saw . . ." *Her*, Brett wanted to say, but he was afraid. Admitting it would make it real. It would take things out of the realm of impossibility, and reality would come rushing into him the way a fist rushes into a body, over and over again, knocking the breath from a dark-haired boy until blood blossoms on his lips.

"I told you," Brett stammered, sweat clinging to his neck. "It wasn't Shane Ferrick. It was—"

"Doll Face." Parker held up her card. *"My name is Doll Face. My weapon is the element of surprise because no one will see it coming. My greatest secret is—"*

"I am already here," Brett finished for him. "Park, I saw her upstairs. Juniper touched her shoulder, and her eyes popped open, and . . . she had his eyes."

"What are you talking about?"

"Shane Ferrick's eyes. Shane Ferrick's rope. Come on, I have to show you, or you'll never believe it."

"Dude. You're freaking me out," Parker said, following him to the stairs. For once, Brett took the lead, and it felt good to be in charge of his destiny. To be solving problems instead of creating them.

He took the stairs two at a time. He was leaping tall buildings in a single bound. Passing the girls' bedrooms in a blur. As he passed his own door, his heartbeat spiked. There, in his peripheral vision, he could see the confetti covering the floor. The sheet he'd draped over the headboard to hide what had been written there. That headboard was curved like a tombstone, and the sheets were a stony gray. When Brett had stepped into the room, he'd thought about just lying down on the bed, seeing how it felt to disappear.

But he hadn't disappeared, and now he could hear the brass knuckles clanking against the inside of his pocket, soft and comforting. A reminder that he was still here. He was still fighting, in his own way, and he would make it through this nightmare.

He would survive.

Then, as Brett entered the fifth bedroom, his stomach dropped out beneath him. In the right-hand chair, where the girl had been sitting, there was nothing. No girl. No doll. Brett's gaze swept to the left. There the boy still sat, dressed in an ebony suit, but his jacket had been torn away. And on every exposed surface of his skin, someone had written words in bright red marker.

Shithead. Deviant. White trash.

Here, on the boy with the startling blue eyes, the words made a certain kind of sense, but not because Brett agreed with them. How many times had Parker leaned in, in the hallways of Fallen Oaks High, and made snide comments about that "white-trash asshole?" How many times had he begged Brett to destroy the "shithead" who'd danced with Ruby Valentine? At first Brett was resistant, because Shane Ferrick had seemed sweet. Thoughtful. The kind of guy you'd like to know. Then, the morning before Dahlia Kane's Christmas party, a video of Ruby had surfaced at school.

And Brett's perception had shifted.

"I did this," he said, gesturing to the doll. "Juniper lured him into the pool, and Gavin wrote on him, but I destroyed him."

"No." Parker's jaw tightened. "He destroyed *Ruby*, and you got him back."

"I didn't."

"You did." Parker held out a hand. Brett's stomach churned, and his vision blurred, but his fingers did what they always did when his friend reached for him. They made a connection. "No matter what happens tonight, I need you to remember one thing," Parker said.

Brett nodded, studying his eyes. He was searching for the gold among the green. The emeralds crackling with light. But Parker's eyes were dark as he whispered, "You did the world a favor."

15.

FORBIDDEN FRUIT

There was something wrong with Shane Ferrick. Parker knew it the day that kid came blowing into town. It wasn't that Shane had arrived in a storm, or that his hair was disheveled and his clothing was torn. The people at this school were throwing themselves at him, and it made Parker sick. Oh, it was subtle, girls offering to walk Shane to class, boys asking him to share a smoke in the park, but Parker saw what the others didn't: Shane Ferrick was a creep, playing on people's sympathies and manipulating them.

He just needed to prove it.

Then Parker was given a gift. It happened on Monday in AP Bio. The task of the day involved slicing up a suffocated frog, and Parker entered the classroom with excitement. He'd been waiting for this, waiting for the hands-on approach to learning that so many teachers claimed was important, but so few actually followed through on. And maybe he was looking forward to slicing something up, just a little. It wasn't as if the thing could feel pain. It was dead.

But Shane Ferrick took one look at the green-gray amphibian, sprawled out like the contents of a mad scientist's bottle, and *freaking cried*. A tear slid down his cheek and splashed on the table. Warmth spread throughout Parker's stomach and slid into his limbs. Finally, after a week of putting up with this guy's bullshit, Parker wouldn't have to hear about the fascinating Shane Ferrick anymore. That kid had revealed himself for what he was.

Pathetic.

Parker cracked his knuckles, waiting for the laughter to start. But something strange was happening. The girls in the classroom were turning to look at Shane, their eyes widened in concern. When one of them hurried over to Shane's side, wrapping him up in a hug, Parker's fingers encircled a glass beaker. He envisioned the glass shattering, like it always did on TV shows when someone was furious. The beaker held. In that moment, he felt this was a perfect metaphor for his existence: Parker was full of passion, full of fire, and there was nothing he could do with it. He was powerless.

That morning, while half the student body yammered about how *sensitive* Shane Ferrick was, *how sweet, he must have an old soul*, Parker skipped third period to go to the grocery store. He picked up apples and cheese and a wicker picnic basket, and yeah, he felt like a total douchebag buying that. But he also purchased a bottle of expensive-as-hell champagne, using the fake ID he'd had since he was fifteen.

Ruby was going to be thrilled.

Twenty minutes later Parker swung into the school parking lot, tires screeching and engine roaring and hair looking fantastic. He swaggered out of his classic Mustang like the king of the universe. Except, you know, a king who carries a cute little picnic basket. But hey, if that was what the girls at this school found sexy, Parker would do it.

He'd do anything to get what he wanted.

He rounded the fat, sprawling oak in the center of the courtyard and spotted Ruby sitting among a cluster of girls. She didn't look up as he approached. She was mesmerized, staring into the eyes of a blue-eyed boy and lifting a grape to his lips. But as the grape neared Shane Ferrick's mouth, he shook his head and moved away. The girls giggled.

Parker cleared his throat.

Ruby glanced up, blinking like the light was too bright to see him. "Park?" she said, her eyes narrowing. "What the hell are you holding?"

This time the girls erupted in laughter. There was nothing sweet or subtle about it. While Shane brought them delight, Parker obviously brought them amusement. He could feel his face reddening. What was happening at this school? Only a month ago, any one of these girls would've thrown themselves at his feet.

It was like Shane had cast a spell over them.

Finally, through all the giggling, Parker found his voice. "I thought I could treat you to lunch," he told Ruby. He was making a point to avoid Shane. He'd never believed in magic, but there was something entirely off about that boy. Something unsettling. Parker didn't want any part of it.

Ruby popped the grape into her mouth, chewing slowly. After an eternity, she swallowed. "I already have lunch plans."

Parker's teeth clenched, his muscles tightening as Shane craned his neck to look in the picnic basket. "Looks like you've got some good stuff in there," he said. And those girls *immediately* shifted focus to Parker's basket, oohing and aahing over the selection of cheeses, whispering about how to open the champagne without being caught. Parker stared at them, trying to understand this sequence of events.

Then, as if in answer, Brianna Ferrick walked by.

She was wearing a white dress. Brianna always wore white, like the lady in that story who'd been stood up on her wedding day and never bothered to take the damn thing off. Parker couldn't remember the specifics, but he remembered the chick was unstable. And Brianna was unstable too. He could tell just by looking at her. She wore about a dozen necklaces, each with a different charm. Crystals and pentagrams and all sorts of devil worship creepery. Every time he saw her, Parker wanted to wrap his hands around those necklaces and pull.

As his gaze followed Brianna across the courtyard, he heard a familiar voice, and he turned. Ruby was giggling, leaning into Shane. "Okay, so you don't like grapes. But I bet you *love* apples."

Parker blinked as she lifted an apple to Shane's lips. The apple from *his* basket! Was she trying to hurt him, or was she actually under a spell? She'd told him she loved him just months ago. Stared into his eyes, so breathless, as she leaned in for a kiss. Now she was chasing Shane with an apple, and Shane was pretending to fight her off, and all of them were laughing so hard, like they couldn't believe how funny it was.

Breathless.

Parker tilted his head, staring at Shane with newfound curiosity. Maybe Shane really had done something to Ruby; maybe he had actual power over her. It sounded ridiculous, but what was more ridiculous—the idea that Shane was manipulating her, or the idea that this gangly-limbed nobody could amble into town and steal the love of his life without even trying?

Shane bumped Ruby's arm, saying, "I told you, I only like strawberries," and Ruby blushed, like they were talking about something *else*. Something personal. Parker fumed. For a minute, he thought about opening the champagne and then telling the principal he'd seen them drinking. He could blame the whole thing on Shane. But no. He was going to do something much bigger, much better than that. He was going to expose Shane for the freak that he was.

For over a week, Parker studied everything he could find on the occult. He learned about the worst things—human sacrifice and ritual torture, and the way evil was always drawn to innocence—and some of the sillier things, like love spells and charms that made you irresistible. He couldn't rule anything out, not until he knew what was real and what wasn't. He'd already learned that half the charms Brianna wore were linked to black magic, and if she knew how to harness their power, she could be involved in some serious crap. But even worse than Brianna was Shane. Shane pretended to be normal. He pretended the girls of Fallen Oaks flocked to him because he somehow deserved it, even though he hadn't done *anything* for the people of this town. He hadn't done *anything* to earn Ruby's affections. Parker supposed it was possible that Brianna was the one with true power, and Shane was benefitting from her abilities. But he suspected the opposite was true: Shane was the truly wicked one, and Brianna had gotten tangled up in something she didn't understand.

He was going to help her break free.

Late on a Wednesday night, Parker drove over to the Fallen Oaks Trailer Park, hoping to spy on Shane through his bedroom window. He could tell something was wrong the minute he climbed out of his car. Something smelled off about the place, not because it was terrible, but because it was sweet. There had been times, in the past, when he'd joked that the scent of Ruby drifted through the air the way the scent of food drifted along in cartoons. He could follow her by her smell. But why was it here? Parker refused to believe the truth of it as he crept between the trailers, seeking the dwelling with the blue curtains and shiny silver door. He'd heard Shane describing his home to people before, always making it sound fancier than it was. The dude was poor, but he spoke about himself like he was some kind of prince. And it wasn't like Parker had anything against poor people, but Shane pretended to be something else.

Rich in love and family.

Everything that guy said was so cheesy, Parker thought, as he arrived at Shane's home. He exhaled in relief when he saw that Ruby's Cadillac was nowhere to be seen. That car was a relic, a hand-me-down passed along from her grandfather to her dad. It had always struck Parker as odd that Ruby's dad had split town without taking his car, but then, maybe the cops could've tracked him that way. Either way, Ruby's father had disappeared, that car had remained, and Parker had swept in to pick up the pieces of her broken heart.

He'd *earned* Ruby's devotion.

Quietly he slipped around the back of the trailer, stopping in front of the first window. He knew it was Shane's, even before he saw the boy sitting inside it. Even before he saw the girl. He recognized the clothes strewn about the space, the wrinkled shirts and ratty jeans that Parker had studied ever since all the females at Fallen Oaks High had lost their heads over this guy. Yeah, the more Parker thought about it, the more he realized Shane *had* to be controlling them.

His eyes shifted left, to the bed. He could see Shane's legs, could see one pale knee poking out from a hole in his jeans. At least he was clothed. Yes, this thought would become very important, as Parker's gaze trailed farther left and took in the sight of long, freckled legs. Legs he recognized. He'd spent countless hours gliding his fingers over those legs, trying to get Ruby to give in to him. He'd memorized her freckles like constellations. He'd trailed kisses up to her thighs, until she was giggling and breathless.

Now, behind the thin pane of glass, Parker could tell she wasn't laughing. She was staring at Shane like he was the goddamned moon. And Shane, that slippery sucker, was leaning in, tucking her hair behind her ear. Parker wanted to bang on the windowpane. He wanted to break through the glass and pummel Shane's face until it resembled the actual moon.

But he couldn't. If he burst into that bedroom, guns blazing, Ruby might think Shane was the victim. He needed to get her away from that asshole without ever letting her know he was responsible.

That meant calling in reinforcements.

Parker returned to his car. But instead of pulling onto the road, he pulled his phone out of his pocket. Dialed information. Asked to be connected to the Valentine residence.

Then he played the waiting game.

It took a couple of rings, but soon a groggy woman answered the phone. Mrs. Valentine. Ever since her husband disappeared, Ruby's mother had become terrified that her daughters would be snatched up in the middle of the night. Now Parker would use that fear to his advantage. He'd get his girl away from Shane Ferrick and back into her own bed.

"Hello?" Ruby's mother whispered. "Who's there? James?"

Parker used his best horror-movie voice. He might as well have fun with it, since his night had gone to hell. "Your daughter is in danger," he warned in a low, throaty voice. "By this time tomorrow, she'll be dead."

Then, a hitch in Mrs. Valentine's throat. A low, strangled sob. Parker started to feel bad. But he couldn't tell her he was kidding without blowing his cover, so he ended the call and put the car in drive.

Back on the road, Parker's heartbeat started to calm. He already knew how things were going to play out. First Ruby's mother would burst into her daughter's room and find the bed empty. Then she'd call her daughter once, twice, twenty-five times. Ruby would answer, eventually, no matter what Shane was convincing her to do, and then she'd go home to find her mother sobbing on the front steps.

Sneaking out would no longer be an option.

16.

POISONED APPLE

Ruby Valentine was coming unhinged. Juniper could see it, even with one eye trained on Gavin. He lay on the black velvet sofa like a four-year-old after a birthday party: arms and legs splayed out haphazardly, dark hair sweeping across his face, chest moving rhythmically up and down.

He looked peaceful.

Ruby, on the other hand, looked terrified. Stumbling over to the window, she tossed the curtains aside, as if ready to make an escape. Unfortunately, she couldn't. Steel bars lined the window, blocking them in. "He's got us trapped."

"Who, Parker?" Juniper asked, heart thudding at the sight of those bars.

Ruby shook her head. She was staring at the window, as if waiting for an apparition to slip through the bars. An apparition with dark hair and startling blue eyes. Long, pale fingers. A deceptive grin.

"Shane Ferrick isn't here," Juniper told her. "He can't be."

When Ruby spun around, her hair rippled over her shoulders like rivulets in a crimson sea. She'd dyed it months earlier, but Juniper was still getting used to it. The girls had grown up together, and she'd grown accustomed to Ruby's ginger tresses.

Once, she'd woven Ruby's hair into a hundred tiny braids, and after they'd been undone, Ruby had looked like a mermaid.

Now she looked like a specter, and that hair looked like blood on a fingertip. Like a stain on an ivory dress. "Like spun rubies," Ruby had insisted, three months ago in the girls' bathroom at Fallen Oaks High. Juniper had been coming out of a stall when she found Ruby standing in front of the mirror.

Then, silence. Always silence with Ruby, ever since things fell apart and the two couldn't look each other in the eye. That day, though, something was different. Ruby was bouncing from foot to foot, grinning at her reflection. "The color suits me, don't you think? It looks like spun rubies."

Juniper just stared. The last thing she wanted was to start a fight, but she hated how pale Ruby looked with that bloody red hair. How wicked. Still, she couldn't stay silent, so she said the nicest thing she could muster: "It makes you look less innocent."

Ruby laughed. For most of her life, she'd had rosy cheeks and a smattering of freckles on the bridge of her nose. She was wholesome as apple pie, or so the boys would whisper, and then they'd imitate *tasting* her. Their tongues would slide between their fingers as Ruby walked by in the halls.

But after Shane's funeral, Ruby had spent so much time indoors, her freckles had faded. She'd lost what color she had. With that crimson hair, she looked less *wholesome* and more *poisoned*.

Now Juniper wondered if that was the point. Wholesome-as-apple-pie Ruby had always been the boys' favorite flavor, and something had always, *always* gone wrong. But if that apple pie looked a little poisoned, they wouldn't beg for a taste anymore. They'd leave her alone and nobody would get hurt.

Nobody would die.

"We went to his funeral," Juniper said, tearing her gaze from the bars on the window. "We watched them lower him into the ground, and we threw rose petals—"

"Closed casket," Ruby murmured, slumping onto the sofa opposite Gavin. She seemed to be having trouble holding herself up, the way a newborn can't quite lift its own head. And Juniper thought, with a fresh wave of self-hatred, that she would hold Ruby's head up if it came to that.

She would give Ruby her blood. Her breath. For now, she knelt in front of the sofa, taking Ruby's gloved hands. "Shane isn't doing this. Think about it, Ruby. If he didn't die, why lock us in a house and torture us?"

"We aren't locked in."

"You're right. The back door is open." She tried to catch Ruby's gaze, but those eyes were as nervous as butterflies, refusing to settle on anything. "We shouldn't be sitting in this room, waiting for someone to come for us. We should be out the door and on the road."

"We can't. A car is the last place we should—"

"Nobody made Shane get into that car! Nobody can blame us for what happened to him. He chose to drive—"

"Did you see him leave the party? Did you see him take the keys from Parker's pocket?" Finally Ruby was looking into her eyes, but that stare was unsettling. It held an intensity that Juniper had never seen before. Ruby was desperate to understand what had happened the night of the party.

But Juniper didn't have the answers she was looking for. "I left before Shane did," she admitted, glancing at the words written on Gavin's skin. "I didn't see Gavin do anything, and I only heard about what Brett did after the fact."

"What about you?" Ruby asked. She said it so gently, Juniper almost thought she could tell the truth. Confess. Wipe the slate clean. But she was still clinging to the delusion that they might rekindle their friendship, and this little bit of honesty would stamp that fire out.

Permanently.

And so, she told a half-truth. The thing she'd been telling herself over and over again since the party. "I never tried to hurt him," she said, still holding Ruby's gaze. Still holding Ruby's hands, amazingly enough. "He came and sat with me, and we had a beer together."

"Shane sat with you?" Ruby asked. She said it softly, like she was caressing his name with her mouth. Juniper didn't understand. According to everything she knew, Shane had done something horrible to Ruby, but if that were true, she wouldn't be speaking his name like that.

She'd be spitting on his grave.

"Okay, be honest with me," Juniper said, glancing at the roaring fire. "You're not staying here . . . You're not hiding in this room because you *want* to see him. Right?"

Ruby lowered her eyes. "If I could apologize—"

"Are you serious?" Heat flooded Juniper's chest. "After what he did to you?"

"What do you think he did?"

"I'm not sure, honestly. All I know is what I saw at school. One minute, you're *feeding* him in the courtyard, and the next, that video is popping up in my inbox, of you . . . Well, I don't need to remind you of what was in it."

"No. You don't," Ruby said, and now her voice was cold. Juniper could envision icicles dangling from her heart. Maybe that was what you had to do when everyone you loved turned against you, or left you, or worse. Maybe you had to take all the warm, bleeding parts of yourself and cover them in a frost.

To survive.

Ruby was a survivor. That much had always been true. In a way, it was what had drawn Juniper to her in the first place. When Ruby fell down on the playground, she didn't cry. When her father yelled at her, she didn't even flinch. And when Shane Ferrick humiliated her in front of the entire school, she didn't seek vengeance.

Of course, she didn't have to. People did it for her. Parker, along with his loyal henchman, Brett. Gavin, apparently. Juniper, too. Now they were here. Five little players in a dangerous game, trying to escape with their lives. And Ruby wanted to stay so she could chat up the boy who'd humiliated her?

"You should hate him," Juniper spat, pushing to her feet. She felt cold without Ruby's hands in hers. "He snuck into your room. He snuck into your bed, and then—"

"He didn't sneak in."

Juniper's heart took a holiday. All night, it had been pounding inside of her, and now . . . silence. Always silence, with Ruby. Always suffering and regret, because Ruby wouldn't forgive, and she wouldn't forget. But she could forgive *Shane*, and she could defend him.

Ruby stood up slowly. In the light of the flickering fire, her hair flashed brighter than poppies, then darker than blood. "He didn't sneak into my room, and he didn't sneak into my bed. I snuck into his."

17.

DESERT WIND

Ruby felt possessed. Her long red hair was wrapped up in a bun on her head, tucked into a knit cap. She was wearing black yoga pants and a matching sweatshirt, which weren't exactly her first choice in seduction attire, but then again, she could always take them off.

And she needed to be stealthy.

She stood beneath the Ferricks' trailer, in the far left corner of the park, and asked herself what she was doing here on a Saturday night. Parker would kill her for this. Then he'd kill Shane, and probably Brianna, just to be a dick.

Parker was that kind of guy. Ruby knew it that night, even if she'd been clueless when they'd started dating. Parker was possessive, and though he had never hurt her, exactly, he'd weaseled his way into every aspect of her life. She felt his presence even when she was alone.

She tapped on Shane's window. She'd only spoken to him a few times since the infamous slow dance in the hallway, but there was something crackling between them, and they didn't need words to find it. That fire had sparked when he'd looked into her eyes, the day of the storm, and Ruby had been ablaze ever since.

Shane opened the window.

Quietly she climbed onto his wrinkled sheets. "I needed to see you," she said, pulling off her knit cap. Her hair rippled around her, and she ran a hand through it, feeling self-conscious.

Across from her, Shane smiled. God, he was pretty. A sliver of hair curved over his left eye, like a black crescent moon in a sapphire sky. Like something you couldn't even see on this planet, but made sense *somewhere*. That was Shane, alien and natural at the same time.

Look at him, leaning so casually on his bed, Ruby thought. *Not even nervous that I'm here.* Nobody treated her this way. Not since she'd started dating Parker. Before she could stop herself, she was speaking the words, "You haven't heard, have you?"

"What, about your boyfriend?"

Four words, so easily spoken. There was no fear in Shane's voice. But Ruby had enough fear for the both of them, and her voice trembled as she said, "He'd hurt you if he knew I was here."

"But you came anyway."

"Yes."

"Because you needed to see me."

"Yes."

His smile deepened. It was sly and mischievous, and Ruby felt stars awakening all over the universe. Galaxies that used to be dark now had light. "Well," he said, scooting closer to her, "that's good enough for me."

"It is?"

He nodded, toying with his sheets. His bedding was cerulean and ivory. His walls, a deep twilight blue. "I've seen you with this boyfriend. I've seen the way you flinch when he touches you. The way you find excuses to slip away, into the places he can't follow. Do you even like him, Ruby?"

Ruby lowered her eyes. She liked it better when he was calling her Strawberry, liked it better when they were both being coy. Playful. All she'd wanted to do was come over here and do something stupid. Take off her clothes and make him lose his mind. Let herself lose hers.

For once.

But now, staring into those sapphire eyes, she decided to do something more dangerous. She decided to tell him the truth. That she'd broken up with Parker *seven times*, and each time, he just kept showing up at her house, playing hide-and-seek with her sisters or making sandwiches with her mother in the kitchen. One night, after a particularly bad breakup, she'd found him in the dining room with a giant carving knife in his hand, standing over a turkey. And she couldn't say anything because, well, there *was* a turkey.

That was the thing about Parker. He might've been a stalker, but he was smart. Everything he did, he did under the guise of protectiveness, of caring. Everything he did included an element of doubt. Like, maybe he was just a sweet, devoted guy who didn't understand that it was over. And he was *so good* with her sisters. Her mother loved him. Maybe she was wrong for trying to break things off.

Now, in the quiet of Shane's bedroom, it all sounded ridiculous. But Shane didn't blame her for Parker's possessiveness. "Every rebellion starts with a small act of defiance," he said, his fingers grazing the inside of her wrist. Ruby felt thunder and lightning coalescing in her veins. "You two eat lunch together, right?"

Ruby nodded. Every day, for the past year, she'd eaten

lunch with Parker, whether she'd wanted to or not. Rain or snow, sleet or storm. Weekend or weekday, Parker was there.

"So on Monday, you'll eat lunch without him," Shane said. "I'll find you after third period, and a bunch of us can sit together."

"Who?"

He shrugged. "Friends I've made." *Girls,* he meant, but Ruby wasn't jealous. Parker would be less inclined to throw a fit if a bunch of girls were watching. "Safety in numbers, right?"

"He'll still follow me home. Corner me at my door. Make me take him back. I'm sorry, I know this sounds crazy—"

"It doesn't sound crazy. I actually kind of hate that word." He looked down, playing with a patchwork quilt at the end of his bed. "It sounds like you've been scared for a really long time. Trust me, I know the feeling."

Ruby's breath faltered. She thought of that day, in the junior hallway, when they'd danced, and Shane's mask had fallen away. The sadness in his eyes had mirrored her own. Now he wouldn't meet her gaze, and he wouldn't stop playing with his blanket. The quilt was made up of multicolored squares, and Ruby caught a glimpse of words woven into the corner.

For Shane, with love.

"Your mother?" she asked, and maybe she was prying a little. Maybe she'd heard rumors at school about Shane's mother *disappearing* in the night. One minute corporeal, and then vapor.

And then wind.

"She made one for each of us," he said, folding the corner of the blanket over, so Ruby couldn't see his name woven into it. She realized she was sitting on one of the patches, and she lifted it out from under her, out of respect.

"Is she . . ." Ruby trailed off, unsure of how to finish the question.

"She left."

"Oh." A beat. "My father's gone too."

"Oh yeah?" Shane ran a hand through his hair. "I was, um. I was being euphemistic."

Ruby's heart tripped over itself. Paused, then quickened to make up for the lapse. For a second, she thought she could tell him everything. The dark, dirty truth about the night her father disappeared. But Ruby had already made herself out to be the victim in the Parker scenario, and even if she *was*, she hated talking about herself like that. Like boys could wrap her up in their sticky little webs and make her do whatever they wanted. Suffocate her. Siphon her blood, bit by bit. She'd broken free of her father's web, and she'd break free of Parker's, too, with or without Shane's help.

Right now, she wanted to help *him*. "You should tell me about your mother," she said.

"I should?" Shane cocked his eyebrow. "And why is that?"

"Because you don't want this weight on your chest." Ruby squeezed his hands. "Trust me, I've been walking around for months, feeling like an elephant was sitting on my chest. And all this time, I've been blaming it on Parker being a stalker—"

"He is a stalker."

Ruby nodded, but the gesture was jerky, more a puppet's movement than a person's. "Parker being Parker, well. That's on him. But I've been keeping it a secret. I've been keeping it a secret *for him*, and I didn't even realize that until I let it out." She looked up, meeting Shane's gaze. "So tell me about your mom."

He laughed, but it faded quickly. "She loved taking us to the circus," he began. "She used to make up stories about the animals, and when Bri worried about the tightrope walkers falling, she told us they had invisible wings." He swallowed, toying with the fraying edge of his T-shirt. It was black, like his hair, and Ruby wanted to peel it off him and wear it to bed. Instead she sat very still, listening quietly as he spoke. "Then we got older, and she started to read about how badly the animals were treated. She said she could see holes in the tightrope walkers' wings. One year, when I was eight, I went to her room, all ready to go, and she was lying in bed, still wearing her nightgown."

"Was she . . ."

"What, depressed?" Shane huffed bitterly. "My mother was the happiest person I've ever known. She was always telling us stories or singing us songs. But sometimes she'd lie down in bed, and it was like nothing could get her out. Like the entire big-top tent came falling down around her, and she couldn't find the exit." He glanced at Ruby. "Like an elephant was sitting on her chest."

Ruby smiled, a soft, feathery thing that fluttered away in an instant. She could almost envision Shane's mother, dark-haired and bright-eyed, trying to explain to her children how depression felt. It was sweet, and it was heartbreaking, and Ruby wanted to slip into the memory and cradle Shane when his mother couldn't.

"I decided not to go that year," he said, breaking into her thoughts. "I told my dad I was staying home, but I didn't tell my mom. I wanted to bring the circus to her. So I gathered up all my stuffed tigers and elephants, and I even put on a top hat, like I was the ringleader." He paused, grinning. But his hands trembled as he said, "While I was setting up, she went to take a bath. Sometimes, on the darkest of days, it helped, you know? To light a dozen candles and surround herself in warmth. But it was weird, because the faucet was on for so long, I thought, it must be cold by now. She must be freezing to death."

Another pause.

"She didn't answer when I knocked. But the lock on the door is fussy, and if you push hard enough, you can kind of, um . . . override it. I pushed, and the door came open, and the entire bath was pink. I told myself that she'd put food coloring in there. She did that when we were kids and Bri would have a fit about taking a bath. Mom would pretend it was the ocean and stain the water blue. Get plastic sharks and dolphins and make them dive into the air. By the end of it, Bri would be laughing and splashing and neither one of us would want to get out."

"It wasn't food coloring," Ruby said. "Was it?"

Shane shook his head. "I probably knew it, deep down. But it's so funny, the tricks your mind plays on you in those moments."

Ruby bit her lip. She knew a thing or two about going into shock. The mind wandered, taking you into curious places, some of them very dark, and some of them weirdly light. "What did you do?" she asked after a minute, sliding her thumb over Shane's finger.

He jerked away, startled. "I called the police and I got all the water out of the tub. I couldn't find any bandages, but she was wearing this long lace dress, and I tore off the bottom of it, to bind her wrists. I kept thinking, 'She's going to be mad at me for ruining her dress,' but by the time the ambulance arrived, I realized I was hoping she'd be mad at me, because if she wasn't . . ."

"That must've been terrifying."

"It was . . . an impossibility come to life," he said. "But so much realer than anything else."

"Brighter, and more vivid."

"Yes." He looked up, into her eyes. "How did you know that?"

Ruby shrugged, suddenly coy. "Same way I knew to wear strawberries the first day we met. The universe told me."

He smiled, looking down at his quilt. In one of the patches, two dark-haired babies held hands, one dressed in white, one dressed in black. "The thing about fear is, it doesn't go away once the most terrible thing has happened. It compounds, so you expect more terrible things to happen. You wait for them."

"Brianna," Ruby whispered, and she wasn't even sure why she'd said it. Brianna wasn't standing on the other side of the window. She wasn't knocking on the door. Still, from the moment Shane had mentioned his mother lying in the bathtub, Ruby had envisioned Brianna floating there. Wearing a long lace dress. Mimicking Mrs. Ferrick the way another girl might dress up in her mother's wedding dress. Pull on a string of pearls. Dance around in too-big shoes.

"Bri's a lot like our mother," Shane said. "Too much like her, if you want the truth. They both shake hands with tree branches, and they both dance at midnight in the garden. They *did*," he corrected, as if remembering his mother had slipped into another plane of existence and wasn't waiting for him in the next room.

Ruby related to this. After her father's disappearance, she'd woken up morning after morning, forgetting he was gone. It happened for days, then weeks, then months.

Eventually, the truth sank in.

"I know that Bri isn't my mother, and she's never once spoken about leaving, but still, I worry about it." He lowered his head. "Every time I hear the bathtub running, I sit perfectly still, listening. I can see her in there, lying in the water, and I . . ."

Ruby took hold of his hands. Just like that, her fingers were gliding up his arms, into his hair. She lowered her forehead to his. "We won't let anything happen to her, okay? I promise."

"I won't let anything happen to you." Shane's hands were warm as they slid over hers. "We're going to stop being scared. Together."

"And then?" Ruby asked, breathless. "After we've stopped being scared?"

Shane grinned. It was a Cheshire cat smile, a crescent moon curving across his face. It was mischief and magic combined. "Then we'll just be together."

She inhaled, fingers curling into his hair. She wanted to protect him. From sadness. From pain. From the absolute horror of knowing that a loved one was never coming back, except in nightmares. "What about Parker?"

Shane leaned in. Lips close to hers, he said, "Parker Addison is a grain of sand in a land of pyramids and gods. All you have to do is wait for the wind, and he'll blow away."

"I've been waiting for the wind for so long. Couldn't we just . . ." She lowered her lips to his neck, and when she exhaled, she *knew* he could feel it.

"Ruby—"

"Is that my name?"

"Strawberry," he drawled, low and sultry, and Ruby's body flushed with heat. She felt like a moon goddess in a land of pyramids and sand, overflowing with light, swelling with longing.

Then Shane trailed his lips along her jawline, whispering,

"Tell me what you want," and her entire body froze. Her heart felt heavy under the weight of desire. Of danger.

She said, "I don't know."

"That's all right." He pulled back, lifting her chin with his fingers. "You don't have to know."

"I don't?" No one, in the history of Ruby's existence, had told her that it was okay to be *unsure*. To not know what she wanted. To give herself space to find out. "Are you mad?"

"Are you kidding?" He laughed. "Ever since I met you, I've been telling myself this story about you showing up at my window. I *knew* it was a fantasy. I knew this impossibly beautiful, impossibly powerful girl wasn't going to climb into my bedroom, just because I willed it so."

"And yet . . ."

"You came." He kissed her nose. "You appeared, and it was so much better than anything my memory could conjure. So much better than anything my imagination could create. You were the opposite of all my nightmares, the antidote to all my fears."

Ruby knew it, in that moment. He was the great love of her life. She could see their future splayed out before them: a grand departure from the city, a list of off-the-wall jobs they'd acquire from town to town. Always discovering new places, eating new kinds of food. Feeding it to each other with their hands. Kids, maybe, way down the line. Ruby wasn't sure yet. But she was sure of him, in a way that she probably shouldn't have been.

They'd only just met.

Still, she knew in her gut they were meant for each other, like she knew Parker would hurt her if he ever found out about them. That was the tricky part. How were they going to get her away from him?

And so, that night, after they'd crawled under Shane's covers, they whispered of liberation. They fell asleep as the sun started to rise. For the first time since her father disappeared, Ruby slept without nightmares, and without waking up terrified. And when she did wake, once, at the sound of a dog barking outside, Shane just followed her body, curving into her. She could feel that he wanted her. As he pressed against her back, his blood shifted. But he didn't try to take. No fingers slipped into the opening of her shirt. No lips moaned, "Please?" He even scooted away a little, to keep her from feeling uncomfortable. But Ruby pulled him back, drawing his hand up to her heart, reveling in the feeling of being safe and wanted at the same time. And she realized that she would do anything to get away from Parker and keep stealing these moments with the love of her life.

Anything.

18.

STORM CHASER

Juniper felt seasick. Her vision blurred, her stomach churning. Of all the secrets Ruby had kept from her, this was the worst. "You were in love with him. You knew Shane Ferrick for all of two seconds, and you fell for him, just like you did with Parker."

"Shane wasn't anything like Parker," Ruby snapped, her voice defensive. "He was my greatest protector, the antidote to all my fears."

"And how did that work out for you? Did he make that video to *protect* you? Did he show it to the entire school because—"

"You don't know what you're talking about."

"Then tell me, Ruby! Tell me *something*. Because all this time, I've been thinking of you as the victim. As the girl who got swept up in a hurricane, until your body was twisted and your clothing was torn and you couldn't see two feet in front of your face. But now . . ."

"Say it," Ruby taunted, stepping closer. "Tell me I deserve what people do to me. Tell me it's my fault."

"I'm not saying that! But my God, there are people who board up their windows when they hear a storm is coming, and there are people who race out the front door."

"And me?"

"You climb to the roof with a pitchfork in your hands. You summon the lightning. You chase the storm."

"See, that's where you're wrong, Juniper. I don't chase the storm. I *am* the storm. I am a goddess in a land of pyramids and sand, and if I want, I can make all this blow away with the wind."

Juniper swallowed, staggering backwards. "He's still in your head," she said bitterly. "You've made him into a hero, like you did with Parker. Like you did with your dad."

"Ah, now we've come to the heart of it, haven't we? The real reason you turned in my father."

"I was trying to protect you," Juniper said, but her chest was flushing with heat. She had this weird, tickling feeling at the base of her neck, like Ruby knew something *she* should know, something she should've known for years. "He was hurting you."

"Yes, but how long had he been hurting me? How long did you know it was happening and do nothing?"

"I didn't!" Juniper insisted, and that was the truth. All she'd ever had were her suspicions. Suspicions, and that same tickling feeling at the base of her neck, telling her she should know something.

Ruby's eyes narrowed to slits. "You waited until I was dating Parker, and *then* you turned my father in. Why?"

"It was a coincidence. Or . . . I don't know, maybe I recognized something in Parker, something that reminded me of your dad. It takes a certain kind of person to toss a kid into a row of garbage cans and then pull you into his arms without batting an eye. Maybe I thought some sort of cycle was repeating."

"Right." Ruby huffed. "Like I'm a chapter in a psychology textbook titled 'Daddy Issues.' Like I'm not a person at all."

"You're a person." Juniper stepped forward. She wanted to

take Ruby's hands again. Pull her close, until they were look-ing into each other's eyes and seeing the truth there. *Feeling* it. "You're the most amazing person I've ever known. You're wild and wonderful and a little bit wicked, and my life has been so much better for having you in it. I would've spent my child-hood curled up in my room, reading about adventures instead of having them. Every time you tapped on my window—"

"Oh, so it's okay to climb through *some* people's windows?"

"Of course it is. If you know them."

"But I didn't know you," Ruby countered, and that was true. The first time she'd tapped on Juniper's window, the two hadn't even been friends. They'd been classmates. But earlier that day, when their third-grade teacher had told them they'd be making family trees for an ancestry project, Juniper had burst into tears and raced from the class. She hadn't heard that Ruby Valentine (the person next to her, alphabetically, on the class list) had been assigned to be her partner. She'd never expected to see that pale face staring through her window, breath fogging up the glass. And, in typical Juniper fashion, she chose not to open the window and risk letting a stranger into her room. Instead she drew a question mark on the glass, like some kind of Batman villain, and Ruby, upon seeing it, started to laugh.

"Let me in," she mouthed in grand, exaggerated move-ments. Then she tapped—*tap, tap, tap*—until Juniper opened the window.

"What are you doing here?" she demanded. "And how did you find my house?"

"I looked you up," Ruby said, climbing onto the bed. "I needed to know why you cried. Was it the family tree project? Are you an orphan?"

"That's rude. You can't just ask that."

"Why not? Orphans are badasses." Ruby said it so casually, like swearing was a normal thing to do on a stranger's bed in the middle of the night. Like they were twenty-five-year-olds about to light up cigarettes. "Harry was an orphan," she added, plucking *The Chamber of Secrets* from Juniper's bedside table. "Ooh, this is a good one. Hey, guess what I did?"

"What?" Juniper asked, not even trying to follow her classmate's train of thought. Instead she watched Ruby pull a stack of photos out of her pocket. "I found these in my basement," Ruby said. "I pretended it was a chamber of secrets and I dug through these boxes and I found these pictures of my great-grandparents in Ireland. For the project!"

Ah, so there was a logic to Ruby's meandering thoughts. Still, Juniper didn't feel better as understanding dawned. Tears were welling in her eyes, and to her absolute surprise, Ruby lifted a finger to her lashes, catching one before it fell.

"Make a wish."

"What?" Juniper was so startled, she stopped feeling sad for a second. "It's not an eyelash."

"Tears are better! That's why they always work in fairy tales. They're, like, pure emotion. That's what my mother says." Ruby smiled, her freckled nose crinkling. "She says crying is, um, bringing your emotions into the light. You can see all your feelings glittering in a single tear, and if you wish on it, the universe will listen, because it knows you feel something honest. So . . . blow."

Juniper did. But tears were heavier than lashes, and no matter how hard she blew, the tear wouldn't budge. Finally Ruby flung the tear into the air, yelling, "Wish!" and by then, the two were laughing so hard, Juniper's sadness was forgotten. So much that, when Ruby asked, "Why were you sad?" she forced herself to answer.

"I don't have any pictures of my great-grandparents," she said. "All of them were destroyed in a fire."

"How did the fire start?"

"Um . . . my great-grandparents started it," Juniper began, her chest tightening in fear. She'd never told anyone this story before. "They were born in Cuba. But it wasn't safe there, so they went on a long, scary adventure, and they ended up here."

"Oh! Happy ending," Ruby said, so simply, like life was a fairy tale. Like every kid had a chamber of secrets in their basement, and seeking refuge in this country didn't come with consequences.

"It was a happy ending," Juniper agreed, staring at her hands. "But it was also dangerous, because if anyone found out they weren't born here, they could've been kicked out, so—"

"Oh! They burned all the pictures."

"Of their family in Cuba, yeah." Juniper let out a long, slow breath. "Things changed, later on. People decided it was okay for them to stay here because of how bad it was back home. But by then, they'd destroyed all the pictures and"—a hitch in her throat—"I'll never get them back. My family tree will be short and stumpy, because I can't even *see* my family in photographs, let alone meet—"

"That's not true." Ruby's hands found hers, and it was startling, how perfectly their fingers fit together. Like they'd been made to find each other. "When we grow up, you can come with me to Ireland, and I can come with you to, um . . ."

"Cuba."

"Right! And we'll be like Indiana Jones, except we'll be

searching for *people*, and then you can meet your whole family. We'll go together, okay?"

Juniper swallowed, breath fluttering in her rib cage. It sounded wonderful. It sounded like a fairy tale, and she really, really wanted to believe it. She wanted to believe they'd travel the world together, and learn each other's history, and be best friends forever.

And they would've been. They would've been in each other's lives, still, if it hadn't been for Parker. Parker had swept in, and Parker had stolen Ruby away from her, and Ruby hadn't even seen how possessive he was. How violent. How familiar.

But Juniper had seen it. And yeah, maybe that was why she'd called the police when she had. Maybe she'd seen Parker gripping Ruby's arm, and maybe it had been like history repeating, and maybe she'd snapped. Maybe she'd stayed up sobbing, late into the night, mentally counting down the days until Ruby landed in the hospital (or worse), and maybe she'd done what was necessary to save her friend's life.

Now she'd save Ruby again.

Reaching out, in spite of the danger of being rejected *one more time*, she took Ruby's hands. "I'm getting you out of here," she said. "We'll have to scream as we're leaving, so the guys hurry back to this room. They'll keep Gavin safe while we go for help."

"But the cars—"

"We won't take the cars. We'll run to the neighbor's house and call the police. They'll get here quickly, this is a nice neighborhood." She led Ruby to the doors and slid the glass coffee table out of the way. "What do you say? Should we go on one last adventure?"

Ruby inhaled. Finally, after a torturous eternity, she nodded. "You promise he isn't coming for us?"

"I swear," Juniper said, pressing her ear to the door. She heard nothing. "The ghost of Shane Ferrick is not coming for us."

"I know. I just . . . I can't stop imagining his spirit slipping through the walls. I can't stop imagining his mother, gliding forward in a white lace dress—"

Juniper's head snapped up. "What did you say?"

"His mother, in the dress—"

"It was white? You didn't tell me it was white."

"What does it matter?" Ruby's brow was furrowed, and there was this little crinkle in the top of her nose, like when she was eight. It would've been adorable, if Juniper's heart hadn't been trying to crawl into her throat.

"There was a doll upstairs," she started, and then stopped. How much should she tell? They needed to get out of there. "She was wearing a white lace dress. I thought she looked familiar, because her eyes were blue, but her hair was pale, and it threw off my theory."

"What theory? Are you saying you've known this entire time?"

"I told myself it was impossible. I was being paranoid, and anyway, you were trapped with Parker and I couldn't go running out the door. I couldn't, and I didn't have to, because that hair was white and Brianna's was black."

"Brianna?" Ruby's cheeks had paled, and her lips were parting. *Damn it.* Juniper shouldn't have said anything until they were out of the house.

She reached for the knob.

And of course, *of course*, Ruby stopped her. "There was . . . a wig," she said, placing a hand over Juniper's. "She was wearing it at the funeral."

"She was? God, I don't even remember. That day is a blur."

"A blur of black. But her hair was white. It was hard to see, because she was wearing that veil, but at some point she was sobbing so hard, it slipped. They both slipped, and I thought I saw skin beneath them."

"Skin?" Juniper narrowed her eyes, disturbed by the image. "Like her hair had fallen out?"

"I . . . I can't be certain, but I know that she was wearing a wig. Why is she still wearing it?" Ruby's teeth tugged at her lip. "We have to warn Parker. Brett can carry Gavin, and together, we can search the house. There's probably a study! We'll find a computer and call the police that way."

"Are you hearing yourself? We shouldn't be going farther into the house! We should be going out the door, and Parker is the last person we should be waiting for. He's determined to keep you here."

"Please, I can't explain it, but I have a really bad feeling about this. If you go out the door . . ." Ruby paused, lowering her eyes. "If you go past the pool, we both know what's going to happen."

"No, we don't." Juniper's voice was clear, but the rest of her was shaking. She didn't want to do this now. She didn't want to do this ever. "*We* didn't go to that party. I went—"

"Along with half the junior class. Everyone saw what you did." Ruby stepped up close, her breath warm on Juniper's cheek. "You got Shane *wasted* and lured him into the pool. You stood over him, laughing, as he sank to the bottom. And when he came up for air, you pushed him back down—"

"That isn't what happened!" Juniper's heart was pounding, and her lungs were struggling for air, as if she was already drowning. Already? *No*, she thought, shaking herself. Brianna couldn't push her into the depths, because she hadn't pushed Shane.

She had *lured* him, though. She'd stolen his breath.

"I don't have time to defend myself," she snapped, glancing at the boy on the sofa. "Gavin needs medical attention, and if you won't come with me to get help, then guard him with your gun. Your *loaded* gun," she added, reaching for the door.

Ruby crossed her arms over her chest. "You won't leave me here. I know you won't, because you always try to protect me."

Just like that, Juniper's hopes deflated. She felt herself going round and round again, trapped in an endless spiral of endangering herself to save Ruby. Why else was she here? She'd had her suspicions about the party from the start, and it wasn't until *Ruby* confirmed she was going that Juniper decided to attend. She'd had more suspicions, up in the hall, about the portraits changing—the people *disappearing* in them—and still, she'd stayed behind, because Ruby was trapped in Parker's bedroom.

Over and over again, she'd chosen Ruby's happiness, Ruby's safety, over her own. Now, at this pivotal moment, she couldn't go farther into the house. She couldn't hunker down and wait for the person who had *every reason to hate her*, had every reason to hate all of them, to come crashing through the doors with a knife. She needed to run, and if Ruby wanted to stay behind, well, Juniper couldn't force her to go. She'd meant what she'd said about the cops arriving quickly in a neighborhood like this. If she hurried, she could make it to the neighbor's house in minutes! She could save Ruby and Gavin, without being foolish this time.

Without putting herself at risk.

"From the moment I met you, I knew that you were magical," she said, not looking into Ruby's eyes. She *couldn't*, or she'd convince herself to stay. "I knew that my life was going to change forever, and it did. And even after I'd lost you, even after my heart was broken, you were still my forever friend. And I love you."

A tear was forming in Ruby's lashes, and Juniper could see it. Even without looking into Ruby's eyes, she could see it. It slid down Ruby's cheek, and Juniper caught it with her fingers.

"Make a wish," she said, flinging the tear into the air.

Then she opened the doors. Into the hallway she went, with only protests on her heels. She could hear that hers were the only footsteps on the hardwood, could hear that no one was pursuing her. With that single thought, she burst forward, racing through the entryway to the dining room. The room was empty, and so was the patio beyond. She was going to escape. She was going to break the rules for once, instead of following them obsessively. She'd almost reached the patio doors when something caught her eye. Something was sparkling under the light of the chandelier. It was Gavin's wineglass, and the sight of its shattered remains bothered her more than she could articulate.

If Brianna was behind the sinister workings of the party, when had she put the drugs in Gavin's wineglass? Juniper remembered sitting down at the table, dazed by the sight of the pool, and staring at the place settings. Those glasses had been empty. Clean. She would've sworn by it, but if that were true, someone else had to have put something in Gavin's glass.

Someone who was already in the room.

Now she felt more than a tickle at the base of her neck. Sharp fingernails were skittering up her spine. She felt breath on her skin, and she spun around, preparing to fight. But no one was standing behind her, and the only signs of life were the footsteps thundering down the stairs. The boys were returning to the first floor, and if Parker saw her trying to leave, he might intervene, like he had with Ruby.

Parker . . . Juniper paused, catching a glimpse of blond hair at the base of the stairs. Parker had stayed at the table when the rest of them had delivered their cell phones to the little tray. Parker had broken the wineglass and found the note in Gavin's pocket. Then, when Ruby had wanted to escape, Parker had reminded her that it was dangerous to get into a car. It was dangerous because, one year ago, Shane Ferrick had climbed into a car and he'd never climbed out again.

And that car? It had been Parker's.

Chills raced through her entire body as she yanked open the doors and slipped onto the patio. Her dress caught in the brambles of a fat potted plant. There was a red sequin lying in the dirt, so familiar it made her heart constrict. Ruby's dress had been clawed by these same branches, and Ruby should be here, now, escaping with her.

She tossed a glance behind her back. Immediately, she regretted it, because Parker was opening the patio doors, and Brett was beside him. Ruby was nowhere to be seen. She hadn't come running after her friend to go on one last adventure. Juniper was alone, like she had been for years.

She kept to the side of the mansion, avoiding the icy pool. Snow dusted the ground, but she didn't falter. She didn't slow. She'd almost passed the patio entirely when she heard Parker's voice. His shouts were unintelligible, garbled by fear or muffled by distance, but Juniper made out a single word.

"Rope."

It was stretched across the patio, a mere two inches above the ground. Juniper didn't see it until she was tripping over it, and then she went flying. Her shoulder took the brunt of the fall. She imagined the bruise that would follow, the purplish-black mark that would darken her skin. Then she didn't imagine anything as a hand grabbed hold of her arm, dragging her toward the pool. Juniper kicked. Juniper screamed. Juniper did everything she could think of to escape, but in the end, she was helpless against her captor.

That fall had stolen her breath.

She looked up, to see startling blue eyes in a moon-pale face. Then Juniper Torres was plunged into darkness, and she saw nothing.

19.

SACRIFICIAL LAMB

Brett had always been quick on his feet. Once, when his mother had started a grease fire in the kitchen, he'd put it out with no trouble at all. At the first hint of smoke, four-year-old Brett had dashed to the pantry, pulled out the fire extinguisher, and doused that sucker until the kitchen was white.

He was wired to act first and rationalize later.

That was what he'd always thought. But as he watched a tall, ghostly girl drag Juniper to the pool, he was rooted to the spot. His mind screamed at him to move, to act, to intervene, but his body refused to listen.

He was as useless as a stone.

Then, with that single thought, Brett scanned the surrounding area for something with the weight of a stone. His eye stuck on the candelabra. It looked heavy, and the breath rushed into him as he plucked the tall black centerpiece from the table. It *was* heavy. It could knock someone out if he hit them just right. Bursting through the patio doors, he hurled the candelabra into the darkness.

Metal met porcelain. A chunk of the mask fell away, revealing a mouth. The girl in white looked up. Brett shuddered as that red, blurry mouth curled into a smile, and he squared his shoulders, preparing to dive into danger. But someone brushed past him then, someone with golden hair and a high-backed chair in his hands.

"I got this," Parker said.

Brett stepped aside. His heart was going *thud, thud, thud* in his chest. Beating against him. Trying to break free. Meanwhile, on the other side of the patio, Juniper had stopped trying to break free. Her body was slumped over the edge of the pool, as Doll Face shoved her head into the water.

"Hey, bitch!" Parker yelled, and Doll Face froze. Her long white sleeves were trailing across the surface of the water. She looked dead. No, undead, like something that had been buried, only to crawl out of the ground after a year of rotting.

Brett shook himself. They hadn't buried a girl a year ago. They'd buried a boy, and thinking about that would only make him sloppy in this moment. He needed to be alert. With Parker taking on the attacker, Brett could focus on pulling Juniper from the pool.

Or so he thought. But after feeling the sharp sting of the candelabra, Doll Face seemed to have no interest in being knocked out by a chair. She took one look at Parker and bolted toward the front of the house.

Brett hurried to Juniper's side. "Let's get her inside, and I'll perform CPR," he said, his voice surprisingly confident as he lifted her into his arms.

"You know CPR?"

"From camp, remember?" For one beautiful summer, Brett had trained to be a junior lifeguard, before his father decided that camp was too frivolous for a Carmichael boy. After that, his summers had been devoted to destroying people, rather than saving them.

But not tonight.

He carried Juniper into the house. Laying her down on the dining room floor, far from Gavin's shattered wineglass, he put his training to good use. *Push. Push. Push. Breathe.* Juniper had never looked so cold. Water dripped from her fingertips, her eyelids, her hair. Brett was shaking as he pushed on her diaphragm, that cold seeping into his skin, chilling him to the core.

"Come on, come on," he muttered, pressing his lips to hers. "Come on."

"Is she . . . ?" Parker started, but Brett wasn't listening. He wasn't stopping. He'd never stop. He was so tired of taking from the universe; he wanted to give something back.

He leaned in, giving Juniper his breath. Giving everything he had. A sound passed her lips, like hinges squeaking, and then she started to cough.

"You're okay," he said, brushing the hair from her face. "I'm going to take you to the living room. You'll feel better on the couch." That was a lie. She wouldn't feel better until they got her to the hospital. But with a wardrobe blocking one exit, and that ghostly girl stalking the other, their best bet was to make Juniper as comfortable as possible. Gavin, too. Ruby, if anything had happened to her in their absence. It seemed strange that she hadn't made a run for it with Juniper. As they entered the hallway, Brett turned to Parker, saying, "Why don't you run ahead? Make sure the others are all right."

Parker nodded, jogging down the hall. When he reached the living room doors, he flung them open, peering inside. But he didn't go any farther. Instead he spun around, his face paler than Brett had ever seen it, and murmured, "She's gone."

"Who's gone?"

But of course, the answer was obvious. Only one person could've made Parker that pale. Only one person could've sent him diving into danger, moments after Juniper went diving into the pool.

"Ruby hasn't been taken," Brett said, leading Parker into the room. "I saw Doll Face before we went upstairs, remember? She was standing on the patio, waiting for Juniper with that rope. Ruby probably went looking for her phone."

Juniper's lips parted, and she pushed out the word, "Study."

"The study?" Brett repeated, nudging the doors closed. Blocking out the hallway, and the danger. "That's where Ruby went?"

Juniper opened her mouth again, but the word that escaped sounded wrong. It didn't sound like her at all. When she said, "Gone," it sounded like someone had crawled into her body and taken possession of her. The voice was breathy, almost ethereal.

It was also male.

"She was gone," the voice said again, and Brett realized it hadn't come from Juniper after all. It had come from the boy with pale skin and dark, glossy hair. Bright eyes. Gavin was sitting up on the sofa, something white crumpled in his hand. "She was gone when I—"

"How long have you been awake?" Parker asked, thundering over to him.

Gavin clambered to his feet. Seeing Juniper, with her dripping hair and bruised skin, his mouth dropped open. "What happened to you? Did Parker do this?"

"Not . . ." Juniper curled over in pain as Brett laid her on the sofa. Meanwhile, Parker glowered, his head whipping back and forth between Juniper and Gavin. "Someone better tell me what the hell's going on—"

"Or what?" Gavin snarled, smoothing his wrinkled vest. He'd given his jacket to Juniper, back at the start of the party, and now his fedora was missing too. "You'll knock us out with chloroform?"

Parker gawked at him. "Dude, you're babbling. Doll Face must've given you the good shit."

"A movie was playing when I woke up," Gavin said, staggering toward the TV. "I don't know who turned it on, but I do know one thing: the movie was familiar."

Gavin picked up a remote and pushed play. Juniper gasped, hands flying to her mouth. Brett's fingers tightened to fists. The movie *was* familiar. Of course, there was a reason for that.

It had been recorded in the mansion.

"Zoom in on our heroes," Gavin said, as if narrating the scene. "They've just arrived in the dining room and are ready for the party to begin. But while four of them scurry off to the kitchen, to hand over their electronics, one of them stays behind."

And one of them had. Parker sat like a king on a throne, watching the others deliver their cell phones to the baby doll. They were gone for less than a minute. Really, it had seemed like the blink of an eye, but that was all it took to stab someone in the back.

Now Brett watched, his heart racing and his mouth dry, as King Parker reached into his pocket and pulled out a bottle of eye drops. But that bottle was a cover, wasn't it? A little protection, in case he got caught red-handed. Smart, if you thought about it. Maybe even brilliant.

Parker squeezed the bottle, dropping the liquid into his cupped hand. In a matter of seconds, he'd coated the rim of Gavin's glass. But that wasn't the end of it. He'd had to be certain the drugs would take, and so, after Gavin had taken a big whiff and tumbled to the ground, Parker dropped down beside him.

"No," Brett whispered. His hands were shaking, and it didn't seem fair that he was burning up when Juniper was freezing.

Looking down at her, he realized she'd scrounged up a pen and notepad from a nearby end table and was scribbling the words *Doll Face* on the little pad of paper. But he didn't care. Honest to God, the words didn't even compute. Because Parker, the one on the screen, was holding his hand over Gavin's mouth. Quietly drugging him, while Brett looked on, clueless. Trusting. Now the Gavin who *wasn't* on the screen stepped forward, blocking the TV from his view.

"The movie was playing when I woke up. Ruby was gone. And this was on top of the TV." He opened his fingers to reveal a card. A character card with *Parker Addison* written across the front.

"*My name is the Human Torch,*" he read. "*I am secretly in love with the Disappearing Act. My weapon is a rope, because then people can't run away from me. My greatest secret is—*" He leapt back as Parker leapt forward. Brett stepped between them, saying, "Keep reading."

Gavin did. With a great amount of flourish, considering he'd recently been drugged, he said, *"I will sacrifice each one of you to get her back."*

"No," Brett moaned, his heart cracking open. "He can't be working with—"

Gavin cut him off. "Ladies and gentlemen," he boomed, bowing deeply to Parker. "May I present to you . . . the Ring-master!"

20.

PATRIOT ACT

Parker's head dropped to his hands, and he took three desperate gulps of air. He could *not* believe he was doing this. But he had no choice. His partner in crime had thrown him under the bus, and every time he closed his eyes, he saw flashes of Juniper falling onto the stones. He saw her plunging into the water, arms flailing. Saw the bruise on her shoulder.

"It wasn't supposed to be like this," he said, lifting his head. Over on the sofa, Juniper was watching him. Gavin stood by the entertainment center. Meanwhile, Brett lingered between them, eyeing Parker with the coolest expression he'd ever seen. Thank God Ruby wasn't here to witness this. Parker was desperate to go looking for her, but first, he would convince the others to keep his secret.

As much as he hated to admit it, he needed their help.

"Three months ago, I got an email from this girl," he began, his voice quavering. "Her name was Abby Henderson, and she was an intern at the Fallen Oaks Psychiatry Center—which is a real place, by the way. I looked it up. I checked out everything before I agreed to work with her. I stalked her Facebook and her LinkedIn."

Juniper snorted. After a minute of scribbling on her little pad of paper, she held up the message: *Stalked. You finally admit it.*

Parker scowled, but he didn't lash out. That was what she wanted: to make him into the bad guy, so she could be the hero. But Juniper Torres was not the hero in this scenario, and neither was Gavin. Neither was Brett. The hero was standing in front of them, making an impassioned plea for their support.

Parker drew in a breath. "Abby was working with a new patient, a girl who'd lost her twin brother in a tragic car accident."

Gavin made a strangled sound, halfway between gasping and choking, and Parker plodded on before he could steal focus. "Abby was only an intern, but she didn't agree with how lax the psychiatrist was being with their patient's case. Brianna was suffering from delusions, convinced her brother had been murdered. Now, I knew that wasn't what happened, but believe it or not, I felt for her. Sure, she was a little creepy, but her brother was the psych—"

"Brianna wasn't creepy," Gavin snapped, his breath coming out short and fast. "I interviewed her for the paper last year. She was running the school clothing drive *by herself,* and she donated a bunch of her mother's clothes, even though it was obviously hard for her."

"Fine, she was a saint." Parker waved a hand. "Then her brother died, and she started rambling about capturing his killers. She wanted to torture you, one by one, until you admitted what you did to him."

Parker swallowed, looking guiltily at Brett. No matter what Gavin and Juniper decided to do, keeping Brett on his side was *essential* in surviving this night. Parker peered into those hazel eyes as he said, "When Abby came to me with her idea, I honestly thought it was the safer alternative."

"Drugging me was the safer alternative?" Gavin demanded, lurching forward. "What if I'd taken a drink from my wineglass? I'm pretty sure chloroform isn't safe to ingest."

"And I'm *absolutely sure* you'd never drink anything I poured." Parker's heart was racing, but he told himself to stay calm. Collected. "As long as you saw me filling the wineglasses, and doctoring up my own with Brett's flask, I knew you'd smell your drink to check for alcohol."

Gavin crossed his arms over his chest. "I guess you have it all figured out. I couldn't possibly have been poisoned, just like Juniper couldn't possibly have been drowned."

"I told you, it wasn't supposed to be like this." Parker held up his hands. "We were going to pull pranks. Perform illusions. Using my money and Abby's creativity, we were going to re-create the night Shane Ferrick died and give Brianna the closure she needed. First you would pass out and she'd write on you. Then she'd push Juniper into the pool. Just one push!" He turned to Juniper, appealing to her for the first time in his life. And he really did feel bad; that was why he was coming clean now. He was the good guy. Brianna was the evil one, manipulating him into helping her and then turning on him.

"Why not go to the cops?" Gavin asked. "From what I heard, Brianna's dad started homeschooling her after the accident. If you'd told the police she was planning to *torture* us, they could've swung by her place—"

"It wouldn't have mattered," Parker exclaimed, his voice cracking. "The night after Brianna confessed to her dark fantasies, someone broke into the psychiatrist's office and destroyed her file. All the recordings and the paper copy. Everything. Abby had no proof, and if she went to the cops, Brianna would've lied. Lied, and then . . ." At this point in

Parker's story, he heard what sounded like a hiccup. A soft hitch in the throat, then another. He turned to find Juniper hunched over, gasping.

She's finally breaking down, he thought, swooping toward her. How great would it look, in that moment, to kneel by her side? Wrap an arm around her? Yes, Parker thought, nearing the sofa, he would brush away Juniper's tears, and they'd all realize he was looking out for them.

But Juniper wasn't crying. She was laughing, as much as she could, with lungs that had already been pushed to their limit. She scrawled out a message on her notepad, then held up the words: *There is no Abby. Brianna played you.*

"I looked her up," Parker repeated, instantly defensive, but now Gavin was shaking his head.

"Just because she exists doesn't mean she contacted you. Brianna could've set up a fake email address, pretending to be from the Psychiatry Center. Maybe Abby really was working with her, but all this?" He gestured to the words on his skin, the water dripping from Juniper's hair. "No professional would agree to this. You got played."

Parker exhaled slowly, his chest flushing with heat. He refused to believe he'd been outsmarted. But Brianna had already played him for a fool, promising to "push" Juniper into the pool, and then drowning her within an inch of her life. He still remembered the *smack* when her body had hit the stones. He remembered, too, the words Abby had emailed to him, the night she'd reached out: *Nobody will get hurt,* she'd promised. *They'll only get scared and confess to what they did. You'll be saving their lives!*

Now, rubbing at his eyes, he said, "I thought Brianna was going to kill you."

"She's still going to kill us," Brett murmured. "Up in my bedroom, she offered to—"

"We're going to be fine," Parker snapped before Brett could say anything incriminating. "As long as I'm running the show—"

He broke off at the sound of scratching. He turned, slowly, to find Juniper holding up a note. *You aren't the Ringmaster. You're the patsy. The Ringmaster doesn't exist.*

Parker's jaw tightened. He was running this show. He *was.* Abby had promised, and even if "Abby" was actually Brianna, he'd keep the reins of the circus in his hands. He would earn the title of Ringmaster, and he'd tame the lion.

"You're right," he said, hanging his head. "She took advantage of my fear. I didn't want her to hurt Ruby and I didn't want her to hurt Brett, so I agreed to help—"

"She offered you something," Juniper broke in. In spite of the pain, she opted to speak the words rather than write them. Parker felt deflated. In one instant, he'd gathered the whip in his hands, and Juniper had snatched it away.

"She offered to spare your lives. That's all!"

"You're lying," Gavin said. "Your Adam's apple pulses when you lie. You have a tell, all of us have a tell. Except maybe Ruby. I can't figure her out."

Brett sucked in a breath. "Ruby," he repeated, and Parker looked up.

"What?" He crept forward, as gently as a hunter approaching a deer. "Do you think we should go looking for her?"

Brett shook his head. "She offered you Ruby."

"No, she didn't."

Brett nodded, a strange light in his eyes. "Brianna wanted answers. You wanted Ruby back. So you made a deal, didn't you? You scare us half to death, and we admit what we did last year. *We* admit it, but you say nothing."

Juniper perked up at that. Gavin, too. And Brett kept talking, spilling secrets he had no business spilling. "The truth was going to come out. *Most* of it was, and then what? You tackle Brianna and she pretends to go down? And Ruby spends the rest of her life thinking you're the only one who can keep her safe? Jesus, Parker, it's brilliant."

"More like evil." Gavin shook his head. "You act like people exist for your enjoyment. Ruby's your sex toy and Brett's your mindless little henchman, tossing people around when they haven't *done anything*—"

"Hey." Brett stepped toward him, his jaw clenched. Parker smiled. He hid it quickly, but he couldn't wait to see Brett knock Gavin across the room. Gavin wasn't small, but Brett was a force of nature, and with the right amount of effort, he could send Gavin into the wall.

Boom.

"That day," Brett began, his voice surprisingly soft, "when we went for a ride . . ."

Gavin snorted, and Parker's eyes narrowed. They were going to talk about *that* now? Weren't there more pressing matters?

Apparently there weren't. Gavin squared his shoulders, making himself almost as tall as Brett. "We didn't go for a ride. You threw me in the trunk of Parker's car. You locked me in there for hours. Man, I wasn't claustrophobic before, but now?" He gestured to the spacious living room. "These walls are closing in."

Juniper gaped at Brett, mouthing, "You didn't."

Brett swallowed. Opened his mouth, as if to defend himself, then turned back to Gavin. "You wrote that article about my family. 'The Crumbling Carmichaels.' You printed it in the school paper, and then you stood by as everyone had a big old laugh at my expense. Did you think it was funny? Oh look, Brett's father can't win a fight. Oh look, his mother got dragged away—"

"I told you, I didn't write it," Gavin said, his fists tightening. It looked like his fingernails were digging into his palms. "You *know* I wouldn't do that. You know me."

Parker stepped between them, holding up his hands. The last thing he needed was some cutesy reminder that these guys used to be friends. Yeah, he knew about it. Parker's mansion sat at the top of Fallen Oaks, and he could see all the way down to the forest below. He remembered the summer that Gavin and Brett had snuck off to the woods to feed a couple of scrawny baby birds. And when those birds were strong enough to fly, the boys held a *freaking ceremony*, where Gavin strummed on a tiny guitar while Brett twirled around the nest.

It was difficult to watch.

Then Brett's mother went away, and the giggling, curly-haired boy changed. He became sullen. He became violent. Gavin didn't know how to help him, but Parker did. He swooped in, offering Brett the things he'd lost. A lavish bedroom to call his own. Dinner with a loving, doting family. Parker's parents thought he hung the moon, but they couldn't have any more children after him, and he knew it broke their hearts. They'd wanted a big family. And so, he'd brought another boy into their home for them to love.

Everyone was happy.

Except Gavin. He didn't like the way Brett was changing, and by their sophomore year in high school, he was writing articles about "the dangers of boxing." The health risks. The emotional toll. Parker didn't get it. Brett was a talented fighter, and with a boxing career, he'd be able to support himself in a way that his parents couldn't. He'd go to college. Build a life for himself. And if that hurt Gavin's feelings, well . . .

Parker would take him out of the equation.

So yeah, he typed up an article about Brett's family and put Gavin's name on it. Snuck into the newsroom after hours. Pulled a little switcheroo. The article wasn't *that* demeaning. Most of what he wrote, people already knew. But Brett had been devastated to see his family secrets splayed out on the front page, and he'd never gotten over the betrayal.

Not then, and not now.

"Listen to me," Gavin pleaded, peering into Brett's eyes. "I did not write that article. I spent all freshman year taking pictures for the paper, just so Mr. Keller would *consider* me for a journalism position—"

"So what? You love taking pictures," Parker said, waving his hand.

"No, I don't. People just assume I do. Can't imagine why."

"Oh, don't you dare." Parker huffed, rolling his eyes. "Don't you dare make this about—"

"Why would I do that? So you can call *me* a racist for pointing it out, and I can literally fall over dead from the irony? No thanks. I'd rather take my chances with Brianna." Gavin shook his head, turning back to Brett. "I almost got kicked off the paper because of that article. But you know what? That was *nothing* compared to what you did to me."

Brett stared at his feet. His cheeks were blazing, his voice feather-soft as he said, "You're the only one who could've written it. No one else knew where my mother was taken—"

"Someone knew," Gavin said, his gaze sweeping across the room. "The same person who *lured* you into this house to get Ruby—"

At the mention of Ruby's name, Juniper gasped. Honestly, Parker was getting tired of the theatrics. But as his gaze followed hers to the entertainment center, he realized that sometimes theatrics were appropriate. The image on the screen had shifted. Or rather, the *room* had shifted, and now he was staring into a dark, grainy space with a single chair. Parker's vision dilated, zeroing in on the girl in the chair. The love of his life. The girl he'd lost his virginity to.

Ruby Valentine, tied up with rope.

Just as his fingers touched the screen, a blur of white appeared in front of Ruby, blocking her out. White hair, white dress. White face, with that broken mask revealing her mouth. Brianna Ferrick grinned, stepping closer, until her smile took over the entire frame. "Hello, darlings. Are we ready to confess?"

It took a minute to realize she was waiting for them to respond. But if they could see her, she could likely see them. Parker knew she'd planted cameras in the main rooms of the house—he'd given her the money to do it. He'd paid for the decorations, and the bars on the windows. He'd dipped into his trust fund for this! Now, glaring at the screen, he nodded begrudgingly. Gavin and Juniper did too. Brett just swallowed, staring not at the screen, but at Parker.

Brianna's lips curled. "Three out of four ain't bad. But don't worry, my little Iron Stomach, I'm coming for you next."

"Leave him alone," Parker snarled, not liking the way she was talking to his friend. Maybe he still felt defensive of the guy, even though they'd grown apart. Or maybe he knew that if Brianna was willing to torture Brett, she was willing to torture Ruby, too.

Ruby was supposed to be off-limits.

"I'll tell you what you want to know," Parker said. He could see the little red light now, blinking above the TV, and he spoke directly into the camera. "I was there for the entire party."

"Oh, I'd love to hear your version of the events," Brianna said, kneeling beside Ruby, "but unfortunately, the story doesn't begin with you."

"I got to the party early! I even put the marker in Gavin's hand. I take full responsibility for it." Parker threw up his hands in surrender, and he felt the vibe in the room shift. Gavin's gaze was trained on him. Juniper's, too. They both thought he was falling on his sword to protect them. But Parker had understood the story of Damocles his entire life, and in that moment, he knew exactly where the sword was hanging.

He wouldn't let it fall. "I arrived at the party around nine o'clock. I was alone, and I wanted to talk to Gavin before—"

"It doesn't start with you," said a voice, and Parker's pulse quickened. That voice was lilting, sweet. Familiar. Ruby stared directly into the frame, her perfect bow lips quivering. "It starts the night before, in my bedroom. You know it does. It starts with Shane, the rope, and—"

"The video he made," Parker said, his cheeks reddening. "The video he showed to the entire school. I wanted to stop him!"

"I know you did. You, Juniper, Gavin, and Brett. The four of you did damage control for me. Or, should I say, you just did damage."

"That isn't fair," Parker said. Juniper looked wounded. Brett and Gavin were silent, watching, listening.

"I'm just speaking the truth. If Shane hadn't crawled into my window the night before the party, none of you would've done what you did. Right? You were seeking vengeance, for me. It all starts with me."

The room fell silent. As much as Parker wanted to gloss over this part, to forget it entirely, he knew they couldn't. Ruby was right. Everything that happened at the party was because of her. Well, everything that happened was because of Shane, and what he did to Ruby on that Thursday night. December 20.

Ruby inhaled shakily, looking at Brianna. "The night before Dahlia Kane's Christmas party, your brother climbed through my window. He was carrying a rope."

21.

TONGUE TIED

I need you. Ruby slipped the note into Shane's locker, hands trembling. She needed him desperately. The two had spent twelve glorious nights together before her mother had noticed her missing and called the cops.

The *cops.*

Ruby had been humiliated, stumbling home in the early morning light, only to be greeted with flashing lights and a gaggle of boys in blue. *Walk of shame indeed,* she thought, running a hand through her hair. Of course, she and Shane hadn't *slept together* slept together (*yet,* she thought, and blushed), but still, her hair was a mess and she was dressed in the clothes she'd worn yesterday.

It painted a certain picture.

But not to Mrs. Valentine. Ruby's mother came charging across the yard, wrapping her daughter up in her arms. She was sobbing before Ruby could even get a word out. It took a good twenty minutes to convince her mom (and the cops and the group of "concerned citizens") that she hadn't been abducted by a serial killer and tortured for sport. She'd simply snuck off to a friend's house, to offer support over a recent breakup.

"But someone called the house," her mother sputtered, freckled hands gripping Ruby's shoulders. "He said you were in danger."

Ruby's stomach tightened. There was only one person who would pull a stunt like that, but she couldn't explain it to her mother without explaining everything else. "Mom, it was a prank. I was hanging out with Juniper." After all, the two used to be best friends. They'd grown up together, told each other secrets, all that little-girl cutesiness. But things had gotten complicated when Ruby started dating Parker, and at the time, she'd thought Juniper was being unfair.

Parker wasn't possessive. He was attentive. Devoted.

That was the problem with dating a boy like him. At first his possessiveness felt a lot like love, like he *couldn't stand* to be apart from her. By the time she realized who he really was, she'd pushed away everyone who might help her get away from him.

That was why Shane was such a godsend. And Ruby wasn't about to let him slip through her fingers just because her mother had become a neurotic mess. Yes, Ruby had sympathy for the woman, and yes, sometimes people did get snatched up in the night, but good God. If she couldn't sneak over to Shane's house, how were they supposed to plot her escape?

Ruby's gaze trailed to her bedroom window. It sat on the side of the house, draped in shadows, even when the sun was high. If Ruby had "trouble sleeping" that night, Charlotte would sleep in their mother's bedroom, and no one would notice Shane climbing through the window.

Hence, the note stuffed into his locker on Thursday morning. *I need you,* it said, without instructions, or a signature. Ruby couldn't risk sending a text. A text could be intercepted, but that note could've been from anyone. And later that day, when Shane passed her in the school park, she leaned in and whispered, "The grain of sand retaliated. Come to me?"

He arrived at midnight on the dot, like a beautiful, mysterious boy should. Ruby opened her window and pulled him inside. At first he didn't say anything, just lifted her fingers to his lips and kissed them, one by one. Ten tiny kisses. She could envision him lifting the eyelet lace nightgown off her body, slowly, so he could drink in every inch of her. Then she envisioned herself doing the same with his clothes, drinking him in. Every inch. Yes.

She blushed and looked down. "We need to . . ." *Come up with a plan,* she thought, as his fingers grazed the tops of her thighs. The nightgown wasn't very long. She sighed, leaning into his touch. "Shane."

"It's okay," he said, brushing her cheek with his lips. She was melting, melting. "I solved our problem."

"What? How?" She'd anticipated weeks of planning, maybe an elaborate contraption. An adult-size mousetrap to contain Parker. A complicated scheme that would land him in police custody.

But as Shane looked into her—always into her, never *at* her—she felt as if cool fingertips were trickling over her skin. Whatever he'd come up with, it wasn't hokey. But it was big. "We can't tell him about us. We can't risk him hurting you," he said.

"Or you."

"I don't care about that," Shane replied, so casually. "But I won't let him hurt you. And I won't let him hurt my family to get to me. Bri's been through enough, and if he starts messing with her . . ."

Ruby swallowed, her hands curling in on themselves. "What are we going to do?" For a minute, she thought he was going to propose a murder, and it startled her, how calm she felt. Maybe it was denial, or maybe she figured he wouldn't really go through with it. But in that moment, she thought, *We can do that. Eliminate the problem and get rid of the body. Never think about him again. Yes.*

But Shane didn't look angry as he peered into her eyes, and he'd have to be, to suggest something like that. He looked, if anything, resigned. "We have to run."

"Run?" Ruby stepped back, more affronted by this suggestion than the one she'd invented in her head. "What about our families?"

"They'll have fewer mouths to feed."

"They . . ." But she couldn't argue. He was right. With three kids instead of four, her mother might actually be able to stick her head above water. And as for Shane's family, well, Brianna would *freak*, but her father would only have to support the two of them. This could work.

"You won't miss them?" Ruby asked finally, tucking a hair behind his ear. It broke free, and she chased it again. God, she loved playing this game. How could she say no to him?

Shane leaned in and kissed her once, twice, three times. "I'll miss them terribly," he said into her lips, and Ruby opened her mouth, so she could draw him closer. "But I'll die without you."

That was it. The exact perfect thing to say, from the exact perfect boy. Ruby could feel herself falling. She *was* falling, landing softly on the bed, laughing, and then he was crawling over her. Laughing too.

His hands slid up her legs, and suddenly Ruby's heart was beating too fast. She was passing over the threshold of excitement and right into fear. Her entire body seized up. Shane must've felt it, because his face fell, and he lowered himself to his side. "Hey, it's okay. We don't have to."

"I want to," Ruby found herself saying, and for the first time, it didn't feel like she was reciting her lines. Playing a character. "I do," she said, rising onto her knees. But instead of creating distance, like she always wanted to do with Parker, she climbed on top of Shane, her legs on either side of him. "Just . . . not like *that*." She remembered how it felt to have Parker crawling over her. Remembered the fear, and the pressure of his body against hers. Pinning her like a butterfly.

"Ruby? I need to know what you're thinking. Come on, walk me through it."

Ruby laughed. Shane had started the "walk me through it" game one week earlier, after a particularly long bout of silence. Ruby had gotten so good at keeping her thoughts to herself, it hadn't even occurred to her that someone would want her to speak, to explain.

But he had. One week ago he'd gotten her to open up about her failed friendship with Juniper Torres, and tonight he'd get her to open up again. Maybe in more ways than one, Ruby thought with a smirk, unbuttoning his shirt, so she could get to his chest. She leaned down and licked him from his stomach to his throat.

Shane groaned. His hands went into her hair, and for a second, she thought he was going to let it go. That was okay. She didn't really want to *talk* anyway. But it made sense that her silence made him nervous, considering all the secrets she kept, and after kissing her for another minute, he pushed onto his elbows.

"You know the rules," he told her.

"I don't want there to be rules between us," she said, pouting. It was a game she was used to playing, everything calculated. She had to remind herself that she could be normal with him, and then she had to remind herself that normal didn't exist. Not when you'd been hiding for so long.

Shane looked up at her sitting over him. "I don't want there to be rules either," he said. "But I will *never* take your silence to mean yes."

Ruby's chest tightened. Tears flooded her eyes. And Shane said, "Baby," brushing the tears away, kissing her cheeks. "Why did that make you sad?" He was looking into her again, into the depths of her soul. Nobody looked at Ruby like that. Not since she'd grown breasts. People wrote songs about her "milky-white pillows, freckled and fair" as if this were medieval times and she should be flattered that they weren't saying "sweater puppets." But Ruby hated being looked at that way. It was like . . .

"Like people wanting to screw you is some kind of compliment," she'd slurred to Parker at a particularly raucous party, where they'd gotten wasted and she'd spent half the night dodging Nathan Malberry's advances.

And Parker, the clueless idiot, had turned to her, saying, "It is a compliment," thinking she was talking about him. Then, when he caught Nathan leering, he and Brett had pounded on the guy until he puked.

Ruby kept her concerns to herself after that.

But now, with Shane's gaze boring into her, she told him what had happened later that night. How she had slept with

Parker, not because she wanted to, but because she'd known, deep down in her gut, that he'd keep going whether she said yes or no. He'd waited *months* for her. And that night, when Nathan wouldn't stop pawing at her, it was like Parker needed a promise that she was actually his.

Ruby had just wanted to go home. She was tired, so tired, and thinking of Nathan curled up on the floor made her sick. But Parker kept looking at her like he'd done her a favor, and she started to get this sinking feeling in her stomach, like what had happened to Nathan had been her fault. So after he'd driven her to his house, and crawled over her on the bed, leering like Nathan had, Ruby finally said, "Okay." Not, *Yes, please. I want you.* Not, *I'm ready now*.

Just, "Okay."

Now, whispering about it in her bedroom, Ruby was thankful for the near darkness. She felt foolish for letting things go so far. She felt foolish for talking about it. Would Shane even want her anymore, knowing what he knew?

He pushed off the bed. Strode toward the window. Peered outside.

"Where are you going?" For the briefest instant, she thought he was going to hunt Parker down. Then, when she realized that was a *Parker* reaction, her stomach dropped to her knees. "You're leaving me?"

"Never." Shane looked back at her, smiling softly. "I just had an idea. Wait here." He slipped over the windowsill. He was gone less than a minute. When he returned to her bedroom, a curious object coiled around his hand, Ruby blanched. She knew it, even without seeing her reflection. Moments ago she'd been swelling with heat, swelling with desire, and now she felt entirely cold.

"What is that for?" She gestured to the rope.

"My dad asked me to pick up a Christmas tree, and I needed this to tie it down. But first . . ." He dropped the rope onto the bed, coiled tightly and fraying on the ends.

"First what?" Ruby crawled backwards, away from him.

"You're going to tie me up."

"I . . . what?" She looked at him like he'd lost all sense of reality, like his brain had tumbled out of his head.

"It's the perfect solution," he said, holding out his wrists.

"Why?"

"Because I won't be able to hurt you. You won't even have to worry about it."

Ruby's chest flooded with warmth. She wanted to hug him. She wanted to do other things too. Still, there were concerns. "I don't want to hurt your wrists."

"My sleeves will protect them." He gestured to the button-down that perfectly matched his eyes.

"We'd have to leave your shirt on."

"You already unbuttoned it." That wry, familiar grin took over his face. Transformed it. He was a creature of love and light, a boy willing to do anything to be with the girl he adored.

"Are you sure about this?"

In response, Shane looped the rope around one wrist, then the other. "All you have to do is tie."

She did, making a grand, elegant bow atop his wrists. It made him look more like a present than a prisoner. Still, her gut was a tangle of nerves, and as she looked at him, she felt she was crossing a line. "Shane."

"I trust you," he said. "Completely. That's the point."

"And I . . ." Did she trust him? Yes. She'd trusted him from the moment they'd met, and making him powerless, just to prove it . . . That was a Parker solution. Parker's wickedness had bled into every aspect of their lives, making them darker. Making them panic. Now they were going to lose their families because of him?

Hooking her finger under the rope, Ruby guided Shane onto the bed. "Tomorrow night, we're going to a party."

"At Dahlia Kane's? It's supposed to be legendary."

"Something big always happens, and people talk about it for the rest of the year," Ruby said, untying the rope. All it took was a single tug, and that bow came undone. "What if, this year, I'm the thing that happens? What if I break up with Parker in front of everyone and then disappear into the forest?"

"Um . . . does Dahlia live in a cabin?"

She laughed, pushing the rope farther away from them. It slithered off the bed, coiling on the floor. "She's on a couple acres of forestland. But there's a road on the other side of it, and if you park there, I could sneak off to meet you after the breakup."

"No, I don't like this. What if Parker sees you going into the forest alone? What's to stop him from following you?"

"That's the point. If Parker sees me sneaking into the woods alone, and he *doesn't* go after me, well, maybe we're wrong about him. Maybe we don't have to leave town. But if he trudges after me, refusing to let me leave him, then running is the right thing to do. The safe thing." Ruby climbed into Shane's lap. "Besides, how fitting would it be for him to chase after me the night I disappear? People will think he made it happen. They'll hold him responsible."

"Karmic justice." Shane kissed her throat. He kissed her neck, trailing his lips to her cheek. Just as he reached her mouth, he asked, "Are you sure about this?" and he could've been asking about the party, or the rope, or the fact that they were about to find each other in an entirely new way.

"Positive." She glanced at the rope on the floor, grinning slyly. "Besides, I hear it's better when boys use their hands."

After that, Ruby lost track of time for a while. Shane pulled off her nightgown, slowly, just like she'd imagined he would, his hands gliding over her skin. She helped him out of his jeans. Finally, when they were both undressed, and both trembling, he looked up at her and she said, "Yes."

"Ruby?"

"Yes. *Please*. I want you."

Shane cupped her face with his hand, kissing her again. When he shifted beneath her, the universe shifted too. She lost sense of herself almost instantly. Then, just as quickly, Ruby crashed back into her body. But instead of skin and muscle and bone, she was made up of pure, liquid honey. Pure, glittering light. The kind of light that could burn away the memory of a scarred, broken girl and leave only a beautiful skeleton behind.

After, he couldn't stop touching her. For hours, his fingers danced over the curve of her hips, circled her stomach, and rose to find her face. She smiled, kissing his fingers. His arm must've been tired, considering everything that had come before, but still, he wouldn't stop studying her. Memorizing her with his fingers. When she got up in the morning, he shook his head and pulled her back to him.

She laughed, falling into his arms.

She was giddy with her love, giddy with her plans to escape. She didn't see anything outside the window. Didn't see the blinking light of a camera. Didn't see a phone. But hours later, when the video popped up in her inbox, Ruby knew all too well that she'd been recorded.

Everyone did.

22.

NORTHERN EXPOSURE

The morning of Dahlia Kane's party, Juniper awoke with no sense of foreboding. No birds flew into her window, their wingbeats fading into silence. Her alphabet cereal didn't spell out *RUN*. Honestly, there was no indication that anything unusual would happen, and by the time she'd arrived in third-period chemistry, she'd resigned herself to business as usual.

Then, giggling. The kind you'd hear in middle school, when someone passed a scandalous note. Nothing for Juniper to worry about, certainly, because she wasn't a twelve-year-old with a crush on a pimply-faced boy. She was practically an adult. She opened her book, flipped to the chapter on atomic theory, and took a couple of notes.

She heard it again. This time the giggling had taken on a sinister quality, the way a beautiful queen might transform, in mid-laugh, into a wicked witch, her lyrical laughter giving way to cackling. Juniper turned, searching for the source. There, in the back of the room, Genevieve Johnson was peering at something in her lap. Her phone. Cell phone usage was strictly prohibited during class, but of course, there were ways around it. Keep your phone on silent. Text with your eyes on the front of the class. Juniper's classmates adhered to a strict code when it came to the rules: if they could be bent, they should be bent, and by the time the third person started cackling, Juniper got a sinking feeling in her stomach.

It wasn't just the laughter's cruel undertone. Plenty of people shared gossip during class. But every time someone glanced at their phone, their gaze drifted to the empty chair in the second row.

Ruby's chair. Ruby wasn't in chemistry today, which was odd, because she hadn't missed a day of school since the weekend her father disappeared. Now, as students glanced from Ruby's chair to the phones they had hidden in their laps, Juniper's stomach tightened. She actually thought she could feel Ruby's emotions. Once, when Ruby had gotten food poisoning at age ten, Juniper had spent the day in bed with the chills before she even knew that Ruby was sick. Logically, she knew the girls weren't psychically linked, but there was a connection between them.

There had always been a connection.

That was why, when the boy sitting next to her chortled, Juniper's face flushed like *she* was the subject of whatever was being passed around. She needed to look at her phone. Now. But she didn't dare take it out in the middle of class, even if Ms. Jacobson was busy scribbling on the board, so she cleared her throat and asked to go to the bathroom. Two minutes later she was locking herself in a stall, trying to calm her heartbeat as she took out her phone.

There was a multimedia message waiting there. The message was titled, *Plowing the Strawberry Fields*, and when Juniper opened it, she found herself staring at a video of Ruby's bedroom. She could only see a corner of the bed. It looked like the video had been taken from outside Ruby's window, and when she pressed play, she had a perfect view of the boy climbing over the sill.

Shane Ferrick, holding a rope.

Juniper gasped, not even caring that she was leaning against the filthy stall. She couldn't stand up straight. It honestly hadn't occurred to her that this could be something *worse* than a sex tape, something darker. And yet, when Shane reached the bed, he dropped the rope onto Ruby's comforter and held out his wrists.

Ruby tied the rope in a bow. Then she pulled him toward the bed, and after a minute, Juniper could only see their feet entangling.

She pressed stop. Well, she *tried* to press stop, but the phone wasn't listening. It took her three tries to realize the screen was wet. She was crying. She was heartbroken, because Ruby hadn't known she was being recorded, and soon the entire school would know, and *oh God*.

How could Shane have done this? Juniper looked down, using her sleeve to wipe off the screen. Now it was dry, but instead of pressing stop, she pressed fast-forward, keeping her thumb over the images as they sped by. She wanted to see the end of the recording. Wanted to see Shane's face as he turned the camera off. Would he smile smugly while Ruby slept in the background?

Would he wink?

In the end, Juniper never got answers to her questions, because she couldn't see his mouth. She couldn't see his eyes. Maybe he was being careful, trying to keep his face out of the frame, but he wasn't careful enough. A lock of hair gave him away.

Black and shining, it curved over the frame.

Suddenly Juniper's hands were moving again, and as much as she wanted to pretend some ghost was possessing her, she knew the truth. She couldn't let fear (or was it pride?) keep her from reaching out to Ruby. If there was even a chance that Ruby wanted to talk to her, she would summon her courage and be there for her ex–best friend.

Ruby, are you okay? she texted.

The response was fairly quick. Juniper's stomach ached as she read Ruby's reply. **He didn't do it.**

Wait, what? Juniper wrote frantically.

Shane didn't make the video, Ruby replied. Was she being serious? It seemed impossible, but when Juniper really thought about it, it made a wicked kind of sense. Ruby's father had hurled her into furniture (or walls? down the stairs?), and Ruby had defended him. Parker had hurled a kid into a row of trash cans, and Ruby had fallen in love with him. Now Shane had hurled her into the spotlight, and of course he was innocent.

I just need to see him, Ruby texted after a minute. **We're supposed to meet at Dahlia's party tonight.**

Oh, you should wear a gown! And Shane will wear a suit, and you can attend your movie premiere together.

Oh crap, had she really sent that? She hadn't meant to do it. She'd only wanted to see it written out. To tell Ruby the truth for once, instead of biting her tongue. But this wasn't the right moment. This was the *worst* moment, and Ruby wasn't writing back.

Not then, and not an hour later. Moment by moment, class by class, Juniper kept hunching over her desk like everybody else. She wrote **I'm sorry** at lunchtime, to no response. On her walk home, the words **I didn't mean that** were greeted by silence.

By the time evening came around, she realized that texting wasn't going to untangle Ruby from Shane Ferrick's ropes.

She needed to take action.

Now, sitting in the Cherry Street Mansion, watching Ruby struggle against her bindings, Juniper knew it was time to own up to those actions. Taking a shuddering breath, she shifted her gaze to Gavin. "I think it's time we told the truth."

And so, at last, they did.

23.

RED HANDED

Gavin was sick of everyone's shit. For years he'd wanted to score an invitation to Dahlia Kane's Christmas party, and now that it had *finally* happened, it turned out to be a trick. Dahlia didn't want to spend time with his fabulous, charismatic self. She wanted someone to take candid shots with an "old-timey" camera.

Well, fine. He would take photos, he thought, as he knocked on Dahlia's door. He would document every down-and-dirty thing that happened at this party, and then he'd use the photos to stop people from treating him like crap. Specifically Parker Addison and his loyal henchman, Brett Carmichael.

But things didn't go as Gavin planned. For once, Dahlia was actually being nice, draping her arm around his shoulder and offering him a beer. It felt good to be welcomed, even though Gavin had no illusions of untapped popularity. He prided himself on not being that shallow. Still, Dahlia's giggle was infectious, and she kept offering him booze, snacks, even trunks to swim in, if the mood struck him—Dahlia's pool was legendary, both for its size and its reputation as a prime make-out spot. He started to feel wanted. He started to feel warm. When Parker burst into the party, waving at Gavin like they were best friends, he thought he'd fallen into a vortex where everything he wanted would fall right into his lap, and he wouldn't have to use blackmail to get it.

He was dead wrong.

Juniper could see eyes watching from the forest. Three tentative steps later, she realized they were Shane's. She recognized that shock of black hair, half hiding his face. She recognized those gangly limbs, angular and sharp-edged as glass. She didn't know what Ruby saw in this guy, but then again, she never knew what Ruby saw in guys.

Maybe that was why she'd come to the party. Looking back, she couldn't quite separate illusion from reality. Was she really trying to protect Ruby from another abusive guy? Or was she pissed that Shane had turned out like the others, and she wanted revenge? Juniper didn't think of herself as a vengeful person, but she'd been angry for so long.

At Parker.

At Ruby's dad.

She approached Shane cautiously. "You came," she said, keeping five feet of distance between them. "Ruby said you would."

Shane inhaled slowly, eyeing her with an animal's wariness. Clearly, he trusted her as much as she trusted him. "She told you about us?" he asked after a minute.

Juniper nodded, wrapping her arms around herself. "She told me something else. She said, um . . ." She chuckled, shaking her head. "She said you didn't make that video."

"I didn't."

No pause. No hesitation. Of course, a practiced liar like Parker wouldn't have waited to think about his story, and

Ruby tended to have a type. "So, a camera just happened to set itself up on the exact—"

"Oh, I'd say there was no coincidence about it."

Huh. She hadn't expected that, and now she was stepping closer, wanting to hear more. This wasn't how things were supposed to go. He was supposed to be following her around, begging for a chance to explain. But he wasn't. He was guarded, locked up tight like Ruby herself, and something about that made Juniper want to get inside.

"Look, you can't stay in the woods all night. Nothing says 'creepy stalker' like a guy peering out of the shadows. If you want people to think you're innocent—"

"I don't care what people think. I only care about her."

"She isn't here."

"But she's supposed to be. Something's happening, Juniper." He stepped forward, and she stepped back. "I don't have all the pieces yet, but last night, somebody made that video to set me up. Now I can't find my phone—"

"Yeah, somebody made the video. Somebody with straight black hair. Like, I don't know . . . yours? Or, hey, maybe your sister did it. You are twins, after all."

Shane huffed, shaking his head in annoyance. Or was it disgust? "My sister's been locked in her room for the past twenty-four hours. It's something she does sometimes. After our mom died . . ." He trailed off, clearly not wanting to share anything too personal. "She'd never do this."

"Who would?"

"Who do you think?" When Shane fixed her with that piercing gaze, Juniper felt the world shift. She felt all the atoms break apart and rearrange themselves, revealing what had been hidden before. Hidden, yet obvious.

"No," she murmured. "No, it's not possible."

"Isn't it?"

"I mean, what did he do? Cut the tail off a horse? Buy a wig from the Halloween store?" The idea wasn't that outlandish. Parker was notorious for trying to tie Ruby down, and seeing her tie Shane up . . . like, literally tie him up . . . could've made him snap.

Still, the world was full of manipulative people, and believing in some grand conspiracy when the culprit was *right in front of her* was foolish. Probably, it was foolish. Oh, crap. She was starting to believe him.

"Look, you don't have to convince me that Parker Addison is a stalker. But why bother with a wig? The video alone would've convinced people you were guilty."

"I never said there was a wig," Shane said, gesturing to the front window of Dahlia's mansion. Her brightly lit foyer was brimming with people. The gold wallpaper made everyone sparkle, and Juniper could barely make out a face among the glimmer of bodies.

But she could make out a camera.

The Polaroid had been purchased in an online auction at the beginning of freshman year. Its owner had gone out for the *Fallen Oaks Forecast*, hoping to become the school's newest reporter, but the faculty advisor had relegated him to photography instead. Two years later, people were still asking him to take pictures.

"Gavin?" Juniper scoffed, still looking through the window. "Okay, if you knew him at all, you'd know how ridiculous—" She broke off in midsentence. An arm was sliding around Gavin's shoulders, guiding him toward the hallway. That arm belonged to a body. That body belonged to a blond.

"Parker hates Gavin. Gavin hates Parker, like he hates—"

"Who, Brett? The guy who's been stationed outside Ruby's house all day?"

Juniper spun around, gawking at Shane. "Brett's over there?" Well, that didn't prove anything. Not necessarily. If Shane had made the video of Ruby, it made sense that Parker would send his muscle over there to keep her protected.

Protected, or isolated.

"We could drive over there together." Shane gestured to the road. "Brett won't attack if—"

"I'm not getting into your car. How stupid do you think I am?"

"I don't. You're not." He held up his hands, backing away. "Just forget it, okay? You have no reason to trust me."

"You're right."

"But what if I could prove it to you?"

Juniper froze. It wasn't due to the low temperature, or the fact that she was wearing a flimsy jacket over her camisole and jeans. She'd been all set to move until he said that.

"Prove it how?" she asked, still keeping her distance. "Parker will never admit to guilt. And I sincerely doubt someone made a video *of* the video being made, so . . ."

"The truth is in there." Shane pointed to the house, though Parker had disappeared from the foyer. Gavin had disappeared too. "If we go inside, and Gavin sees us together, you'll be able to read his reaction."

"I don't know," she said, but deep down, she suspected he was right. Gavin liked staying on her good side. If he knew anything about the video, he wouldn't be able to hide it. And honestly, it wouldn't be so terrible to attend a party. To pick up a beer and pretend to be like everyone else, when all the while, she'd be watching. Watching Parker. Watching Shane.

"I'll stay for one drink," she said finally. "If you haven't convinced me by then, you're on your own."

By the time Parker arrived at the party, Gavin was drunk. He'd only ever had a couple of beers before this. When Parker waved at him, Gavin narrowed his eyes, looking behind his back.

Parker laughed, mouthing, "You."

Gavin turned all kinds of red. He could feel it, as Parker made a beeline for him. Draping one arm over his shoulders, Parker boomed, "Dude! I need your help with something. Can you follow?"

Gavin was perplexed, but caught up in Parker's half bear hug, he didn't have much choice but to stumble along to the closest bedroom. Parker closed the door behind them, making Gavin's stomach drop. "What do you—"

"What the hell is that punk doing here?" Parker demanded, pointing toward the window.

Gavin was confused. *He* was usually the punk on Parker's bad side. "I . . ."

"First he defiles my girl, and then he has the nerve to show up at my friend's party? Like, what the hell is he thinking? We have to teach him a lesson."

"We?"

"Duh." Parker knelt in front of Gavin, who'd plunked onto the bed to keep the room from spinning. "You and me."

"Where's your friend? You know, the bald, pummel-fisted *traitor*?"

"Oh, him?" Parker said, not even flinching at Gavin's drunken honesty. "He's taking care of my girl. She's trying to be brave, but . . ."

"What happened?" Gavin asked, smiling when the room

righted itself. He wasn't *that* drunk. He just needed to eat something. "Did he really—"

"Yes, and worse," Parker confirmed. "I don't want to get into what she told me. It's too messed up." His fists tightened, and Gavin thought Parker might hit him. But tonight, for once, he wasn't Parker's target. An actual asshole was. A guy who deserved to be hit.

"Why should I help you?" Gavin asked. He looked around the room for something to pop into his mouth. Someone had been eating pizza rolls earlier. Then he remembered they were in the bedroom and the food was out *there*.

"Don't do it for me. Do it for Shane's next target," Parker said, striding to the window. He parted the curtains, beckoning Gavin closer. "Notice anything?"

Gavin's heart dropped to his knees. There, on the edge of the forest, was Shane Ferrick, and he was talking to someone all too familiar. Juniper Torres. "She's probably telling him off," Gavin said, waving a hand dismissively.

"Doesn't look like she's telling him off."

It was true. Juniper was inching *toward* Shane, rather than away from him, and after a minute, the two made their way to the house. Together. "Well, maybe she's getting his side of the story," Gavin reasoned. "Just to poke holes in it, you know? Expose him."

"What if we exposed him first?"

"How? I'm not going to attack the guy."

"You don't have to attack him. You just have to make sure he gets good and drunk, and then . . ." Parker dug around in his pocket, tossing a bright red Sharpie into Gavin's hand. "You mark him as a deviant. Then he can hit on whoever he wants, and they'll see *exactly* who he is. He won't be able to hide it."

"Huh," Gavin said, turning the marker over in his hands. That didn't sound so bad. Barely a middle school prank, really. And Shane had done much worse. Still, as Parker opened the door and ushered him outside, he had the feeling that something was being kept from him.

Something big.

Juniper was drunk. Yes, she could admit it. But Shane was freaking *wasted*. She'd never seen anyone get drunk so fast. And even though he was entertaining her with animated stories about his childhood, she felt an undercurrent of nervousness every time someone at the party looked their way. It was like everyone was waiting for her to step away for one second, so they could descend on Shane. Tear him to shreds. She'd come to this party to prove he wasn't who Ruby thought he was, but she found herself growing *protective* of him.

She wished Gavin would make an appearance. As soon as he saw her sitting with Shane, she'd be able to read the innocence on his face, and then she could go home. She had no business being at this party. She certainly had no business enjoying herself.

But she couldn't help it. Shane was in the middle of a story about the time he and his sister spray-painted *Ferricks' Traveling Circus* across their trailer and spent the day performing acrobatic tricks before their father came home and shut the organization down. All his stories were like that: the time Shane and Brianna conned a local priest into feeding their family for a week, the time they dressed in white wigs and white clothing and walked around the town wailing like ghosts. Beneath the stories of gaiety, Juniper could see the common thread of a couple of scared, starving kids doing everything they could to keep their family afloat. Maybe Ruby had been right about Shane. Juniper thought about texting her, but when she pulled out her phone, it started to buzz.

Ruby was texting *her*! No, wait, she was texting *Shane* through her phone. Juniper got pissed all over again. Meanwhile, Shane saw the message on her screen (**Are you at the party? Can I talk to him?**) and made a desperate grab for the phone.

"Hey!" She jerked the phone away from him.

"Please," he said, fingers swiping at the air. "Please let me talk to her."

"Tell me what to write. If it's appropriate, I'll send it."

His lips twitched at the word "appropriate." But he didn't smile, because he was too close to getting what he wanted. "Tell her the winds are still blowing," he said quickly. "Tell her . . . tell her the grain of sand is eroding the pyramids."

Juniper typed out the message. Stared at it a second, waiting for the words to stop blurring, then hit send. Ruby's reply chimed almost instantly: **The goddess is tipping the hourglass. When time runs out, doubt will creep in. Come now.**

Shane shot up from the couch. Swayed a little, then bolted for the door. If somebody had asked Juniper later what took her so long to get up, she would've blamed the booze, but the truth was, she was sick of being their go-between. Ruby had only texted her to get to Shane, and Shane had only been nice to her to get to Ruby. Now that they had each other, they didn't need her anymore.

Juniper shook herself. Shane was wasted, and it wasn't safe to leave him alone. There were six beer bottles on his edge of the table, and she didn't even remember him getting half of them. They'd just appeared, like magic. Pushing off the couch, she caught him at the front door.

"Wait. Shane, wait! You drove here, right?"

He yanked the door open. He looked possessed, paler than usual. "I had to park on the other side of the forest," he said, thundering down the steps. "In case Parker decided to—"

"Mess with your car. Right." Again, Juniper felt protective of him. She followed him across the lawn.

"It wasn't supposed to be like this." He lumbered toward the tree line. "I wasn't supposed to go inside."

"Hey, it's fine. I can call my mom, and she can drive us both—"

"I wanted you to like me. I thought if you liked me . . ."

"Why would it matter?" Juniper asked, pulling out her phone. It didn't take long to find the name *Mom*, even in the darkness.

"Because she cares what you think. She likes you, Juniper Junebug. She—"

"Hello?" Juniper cut him off when a familiar voice picked up. "Mom? I need a ride. Now."

Shane turned, trudging through the underbrush as she ended the call. "There isn't time. I have to go."

"You can't go. You're totally blitzed." She hurried after him, almost falling in the process. "But my mom's on the way—"

"This whole thing is a setup. Why didn't I see it? I shouldn't have come in with you. You—" He spun around, peering at her in the darkness. His eyes were narrowed, like two of her were dancing before him. "You were a part of it! I never should've trusted you."

"No. Shane, I—" But maybe she had been a part of it without realizing it. Everyone at the party had been out to get Shane, and she'd gone and delivered him on a drunken platter. Now he was bolting through the forest, and she was chasing after him, her shin banging into a fallen log. But Shane had to one-up her: he tripped over a root and went flying. As he tumbled, his keys fell out of his pocket.

Juniper snatched them up. "I'm really sorry, Shane, but you aren't driving tonight."

He stared at her, his sapphire eyes stretched wide in the moonlight, and the look on his face was pure anguish. Juniper considered trying to drive his car. But she could barely see straight as she trudged back to the party, the keys curled into her fist. She could hear Shane chasing after her, and she half hoped he'd fall down in the bushes and take a short nap.

There, in the darkness, he would be safe.

Shane didn't fall. Instead he raced after her more deftly than she would've thought possible. He'd almost caught up to her when she reached the front steps. Rather than pushing through the swell of bodies, she turned right, slipping through the gate to the side yard and heading toward the pool.

There it sat, sparkling and beautiful. There, like an oasis in the desert. Juniper chucked the keys into the deep end as Shane passed through the gate. He screamed. Then, to the surprise of everyone cluttering the deck, Shane kicked off his shoes, pulled off his jacket, and jumped into the pool.

Even the spray was ice cold. Juniper had assumed the pool would be heated this time of year, but one glance to the right showed the folly of her thinking. Dahlia's hot tub was packed to the brim, filled with horny, drunken students now taking bets on how long Shane would stay under the water. When someone yelled, "Forever!" the group erupted in raucous laughter. Juniper felt ill, and she stepped up to the lighted pool.

Shane hadn't come up for air. But she could see his body moving under the water, could see his hands searching for the keys. *No, no, no.* She hadn't thought he'd actually go after them. But love made people desperate. She could see that now as he surfaced once, took a big gulp of air, and went down again. Three more tries, and he still hadn't reached the keys. Juniper thought he was going to drown himself. She started looking around for a net, a pool toy—*anything* she could use to retrieve the keys or offer to Shane as a flotation device.

She came away empty-handed.

Frantic, she started to kick off her own shoes as he surfaced again. He sputtered and coughed, then went under the water. Down, down, to the bottom of the pool. Nine feet. Juniper was poised to jump when Shane's hand circled the keys. Soon he was racing toward the surface, his face practically purple as he sucked in a breath. All around him, people were laughing, snapping photos, and taking more bets on whether he'd pass out.

Juniper knelt down, reaching for him.

Shane pushed her hand away, going under again. This time, when he came up for air, he scrabbled for the pool's ladder. He barely made it to the concrete before losing control of his limbs. For a second, Juniper thought he'd passed out. But as she knelt beside him, brushing the hair from his face, he blinked up at her, water slipping from his lips.

"Are you trying to kill me?"

"I . . . I didn't think you'd . . ." Her phone started to ring. Juniper's first instinct was to silence it and keep talking, but then she saw the name flashing across the screen. "Oh, crap. My mom's here. I forgot we called her."

Shane huffed, as if to say, *We didn't do anything together.* Then he erupted in a coughing fit.

"I'll be right out," Juniper said into the phone. "I'm bringing a friend, too."

"I'm not going anywhere with you," he snarled, his chest heaving. "Just stay away from me."

"We can give you a ride. We'll go by Ruby's and—"

"Get away from me," he screamed, and Juniper stumbled back. Here was the boy she'd been afraid of, the kind of boy who always ended up with Ruby.

She blinked, trying to separate fear from rationality. But Shane was glaring up at her, and his hand was bleeding where he clutched the keys too tightly. "I have to go now," she said as her phone rang again. "We can still drive you."

Shane lowered his head to his arm. He looked, for a moment, like he was sleeping. As Juniper's phone rang for the third time, Gavin stepped onto the patio, a concerned look on his face.

Parker was nowhere to be seen.

Holding her hand in front of Shane's mouth, to make sure he was breathing, Juniper answered her phone with her free hand. "I'm coming. It's just going to be me." She pushed off the ground. And she backed away from him as Gavin stepped closer, his eyes widened in shock.

"I have to go," Juniper told him. "My mother's here. Can I trust you to—"

"I'll take care of him," Gavin promised, and Juniper smiled, barely registering the sight of the bright red marker in his hand. A car honked in the distance, her phone started to vibrate, and she disappeared into the darkness.

After that, the night revealed itself in flashes. Gavin remembered the sound of Juniper getting into a car. He remembered Parker throwing ice cubes into the hot tub, while yelling, "You've been pranked, suckas!" and then everyone scattered.

The patio was theirs.

The night was theirs, and Parker was huddling in the bushes, giggling like a ten-year-old, as Gavin wrote *shithead* on Shane Ferrick's arm. Then a chunk of time went missing. When Gavin looked down, he thought Shane was covered in slashes, and he had to blink several times before the world came into focus.

"Write 'douchebag deviant,'" Parker hissed from the darkness. "Write 'white trash piece of shit.'"

Gavin's stomach turned. He wasn't sure if Parker's instructions were causing it, or the fact that he'd ingested more beer in the past two hours than in all his previous hours on earth. There'd been a tequila shot in there too. He had the vaguest recollection of noshing on chips and artichoke dip, but that had been forever ago. A lifetime had come and gone since then.

No matter, he thought, stumbling away from the body. He'd remember his last meal soon enough. It was about to come up, and if Gavin wasn't careful, both Parker and Shane would bear witness to it.

No, not Shane, Gavin realized, pushing past Parker into the darker part of the bushes. Shane was passed out, and someone else was trudging across the lawn. Then Parker was picking up the marker, writing *white trash* in the crook of Shane's arm, and the boy with the bald head was stepping into the moonlight. The last thing Gavin remembered was mumbling the words, "We exposed him," to Brett Carmichael, before opening the patio doors and slipping inside.

24.

WILD HAIR

Ruby's breath was ragged, like she'd raced through the forest with a beast on her heels. That was how she felt in this moment. Like she'd been running from something horrible all night, and now she had to face it. But when the monster turned to her, she found its face was sweet. One of its faces was.

"You weren't trying to kill him," she breathed.

"Of course I wasn't," Juniper said, knowing immediately that Ruby was talking to her. They couldn't exactly make eye contact through a camera lens. But here, in this dark passageway, Ruby had no choice but to address the camera on the wall. Below it, a screen revealed her classmates lounging in the beautiful, spacious living room. A room with sofas to sprawl out on.

Ruby cringed. She hated being confined, hated being lashed to a chair with a rope. Still, that was nothing compared to the sight of her childhood friend slamming into the patio stones as Brianna Ferrick stood over her, grinning.

"Juniper doesn't belong here," Ruby said. "You should let her go."

"*Juniper* lured my brother into that house," Brianna drawled, and Ruby thrashed against her bindings. "*Juniper* lured my brother into that pool and left him, half-conscious, at a party where everyone hated him."

"She was trying to keep him from driving! It's wrong to punish her for that."

"Wrong?" Brianna smiled, slow and eerie, and it was so much worse than the doll's smile had been. Her lips were a blurry red. "All of this is wrong. My brother is dead. First drowned. Then branded. Then bludgeoned, if what I suspect is true. But until I know for certain, I need everyone present. Do you understand?" Her gaze narrowed, settling on the boy with hazel eyes. "Brett," she said, clucking her tongue. "You know you're next."

Brett shuddered, shaking his head. "You know what I did," he murmured, just loud enough for the camera to pick up his words. "I thought nobody could see me from the house, but some of them did. Some of them saw me through the windows."

"I've heard rumors," Brianna agreed. "But if that's all you're hiding, why the blush in your cheeks? The fidgeting? I've got a wild hair to prove that you're protecting somebody, and you don't love yourself enough for it to be you. Is it Juniper? Gavin? Our darling Ruby?"

"He won't tell you," Ruby said calmly. "Not without Parker's permission."

Brett glowered, now that Ruby was taunting him. Pulling at the threads that barely kept him together, like a sweater that had been unraveling for a very long time.

"Parker's the only one who loves him," Ruby explained. "His father's given up on him. His mother disappeared long before I lost my dad. Then Parker came along and scooped you up, didn't he, Brett? Made you into a monster. Can you even look at yourself, after what he's done?"

Brett was gritting his teeth. Ruby could see it, even from a distance. And, because she was getting to him, she gave him one more push. "But you know what's funny, Brett? Parker *doesn't* love you. He only loves me."

"You don't know what you're talking about," Brett said, glaring into the camera.

And Ruby, lashed to a chair with rope, simply shrugged. "What if we could prove it? What if we could prove, beyond a shadow of a doubt, that Parker Addison is a self-serving liar who's thrown every one of you under the bus? You already know he funded Brianna's party to get me back."

"He wanted to keep you safe," Brett said, softly enough that Ruby had to lean in to hear him. "He didn't want you tied up like a prisoner."

"Yet, here I am. Tied up, like a present to be delivered, and none of it would've happened without Parker's help. He *designed* these punishments with her, first Gavin's and Juniper's, then—"

"No." Brett leaned against the wall, and Ruby could tell he was holding himself up. "They were supposed to be pranks."

"Maybe the first two. The writing on Gavin's skin and Juniper's tumble into the pool. Oops, you're all wet! Let's have a laugh about it." Ruby's lips twisted. "But your punishment, Brett? The boy who pulverized Shane Ferrick with a flurry of fists? How does one fashion a prank after that?"

"He wouldn't have agreed to it if he thought I'd get hurt."

"He knew you'd get hurt!" That was Brianna, and it was obvious she was feeling left out of the fun. Ruby needed to be careful. She didn't want to step on any toes. But rope be damned, the girls made a pretty good team when it came to exposing Parker. Still, the best was yet to come, wasn't it?

Brianna was gearing up for something. "In a proper court-room, each side presents arguments, along with exhibits. What do you say?" she asked, the joy returning to her voice. "Should we put Parker on trial?"

"All rise!" Ruby agreed.

Brianna fussed with the TV, pulling up a split screen. On the left, Ruby saw the live feed of the living room, just as she'd seen before. On the right, she saw Parker's lavish bedroom. The four-poster bed. The gilded mirror. But the video must've been taken earlier in the night, because someone familiar was entering the room: Ruby herself. Parker pulled her through the door, and then he was locking it, blocking Juniper out. As Ruby sat on the black satin sheets, he told her he'd been asked to bring a rope to the party.

"And you didn't do it?" Ruby heard herself ask in a ridicu-lously breathy voice. And Parker, his pretty eyes wide, said, "I left it in my car."

Brianna pushed another button, rewinding the scene. This time, she pushed play a couple of minutes before Ruby entered the room, when Parker *pulled a rope out of his bag and hid it in a drawer.*

"Any questions?" Brianna asked with a smirk.

Ruby's gaze zeroed in on Parker, the blood rushing through her ears. "You looked me in the eye and told me you hadn't brought the rope. How could you do that? How could you leave it for Brianna to find?"

"That isn't what happened!" Parker exclaimed. "Yes, I brought the rope into the house, but I didn't hide it *for her*. I hid it in case we needed to defend ourselves."

"I could pull up the emails," Brianna replied, and that shut

Parker up. "I could pull up the part where we discussed hiding the rope from Ruby. But I won't, because there are more important things to discuss. The reason we're all here. My brother, with his rope. My brother, making a video of our fair Ruby, and sharing it all over school. Or so it seemed. After all, Shane had that ebony hair. We both did, actually."

Parker clasped his hands over his mouth, staggering backwards. "*You* took the video. Everyone blamed Shane, because of that dark hair, curving over the frame—"

"But it was mine," Brianna admitted. "When you're right, you're right."

Juniper gasped, and all the color bled out of Gavin's cheeks. Brett closed his eyes. But Ruby's eyes had grown wide at the sound of Brianna's confession, and she stared at the girl in the mask, her gaze unflinching. "When did you start wearing the wig?"

"Oh, I think you know the answer to that question." Brianna reached up, scratching her head. "Did you ever see the movie *The Witches*? Remember how they scratched their wigs before they revealed themselves? Their true faces?"

Ruby remembered. She'd seen *The Witches* and read the book when she was a child. She'd seen the movie *Clue* and played the game whenever she had the chance. She'd seen *Scream* and *I Know What You Did Last Summer*. She loved scary movies, as long as they weren't too gory.

Psychological torture was better, anyway.

That was what she'd always thought. But now, with Brianna scratching that wig, Ruby's guts clenched. She imagined a hideous sight hiding beneath that hair. Imagined a skull covered in third-degree burns. And she held her breath as the wig fell away, revealing the secret Brianna had been keeping.

Each one of them had a secret. Each one of them was wearing a mask. And one by one, those masks would fall away.

"Parker?" Brianna asked, looking small and vulnerable without her wig. Her head wasn't bald, but rather, had the first downy curls of a newborn's growing out of it. Dark and beautiful and soft. "Would you like to tell them what happened?"

"Hey, if you decided to shave your head, that's your problem." Parker shrugged, crossing his arms.

"Actually, I did. Two months ago," Brianna added. "It wouldn't grow back even, after the burns." She ran her long, lithe fingers through Ruby's crimson tresses. "You have beautiful hair, you know that?"

"I . . . Thank you," Ruby managed. Her heart was a wild thing, feral and thrashing. Blood pulsed in her palms.

"It's really a pity, what I have to do now."

"Leave her alone," Parker snarled, storming up to the camera.

"Of course, you could stop it." Brianna turned, rummaging around in the darkness. She'd confiscated Ruby's purse, but she also had a bag of her own. "If you told them the truth, I might let her go."

"Might," Parker repeated. That was the word he stuck on. Not "let her go." Not "the truth." Just "might." Without a guarantee, he'd let Ruby burn. *Literally*, she thought, as Brianna lifted a matchbox from her bag.

"Parker, please," Ruby begged. "Whatever happened, I promise I'll forgive you. Please don't let her kill me."

"I'm not going to kill you. I'm just going to . . ." She struck a match and lowered it to Ruby's hair. "Where should I start? The ends will go up more quickly, but the roots will have more of an impact on the audience."

Parker made a sound like choking. Opened his mouth, as if to spill the dark, dirty secret he was keeping. Then, just as quickly, he fell silent. He wasn't going to sacrifice himself to save Ruby.

As usual, she'd have to do it herself.

Ruby slammed her head backwards. There was a sizzling sound, as fire met flesh, but that was nothing compared to the sound of her skull meeting Brianna's mask. Porcelain cracked, and when Ruby twisted around, she found a long, crooked line running down the center of the mask. She could've whooped in triumph. Instead she pushed to her feet, the chair still lashed to her body, and pivoted left, slamming it against her captor.

Then, a thud.

Then, scampering as Brianna struggled to find her footing, but Ruby didn't stick around to watch. She bolted up a set of stairs, seeking the door at the top. She turned the knob. Pushed and pushed. The door cracked open, just enough to squeeze through, and then she was standing in the playroom with the life-size doll. Someone had written on his skin. Someone had drenched him from head to toe, and now he was dripping water onto the floor. Ruby's heart clenched, and she fought off the dark, desperate desire to protect him. This was only a doll.

The real Shane Ferrick was gone.

Tearing her gaze from the boy so familiar he knocked the breath from her lungs, Ruby lunged for the playroom door. She was halfway down the hall when she heard footsteps behind her, slow and measured, as if Brianna had all the time in the world.

Ruby didn't. When she reached the top of the banister, she slammed the chair against it. Wood splintered but didn't crack. She slammed it again. The rope was burning her skin, but still, she hurled that chair against the banister until it broke. It didn't come apart entirely, but it came apart enough, and then Ruby was wriggling out of her bindings.

She was free.

Or so she thought. But the others had gathered at the bottom of the stairs, and they were screaming at her to turn around. She spun just in time to see Brianna reaching for her. No, not reaching. Pushing. Ruby stumbled backwards, and she barely had time to drop to her knees before she was falling. She wasn't a girl escaping a beast. She was skin scraping and bones bruising and lungs crying out for release. But Ruby was a survivor, and this wasn't her first time falling down the stairs.

She wouldn't let it break her.

When she passed the middle of the staircase, Ruby reached out, her hand slamming against the banister. She shrieked, cursing the wrought-iron structure, and gravity, and any god that still cared about her. New bruises blossomed on her skin, but she didn't pull back her hand. Instead she grappled until her fingers curled around the banister and her body stopped falling.

Everything stopped.

Then, a homecoming party. A welcoming like she'd never known. Parker and Brett were cheering at the bottom of the stairs, and Gavin had some color in his cheeks. Only Juniper failed to grin, and Ruby didn't have time to ask why as she hobbled toward them.

She felt the rope slide around her throat. Felt herself lift into the air, her hands going instinctively to the rope, but she couldn't pull it away. She couldn't free herself. The last thing she saw, before spots eclipsed her vision, was Parker's mouth opening. "It was me!" he shouted.

Then another thud, as Ruby's body hit the first-floor land-ing. Her hands clasped her throat. She was crying, her eyes stinging like her skin, and when she looked up at Parker, she found his lashes were wet.

Ruby reached for him. He pulled her from the ground, cra-dling her in his arms. And Brianna, curiously, moved back.

"Park, you can tell me," Ruby said softly, curling into him. "Whatever you did, you can tell me."

Parker peered at her. Those green eyes, which had always seemed like emeralds glittering, had a curious light to them. A wicked spark. He brushed the hair from her face, kissing her forehead tenderly, and whispered, "I made the video of you and Shane."

25.

God's honest truth, Parker only half remembered that day. He thought he'd taken care of the problem. Thought cutting off Ruby's access to Shane's bedroom would be enough, and the spell would unravel.

He'd been wrong.

The morning after he'd sent her mother into hysterics, he spied Ruby at the edge of the school park, her fingers sliding into Shane Ferrick's hair. Parker's fingers curled into fists. He wanted to charge into those trees and knock the forbidden fruit right out of Ruby's hands, but that would only make it more tantalizing to her.

He needed to cut Shane off at the roots.

Later that day, he found himself stalking the aisles of one of his father's grocery stores, searching for chemical hair remover. Parker could remember the summer when Ruby had tried that stuff on her legs. Tired of shaving (and too proud to let Parker pay for a waxing), Ruby had opted to burn the hair off her legs. The result had been red, splotchy skin with the occasional tuft of hair sticking out.

Parker had burst out laughing at the sight of it.

Now he almost did it again, envisioning Shane's bald,

splotchy head, but there were cameras all over his father's stores. He didn't want to get caught acting suspicious. Calmly, he plucked a razor from one of the shelves, to give the illusion that he was shopping for himself, and then he slipped a bottle of that chemical crap into his shirt while he was bent over.

The evening passed in a blur. Before he'd even realized where the time had gone, he was climbing out of his car at the Fallen Oaks Trailer Park, approaching Shane's trailer in the dark. The bathroom window was cracked. It led directly into the shower, and Parker reached inside, easily locating the bottle of shampoo on a hanging rack. He knew, from conversations at school, that Shane liked to take showers "when the moon was bright."

He rolled his eyes at the thought, filling the bottle with hair remover.

Then he waited for Shane to arrive. It took a good hour and a half, and when the door to the Ferricks' bathroom opened, Parker jumped back. From the safety of the darkness, he caught a glimpse of sickly pale skin and stringy dark hair.

He grinned.

And time began to speed by. Maybe it was because Parker was enjoying himself, or maybe the universe was conspiring with him, speeding past the unimportant moments to get to the good stuff. Yes, that had to be it, because time slowed down again when a shriek came from the bathroom.

Parker stepped closer, pulling his phone out of his pocket. *A picture is worth a thousand words*, he thought, creeping up to the glass. But what he saw there stilled his breath and knocked the smile from his face.

Shane Ferrick wasn't standing there in a towel, sobbing into his hands. It was Brianna. Then someone was knocking on the bathroom door, and Brianna was wrapping another towel around her head to hide what had happened.

Parker raced for the parking lot. He'd almost reached his car when a door slammed open. He could hear it at his back, and he froze, telling himself he wouldn't be seen. If anything, the light coming from inside the trailer would make the surrounding area darker.

He turned and looked.

And there, coming out of the Ferricks' front door, was Shane. Did he know Parker was there? No, Parker realized, sliding into his Mustang. Shane didn't look angry. He looked excited.

He was carrying a rope.

He's going to see Ruby, Parker thought, as Shane slipped behind the wheel of his car. He didn't know where the thought had come from, or why he felt so certain of it, but he did. He had hurt someone Shane loved, and now Shane was going to hurt someone he loved.

He tailed the guy all the way to Ruby's block.

When Shane disappeared around the side of the house, Parker pulled out his phone. He wanted to record Shane standing in Ruby's room with that rope. Wanted to show the world who Shane really was before he kicked his ass. Activating the camera, he set it to record, then hurried across the lawn. There was an old, fat cherry tree outside Ruby's window, and if he set the phone in just the right crook, he could get part of her bed in the frame.

So he did.

Then, creeping around the tree trunk, he peered through the open window. Ruby was sliding off her bed, dressed in a tiny white nightgown, while Shane stepped toward her, whispering about leaving town. And Ruby . . .

The love of his life.

The girl he'd lost his virginity to.

Ruby leaned in and *agreed*. Soon she was kissing him, and they were crawling all over each other, and then . . .

She stopped.

The breath rushed into Parker's body. She stopped! Finally, after all his plotting, Ruby had shaken off Shane's spell on her own. Now Shane was moving to the window, ready to slip into the night and out of Ruby's life.

Parker slid into the shadows with no trouble at all—that, he was getting very good at—and he waited for Shane to climb into his car and peel away. But Shane didn't. He simply plucked an object from the passenger seat and returned to Ruby's window.

What the hell?

Parker waited for Ruby's strangled cry. He waited for the exact perfect moment to swoop in and be her white knight. He was even wearing white! His crisp white T-shirt was in perfect contrast to Shane's dark button-down, and he felt a thrill of excitement at the thought of defending Ruby's honor.

But something strange was happening inside of Ruby's bedroom. Parker took one step closer, then two. By the third step, his heart had cracked open and his brain had turned off. When he came to again, he was kneeling on the ground, the rope had been discarded, and so had Ruby's clothes.

Then he remembered the phone.

He'd been recording the entire time, and he'd never once stepped in front of the camera. But would it be enough? From the looks of things, Ruby and Shane were just getting started. If Parker played this right, he could still pull off a major coup, humiliate Shane Ferrick in front of the entire school, and win back the love of his life.

But he would have to be quick. He raced down the street, pulled open the door to his car, and practically tumbled inside. After taking three painful breaths, he turned the key in the ignition.

Then Parker drove off into the night.

Fifteen minutes later, when he was squeezing through the Ferricks' bathroom window, he wondered if the universe was testing him. In fairy tales, the knight in shining armor always had to endure some great and terrible trial. In order to rescue the princess, and be worthy of a kingdom, you had to be fierce. You had to be strong. Gathering a few strands of Brianna's hair, Parker felt invincible.

He drove back to Ruby's house.

This time, he parked halfway down the block, jogged quietly to Ruby's window, and hid behind the cherry tree. But he didn't stop the recording yet. He needed to wait for Shane to leave, and then he could dangle that ebony hair in front of the camera. The evidence would be irrefutable. Shane would be exposed for the deviant that he was. And Parker would swoop in, comforting his princess and securing his rightful place on the throne.

26.

KNOCK OUT

Ruby stared at Parker, her mouth hanging open. She was trembling, and she didn't imagine it would stop anytime soon. "You . . ." She pushed out of his arms. She thought that if Brianna snuck up on her in that moment and slid a knife across her throat, she wouldn't feel a thing.

But Brianna didn't sneak up on Ruby. Brianna wasn't even there. During the course of Parker's confession, she must've slipped down the hallway. Now Ruby could see a blur of white watching them from the dining room, while the rope remained at Ruby's feet.

She lifted it from the ground. Beckoning the group into the living room, she bound the doorknobs carefully, the way she'd done with Shane's wrists one year earlier.

Then she hurled herself at Parker.

Her first blow knocked his face to the side, and she could already see a welt. But she didn't stop to savor the sight. She caught him with a left hook, pushing off with her heel, the way she'd learned to do after her father disappeared. Mrs. Valentine had insisted the older girls in the family learn self-defense, and Ruby had taken to it instantly. There was so much fire inside her, so many things she'd held back over the years. It had been nice to let it out.

It was nicer now. Parker lumbered backward, smacking into a sofa, and Ruby actually thought he was going to go down. She tossed a glance at Brett, as if to say, *This isn't so hard*. But Brett was coming closer, and while Ruby didn't think he'd knock her out to protect his precious Parker, she could envision his arms wrapping around her, lifting her as if she were weightless.

She got in one last kick before she walked away, hands in the air. A false surrender. Once Brett let his guard down, she could go after Parker again. She could really make him pay.

Down on the floor, Parker was kneeling, hands scrabbling for the edge of the sofa. "What the hell—"

"You're the reason we're here," she spat, hands shaking. He was staring at her, red-faced, panting, like he didn't even know who she was. *That's good*, she thought, gritting her teeth. *He has no idea who I am. But he will.*

"Brianna's the reason we're here," he said, finally regaining his composure. "She tried to kill you. She tried to drown your friend."

Ruby glanced at Juniper, curled up on the sofa. Gavin sat beside her, keeping her warm. A surge of empathy rushed through Ruby, and she hurried over to them. She was so, so angry, ready to rip Parker's face off, but seeing them huddled together was tugging at her heartstrings. Tugging at what was left of her. Sometimes, she thought only a piece of her had remained after the night of the fire.

Like her soul had slipped away with Shane's.

She winced, sitting gingerly on the sofa. "That morning, I had the most wonderful smile on my face. The kind that sends energy all through your body, down to your toes. Then I looked at my phone, and that video was waiting for me." She squeezed her eyes shut. "God, Parker, how could you do that?"

"I needed you to see who he was."

"That isn't who he was! That's who *you* are." Ruby's fists tightened, and Juniper reached out to stop her from attacking again. For a moment, the girls had a conversation without words. Ruby could see the remorse in Juniper's eyes, and she could only imagine how sorry her old friend was. Everyone at school saw the video of Shane carrying a rope into Ruby's bedroom.

Everyone thought he was guilty.

"I didn't want to believe it," Ruby whispered as Juniper studied her. Gavin studied her too. Even Brett, who'd been glued to Parker's side all night, couldn't tear his gaze from Ruby.

He slumped against the doors. "Parker told me Shane made the video. He said Shane was laughing about it that morning, bragging in the locker room—" Brett choked off, clutching his head in his hands. His brain just didn't want to stay inside.

And Ruby shook her head, cluck-cluck-clucking her tongue. "Oh, Parker. That's a rookie mistake. You *never* lie to the best friend."

Parker scowled, not even bothering to appeal to Brett. Always, he appealed to Ruby. "Nobody understood what Shane was doing. He was manipulating you."

"Do you hear yourself? He wasn't doing anything to me. I wanted him." Ruby wandered over to the window, savoring the memory of Shane's lips pressed against hers. She remembered leaning over him, learning to move her body in an entirely new way, melting into someone, rather than always pulling away.

"And you know what? He was good. *We* were good. I knew he couldn't have hurt me like that. But there was this moment, watching the video, when I just . . . didn't trust myself anymore. Didn't trust my memories, didn't trust my instincts." She turned, catching Parker's gaze. "I haven't always made the smartest choices."

Parker flinched, looking to Brett for support, but Brett wasn't having any of it. Ruby smiled at the rift growing between them. Finally, *finally*, people were showing their true faces.

"All day, I tried to get ahold of him," she said, remembering her desperation. She'd texted and she'd called, doing everything short of visiting Shane at home. "What did you do, steal his phone?"

Parker's gaze hardened to stone. "It fell out of his pocket when he dropped his pants on your floor. And he didn't notice it when he left, so I reached in and picked it up while you were taking a shower. I sent the video *from* his phone, then I sent Brett to your house to keep you from doing something reckless. Right, Brett?"

Parker turned to the doors, where Brett had been standing a moment ago. Now there was only empty space, and a hastily tossed-aside rope. Ruby had, after all, only tied it in a bow, in case they needed to escape.

"What the hell?" Parker darted across the room. "He's gone."

Gavin cursed, staring at the space where Brett had been. "He's going to run. She's going to catch him and—"

"Maybe not," Ruby said, holding Parker's eye. "Maybe he's going to confess."

Parker's face reddened, and he yanked open the doors. Before anyone could stop him, he'd bolted into the hallway, leaving the others in his dust. The doors swung shut behind him.

"We have to go after them," Gavin stammered. "If Brianna gets her hands on Brett before Parker can reach him—"

"She won't," Ruby said, gathering the rope in her hands. Juniper stood with Gavin's help. Together, they followed the sound of shouting to the dining room. There, Parker was engaged in an epic battle. A battle with the patio doors. He was screaming at them, trying to yank them open, but they must've been locked from the outside.

Brianna must've locked them.

Ruby could see her now, inching slowly across the patio in the darkness. There was something unusual about her ensemble, a splash of red among the white. Was it blood? No. It was a little red can. Not unlike the watering can Ruby used to feed the vegetables in her garden at home. Except, well, that can held a life-giving substance, and this one could take life away in an instant.

All you had to do was strike a match.

"Brett," Parker yelled, banging on the doors. "Brett, get back here!"

"He's not out there," Ruby said. "None of us is going anywhere." When she stepped up to the glass, she could see that Brianna was just completing her project. She must've been busy while Ruby was punching Parker in the face.

Now, with a line of gasoline drawn around the house, Brianna pulled a matchbox out of her pocket. Such a small thing, to take down a person. A single match! It was kind of pathetic, when Ruby thought of it like that. But the tiniest of sparks could give life to the greatest of fires, and Ruby watched, mesmerized, as Brianna stepped up to the patio doors.

She wasn't lighting her wicked circle. She was writing something on the glass. But she hadn't perfected the art of writing backwards, so it took Ruby a minute to decipher the message.

> *The Iron Stomach's gone rogue*
> *The situation looks dire.*
> *If he leaves without permission . . .*
> *This party ends in fire.*

27.

ELECTRIC LOVE

Parker reacted first, because, like always, Parker had to be the center of attention. He had to keep the spotlight on his face. Spinning away from the patio doors, he raced toward the hallway, shouting, "Brett! Damn it, get back here. I can't—"

Then, silence. Gavin tried to fill in the blanks. *I can't protect you* seemed too thoughtful for Parker Addison. *I can't fool Brianna without you* seemed too honest. Was Parker trying to fool Brianna? Still? He looked frazzled, even in that crisp green suit, and his usually tousled hair was a little flat, like he'd been sweating. Clearly, he knew more than he was telling, but if he'd done something to Shane Ferrick the night of the party, he'd take that secret to his grave.

He'd take all of them.

"We're going to burn," Ruby said, her breath fogging up the glass door. In that long red dress, she looked like Jessica Rabbit. All she needed were the gloves. Well, she *had* gloves, but Jessica's were purple, and Ruby's were red, to match her slippers.

Which movie was this?

Gavin shook himself, but his mind kept meandering. He was desperate to believe they were in a movie. A million-dollar

production called *Who Framed Shane Ferrick?* where Hollywood
directors told him where to stand and what to say. And, after
it was over, the director would yell, "Cut," and the actor playing Shane would jog out from behind the scenery, waving and
grinning.

Then they'd all go out for drinks.

In the real world, Gavin's eyes trailed to his skin, and he
had to stop himself from throwing up. Shane Ferrick hadn't
done anything to Ruby. He hadn't done anything to anyone,
and still, they'd tormented him until he was too messed up to
see three feet in front of his face. Yes, if Gavin was very honest
with himself, the truth about that night was clear:

They'd killed an innocent boy.

Maybe they even deserved to be punished. But how much?
That was the question, and it was a tricky one. When Brianna had scrawled on his skin with a marker, an eye for an eye
hadn't seemed so horrifying. It hadn't been *great*. In fact, it
had all-around sucked to wake up like that, head pounding and
body looking like Banksy's drunken cousin had gotten ahold
of it. But Gavin would allow himself to be written on, if that
was what it took.

To make up for what he'd done.

Then Juniper had almost drowned, and Ruby had tumbled
down the stairs, and an eye for an eye had taken a terrifying
turn. Gavin wanted to stop it. He wanted to save the girls, and
Brett, too. Even Parker, if the guy stopped talking for the rest
of the night. Every time he opened his mouth, Gavin's hands
balled into fists. Ruby was practically chanting "Redrum" at
this point. Parker was dragging them down, and while Gavin
didn't approve of setting the guy on fire, the longer they stayed
together, the greater the risk of Parker fanning the flames.

He needed to get Parker out of there, and then he could conspire with the girls. Share knowledge about the house. So he did the one thing that would *guarantee* Parker's exit from the dining room.

"We need to stay where we are," Gavin said, his voice filling the space. He sounded confident, strong. That would really piss Parker off. "Every time we go running off on our own, Brianna strikes. The only way to ensure our safety—"

"There is no way to ensure our safety," Parker spat. "She's going to burn the house down!"

"That was a bluff. She's going after Brett, and you know it. She thinks he knows something."

"He doesn't."

"Then you don't have anything to worry about," Gavin reasoned. "I'm telling you, the only way she lights that fire is if she has *proof* one of us put her brother into that car. She's doing to us what we did to him."

"It . . . kind of makes sense," Ruby said, from her place by the doors. She wouldn't even look at Parker. "Brianna wants justice, which is why she's drawing out our stories, one by one. Some of the stuff, she must've heard around town. I heard plenty of rumors." Her gaze flicked to Juniper, and Juniper winced. "But until tonight, I didn't know what you guys really did. I think you're right. I think she's going after Brett next, but she's not going to attack until she knows what really happened."

"You guys are crazy. She's going to hunt him down and—" Parker broke off, pretending to be choked up. Gavin knew he was pretending at this point. Parker only admitted to guilt when he'd already been caught, and even then, he defended himself.

All this horror, all these lies, and still, he hadn't said he was sorry.

Now, wearing remorse like a mask he could shed at any moment, he told them, "She's going to torture Brett. She's going to *torture a person*, and you don't even care. Whatever. Stay here and cower. I'm going after him."

With that, Parker raced to the stairs, his footfalls pounding against the hardwood floors. The house shook with the force of them. And Gavin, a little too pleased with himself, turned to the girls with a smile. "Well? You ready to get the hell out of here?"

"Oh my God. Yes!" Ruby clapped her hands. "But what about the guys? Brianna *will* hurt Brett if she finds out what he did."

"I know." Gavin's stomach dropped, and he told himself that he could save all of them. He would. "But if Brett locks himself in a room, it'll take Brianna time to get to him. And by then . . ."

"We'll have called the police. But how do we get out of the house? There's only one exit."

"As far as we know." He stepped closer to Ruby, speaking softly. "But Brianna knows things that we don't. Where was she hiding you, before?"

"There's a secret passageway. It leads from the study to the master bedroom upstairs," Ruby said, toying with her rope. "If she used a ladder to climb up to the balcony, she could slip in and out of the house whenever—"

"What balcony? Where?"

Ruby pointed out and up. Over the patio. Gavin's body flooded with heat. Meanwhile, Juniper was shivering, her arms wrapped around herself. His heart sank, thinking of what it would take to get her out of this house.

He hurried to her side, sliding an arm around her waist. "How you doing, Bambi?"

"Bambi?" she asked, her voice a little stronger than before.

"You know, shaky fawn's legs. Baby steps."

"Funny." She scowled, but he knew it was playful. Just like she knew his joking came from a place of affection. That, and a desperate desire to keep from panicking. As long as they could joke, they could survive.

"How about you?" he asked Ruby. "You doing all right?"

"I thought you'd never ask," Ruby gushed, following his lighthearted lead. There was a pause, as she surveyed her bruises. "I'll live."

"Good." He offered his free arm. Ruby took it, and together, the three of them returned to the hallway.

"Do you think there are cameras out here?" Ruby asked, her cheeks still flaming from her encounter with Parker. The girl had a mean left hook. "God, do you think he installed them for her?"

"Probably," Gavin muttered bitterly. He needed to keep her mind off Parker. He needed to keep *his* mind off the guy, because every time he thought about Parker's manipulation, and what he'd done to the Ferricks, Gavin found himself sympathizing with Brianna.

And that wasn't good.

"Look, we can figure it all out later." He led them toward the long, twisting staircase. "We can analyze the whole thing when we're sitting in my living room, in front of the fire. Scratch that, no fire," he corrected. "Hot chocolate and blankets."

Juniper cooed. Her hair was still wet from the pool, and Gavin wished they could stop by a bathroom and get her a towel. It was a foolish thought, considering where he was leading them, but he wanted that for her, in that moment. Comfort. Warmth. Besides, there were practical reasons for making a detour.

"Anyone else have to pee? We've been here, what, two hours? Three? And if Brianna keeps popping up out of the shadows . . ." Gavin paused, smiling slyly. "Well, let's just say we don't need an accident on top of imminent death."

"It's there." Ruby pointed to a door at the end of the hall. "I found it when I was looking for the study. Oh my God, you guys, Brianna came out of the walls! I'd just come into the study when an entire bookshelf swung forward, and I felt fingers tickling my neck." She swallowed, clearly thinking about what had happened next. The dark room. The rope. It was kind of a miracle that she'd broken free.

Quietly they hurried to the bathroom. Slipped inside. Scanned the room for signs of a threat. But all they found were white tiles and brass accents, and a door that actually locked.

They closed themselves inside.

"Well," Gavin said after a minute, "you'd think we'd be bonded after everything that's happened, but . . ."

"Feeling a little shy?" Ruby teased. Then, to show she was a good sport, she reached down and turned on the bathtub, creating noise. She even plugged up the drain, so steam would fill the room.

Gavin was thankful. The house was big, old and drafty. Soon he started to feel warm. As the girls took care of their business (of course they wouldn't be shy around each other), he searched the cabinets for towels. He found a hair dryer and curling iron, but nothing fluffy. Nothing soft. Still, the room was steaming up, and after they'd all relieved themselves, they huddled together beside the tub, listening to Gavin's plan. When he'd finished talking, Ruby turned to Juniper, asking, "Are you up for it?"

Gavin held his breath.

Juniper didn't make him wait. Her limbs were trembling and her hair was plastered to her face, but she said, "Yes." Immediately, she said, "Yes." His chest tightened. This was what he loved about her, what he'd always loved about Juniper Torres. Her bravery. Her refusal to give in.

Maybe, after tonight, he would tell her.

For now, he stuck to the basics. "When we leave this room, there's no going back," he said, sliding off his shoes. The girls followed suit, Juniper kicking hers across the room. "We'll go as quickly as we can. And if she figures out what we're up to, and sets the house on fire in an act of desperation, we'll take a leap of faith—"

"An act." Ruby gasped, looking up. "All of this is set up like a circus. A grand, dramatic show."

"You're not telling me anything I don't know," Gavin said.

"Well, how about this?" She pulled the hair dryer out of the cupboard. The curling iron too. "What if you could actually become the Invisible Man?"

"Why would I want that?" he asked, as Ruby plugged in the styling tools.

"All night, we've been trying to escape the identities she made for us, but maybe they're exactly what we need to shut the circus down." Now that the electronics were plugged in, Ruby guided them toward the huddle. Toward the tub. "You have to become invisible. Juniper has to make friends with the depths."

"And you?" Gavin cocked his head.

Tucking the hair dryer under her arm, Ruby pulled something out of her dress. Like a saloon dancer in an old western, she reached right into her cleavage and procured the card marked *Ruby Valentine*. Opened it up. The three of them read it together.

1. My name is THE DISAPPEARING ACT.
2. I am secretly in love with A CORPSE.
3. My weapon is a REVOLVER because I HAVE A KILLER'S INSTINCT.
4. My greatest secret is I MADE AN ENTIRE PERSON DISAPPEAR.

"Um. Hold on a minute," Gavin said, pointing to number three. "You have a revolver? Is it loaded?"

"Would you bring a loaded gun into a house with Parker?" Ruby huffed, shaking her head. "I wouldn't, and it's a good thing too, because Brianna confiscated my purse in the secret passageway. But let's focus on number four, shall we? Apparently, I made a person disappear."

"Shane." Juniper bit her lip. "She blames you as much as anyone."

"I was supposed to go to the party. I left him alone. I made him disappear. And now . . ." When Ruby looked down at the swiftly filling tub, the red of her dress reflected in her eyes. Red eyes. Red hair. Red gloves. She looked possessed. Stepping closer to the bathtub, she lifted the electronics over the water. "I'm going to make the entire circus . . . disappear."

28.

KEY WITNESS

The bedroom was colder than Brett remembered. Maybe his body had acclimated to the temperature of the living room, with its blazing fire and tangling bodies. Or maybe he was simply panicking, and his body was going haywire as a result. What he knew for certain was that he needed to be alone, in the quiet.

He closed the door and stumbled to the bed.

He couldn't believe that Parker had made the video. He honestly couldn't, and his mind kept trying to find a hole in the story. Parker had lied about so many things. Maybe this was all part of the game, and Parker was still working with Brianna, and the lie about the video was supposed to send Brett into a tailspin from which he would never return.

If that was their intention, those two were geniuses. Brett was coming undone. He felt as if his skin was unraveling, and whatever remained of his soul was trying to climb out, to get away from the person that he'd become.

"I was never supposed to go to that party," he said, speaking to the camera he assumed was there. It made no sense to bug the common rooms but not their private spaces. *This* was where the magic would happen. Where they would slip away, alone or with a partner of their choice. Where secrets would unfurl.

"I was supposed to watch over Ruby, to make sure she didn't leave the house. Parker thought she might try to confront Shane at the party and humiliate herself. That's what he told me, anyway." Brett swallowed, running his hand over his head. When he was a kid, he'd had soft, chestnut curls, just like his mother, but after she'd left, his father had been unable to look at him. Not with that hair. It had been impossible, and after months of seeing his father wince at the sight of him, Brett had taken a pair of scissors to those curls.

Now, in these final moments, he missed them. He missed her.

What would she think of him? When he was a little boy, he'd believed his father's stories about growing up strong. To save her. To bring her back. But Brett's mother had never been as happy as she was in the moments when she was dancing with him. Sharing secrets. They'd been best friends and they'd been kindred, and his father had taught him to hate the parts of himself that were like her. To cut them out. To pummel them with invisible fists until no softness remained.

Still Brett cried in the dark of the night, when he was alone. And now, with only a pale, ghostly girl watching, he felt tears stinging his eyes. He lowered his head.

"I didn't *want* to go to the party," he admitted. "I hate those things, if I can be honest. Parker always starts shit that he can't finish, so I step in to protect him. But I knew that night would be different."

He'd known it, deep in his bones, long before midnight, when Parker's text had come in. **Ruby still at home?**

Brett wrote back, **Yep. She'll probably be going to bed soon. So . . .**

So, get your ass over here. I've got a present for you.

Brett almost told him no. He was tired, and he wanted to go home. But there was work to be done, and he told himself that after that night, Shane would never hurt Ruby again.

He'd never hurt anyone.

And so, Brett made his way to the party in the hills. He arrived just in time to see Gavin staggering into the bushes. That was a surprise, but Parker was full of surprises, and it was a night of unusual allegiances. Parker and Gavin. Ruby and Brett. Of course, Ruby didn't know that Brett was looking out for her, but that wasn't the point of doing a good deed. You protected people because it was the right thing to do, and because they needed it. Ruby may not have been the angel that people thought she was, but she wasn't violent. She wouldn't hurt Shane, and right now, Shane needed to be hurt in order to learn his lesson.

For doing what he'd done.

Brett had felt certain of that, trudging across Dahlia Kane's lawn. Then he saw Shane passed out on the far end of the patio. Someone had written all over him, and the guy was dripping wet. "What happened?" he asked.

Parker slid out of the shadows, flashing a grin. "Juniper Torres tried to drown him."

"Um. What?"

Parker laughed, clearly delighted at the strange turn of events. "You know how she feels about my girl. Of course, she had the good sense not to sneak into Ruby's bedroom—" He choked off, his jaw clenching. "You ready to do this?"

Brett's stomach tightened. He wanted to feel excited, wanted to believe he was a hero meting out justice. But as Parker lifted Shane's limp body from the ground, all he felt was dread.

"We should wake him up," Brett suggested, forcing a smile. He knew if he said it like that, Parker would think he was being devilish, wanting Shane to experience every moment of pain. In reality, the thought of pummeling an unconscious boy made him want to throw up, even knowing what he knew about Shane.

What he thought he knew.

And so, before the flurry of fists, Brett slapped Shane in the face. Parker was already laughing. And Brett tried to get into it, tried to pretend he was in an old-timey movie, where men slapped each other and said, "I challenge you to a duel!"

In reality, there was no challenge, and this was no duel. But Shane did wake up, after the second slap. When he realized that Parker was holding his arms, and Brett was standing in front of him, he did what anyone would do. He struggled. He screamed.

No one came for him.

Maybe the party was too loud, or maybe the distance was drowning out the noise. Brett sucked in a breath. He felt like he was waiting for something, and he couldn't summon the energy to lunge until Parker whispered in his ear, "He recorded her without her permission. He exposed her to the entire school. What kind of man does something like that?"

Brett's fingers curled into fists. He knew *exactly* what kind of man used a person's most vulnerable moment against them. That was why his mother had been taken away in the middle of the night. Because his father had recorded her, drunk and stumbling, and used the video as evidence to lock her up.

Something inside of Brett broke. All his hesitation fell away, leaving only fury behind. Rage. By the time blood appeared in the corner of Shane Ferrick's mouth, the party was winding down.

"I hit him, over and over again," Brett said into the cold, gray bedroom. There was a sheet draped over the headboard, to hide what had been written there, but he felt the words pressing into him, warning of what was to come.

"And then?" a voice said, and Brett looked up, to see a figure slipping into the room.

The door closed, blocking them in.

29.

When the world went dark, Ruby's heartbeat calmed. For the first time all night, her fingertips ceased to buzz. Her nerves untangled and her breathing slowed. The circus was coming to an end, and she could feel it.

It felt good.

The inside of her mind mirrored the dark, quiet corridors of the house as she slipped out of the bathroom. Gavin had wanted to go first, but with a touch on his arm, Ruby had stopped him. She'd been up and down these halls more than anyone. Tucked away inside a secret passageway, and pushed down the stairs.

It made sense for her to lead them.

And so, she did. On lithe limbs she glided across the floor, her feet a whisper in stockings and no shoes. The rope was looped around her arm. At the foot of the stairs, she paused, waiting for the others to catch up. A part of her wanted to take each of their hands in hers and walk up the stairs as an impassible wall, but of course, it made more sense to press against the banister. To take up as little room as possible, in case Brianna was lurking nearby. Ruby suspected she wasn't. Right about now, she'd be guarding the patio, or listening in the secret passageway while Parker convinced Brett to stay quiet. Still, it was foolish to take up more space than necessary. In single file, they kept to the side of the stairs, and their steps made no sounds.

This was happening. This was *working*. Ruby grinned as they reached the second floor, her eyes acclimating to the darkness. She couldn't see much, but she could make out the emptiness of the hallway. The lack of a murderous doll. To add to their luck, the door at the end of the hall was open, along with the balcony doors beyond. Ruby could see the moonlight pouring in, surrounded by an indigo sky, and it was the most beautiful thing she'd ever seen. She wanted to rise up into the darkness and never come down. Of course, being a girl, and not yet a ghost, her body was subject to gravity, and thus, she could not go swimming in the sky.

But she could go swimming in the pool.

Yes, Ruby thought, *we are coming to the end.* She could feel it in her bones as they passed Juniper's open door. In spite of her desire to keep moving, she turned, peering at the photographs inside. Photos of two smiling girls at age eight, twelve, fourteen.

Ruby and Juniper.

Her heartbeat went erratic, and before she could stop herself, she was plucking a picture from the wall. A grainy shot of Juniper and herself, surrounded by cupcakes. Red velvet, because that was Ruby's favorite—not that it mattered in her family. Ruby never got to pick out her own cake. Three of the four Valentine girls had August birthdays, and by the time Ruby was in second grade, she was splitting her cake three ways. Splitting her presents. Splitting her party. And even then, she didn't really mind, until her mother brought home a Reese's

Pieces cake, forgetting Ruby's allergy to peanuts. That, Ruby had minded. Still, she'd sat through the party, helped her sisters open their gifts, and then quietly slipped into the bathroom to cry. She couldn't cry in her bedroom, because it wasn't *hers*, like everything else in the house. The bedroom was shared with Charlotte, and the birthday was shared with Scarlet and May, and nothing, absolutely nothing, had been Ruby's.

Until that birthday.

Back then, Ruby and Juniper were joined at the hip, but halfway through the party, Juniper had started to feel sick. At least, that was what she'd claimed. But two hours after her sudden departure, a knock had sounded on Ruby's window, and Ruby had rushed over to see her friend holding something on a tray.

Cupcakes. Twenty-four red velvet cupcakes, each with the name *Ruby* scrawled across them in pretty red frosting. "They're all for you," Juniper had insisted with a smile.

Now, as Ruby stared at the photograph, her chest ached and her eyes stung with tears. She wanted to pull Juniper into her arms. No, she wanted to build a workable time machine and go back to the moment before things fell apart. If Juniper had been her friend all these years, would she still feel like a person, instead of a cracked, porcelain replica of herself?

It was impossible to know, and it was foolish to be wondering about it now. The past was the past. But with the future uncertain, and altogether *empty* without Shane, Ruby kept searching for the last time she'd felt human. As she hurried into the fifth bedroom, the photograph clutched in her hand, she found herself face-to-face with the answer.

He was sitting in a chair, red markings covering his skin. His hair wasn't dripping anymore, but his shirt was open, like he was waiting for a flurry of fists to knock the breath from his lungs. Waiting for fat purple bruises to cover his chest.

"I'm taking him," Ruby said, looping an arm around the doll. When Juniper turned to her, eyes widened in concern, Ruby explained as best she could. "This story ends in fire. You know it does. And I know he's made of porcelain, but I'll be damned if I'm going to watch him burn a second time."

Juniper nodded as Ruby dragged the doll across the room. If she was worried about Ruby's state of mind, she didn't show it. There were more important things to consider, like, for example, their death-defying escape. Once upon a time, in the dead of night, Shane and Ruby had made plans for a death-defying escape. A way to break free of Parker, together, and stop being scared. And then . . .

"We'll just be together," Shane had said, grinning like a Cheshire cat, and Ruby had melted.

Now, hurrying across the balcony, Ruby thought of other things that could make you melt. She could see the line of gasoline snaking around the house. It *didn't* snake around the pool, but if Brianna struck a match soon, there wouldn't be time to leap to safety. Ruby would go up in flames like Shane had, one year earlier.

They would all burn.

For the moment, the patio was dark. Ruby saw no hint of white, no garish red lipstick. "We can jump together," she said, binding the balcony doors with the rope. This time, she made a knot. No bows. "We'll have to climb over the railing, then push off from the ledge. Otherwise, I'd say we should hold hands."

"We can hold hands now," Juniper said, entwining their fingers for the briefest of seconds. When the girls pulled apart, she was clutching the photo that Ruby had taken from the house. "You saw my bedroom?"

Ruby nodded, watching her in the moonlight. "Of all the things you could've wanted, you wanted me."

"Back in my life, yes."

"I want to be," Ruby said, and it was the truth. She was deathly tired of lying. Deathly tired of wearing a mask. Before she could stop herself, she threw her arms around Juniper, whispering, "I've wasted so much time—"

"Um," Gavin broke in. "I don't want to be *that guy*, but you're wasting time now."

"Shh." Ruby held a finger to his lips. "We're having a moment." And they were. They were holding each other, for what might be the last time. They were even swaying a little, and Ruby thought it was perfect, that it should end like this. Two princesses on a balcony, dancing in the moonlight. Two knights reunited after a long and painful war.

Then, just as Ruby *felt* the illusion, Gavin's voice broke into their bubble again, shattering the fantasy. "Well, I'm going to jump. You guys can—"

He wasn't able to finish his thought. Spinning away from Ruby, Juniper took his face in her hands. "Oh my God. Shut your beautiful face."

Then, under a million twinkling stars, she kissed him. It was ridiculously innocent. *A perfect Juniper kiss,* Ruby thought with a grin. Soft and tentative and ending as quickly as it had begun, but still, it did the trick. Gavin came away with a smile on his face, and then he was part of the fantasy. All three of them had slipped into an alternate reality, where the world was beautiful and terrifying, and you had to see both sides in order to survive.

Together, they climbed over the railing. Inside the house, footsteps were thundering on the stairs, but it didn't matter, because the plan was in place. The players were poised to jump. Fingers curling around the railing, Ruby turned to Gavin first, saying, "Ready?"

He nodded.

"Junebug?"

"It's now or never," Juniper said, and her voice wasn't shaking that badly. "On three?"

Ruby nodded. It made sense to do it together. Together, they'd count. Together, they'd leap. And then, hours from now, when the fear was gone . . .

We'll just be together.

Tears streamed down Ruby's cheeks. It wasn't supposed to happen this way, not without Shane. There was no *together* anymore. Reaching over the balcony, she lifted the doll into her arms. "One," she said.

Juniper swallowed beside her, saying, "Two."

"Three," they shouted together, leaping into the sky. Then flight. Then gravity, pulling them down faster than Ruby thought possible. She hit the water hard. The blue-eyed, pale-skinned boy slipped out of her grip almost instantly, and she found herself reaching for him before she tried to breathe. Then the moon was hurtling toward her. For a moment, she thought she was seeing double. *No, triple,* she amended, staring at the lifeless face of Shane Ferrick, the luminous moon in the sky, and the girl stepping out of the shadows, clad only in white.

30.

HAIL MARY

Parker slipped into Brett's bedroom. The place was ominously gray. Torn photographs littered the floor, hinting at Brett's secrets, but Parker didn't give them a second look as he closed the door behind him.

All he cared about was the boy on the bed.

"Leave me alone," Brett said coldly. His skin looked as gray as the walls. He was holding something in his shaking hands, something shiny and metal.

His brass knuckles.

"Look, I messed up with the video." Parker stepped closer, running a hand through his hair. "I lost my head, seeing Ruby with *him*. I mean, can you imagine? If you'd walked in on me and her, wouldn't you have—"

"Don't."

"I'm just saying, it would suck."

"You don't get to talk to me like that. You don't get to act like you understand. All my life, everything I've done . . . It hasn't been to trap you. It's been to protect you. And yeah, if I saw you with her, it would've sucked, but guess what? I'm a big boy, Parker, and if I found you with a rope, the last thing I'd do is tie you up."

"Bullshit," Parker said, advancing on him. "What did Brianna offer you? You've been trying to tell me, haven't you? Trying to turn my gaze to your bedroom? Why? So you could lure me in here—"

"I didn't lure you! You lured *us* to this party. That's literally a thing that happened."

"All you people can do is throw dirt at me. Well, guess what? I made you into something. I made *her* into something. Gavin's dying to be me. Juniper, too. Don't hate me because I have what you want, okay? If you'd just played along . . ." Parker leaned over him. Then they were staring at each other, and Parker was reaching for Brett's collar, and . . .

"No." Brett crawled backwards, away from him. "No, I don't want you like that. I don't want you at all."

"You're lying."

"I don't! She didn't offer you, because she knew I wouldn't take it. She knew. She knew." Now he was rocking, and Parker was starting to feel nervous. Of course Brianna had offered a little taste of Parker, in order to keep Brett cooperative. What else could his friend possibly want?

Parker snorted, shaking his head. "She put my picture in your room. She covered your walls with my face, and you tore up every single—"

"Believe it or not, Parker, there's something I want more than you. Something I can actually have." Brett reached up, pulling the sheet away from the headboard. That thing curved like a tombstone. Across the front, words had been written:

Brett Carmichael

Rest in Peace

"What the hell is this?" Parker demanded, gaping at Brett. "This is what she offered you?"

Brett covered his face with his hands, voice cracking. "It's what I wanted."

Parker's first instinct was to leave the room. To give Brett the space to pull himself together. Still, he waited. He'd made so many snap judgments tonight, and in the weeks leading up to the party.

"Why would you want this?" he asked.

"Because of what I did," Brett managed. "All year, I've been trying to push it away, but I can't."

"So she offered to make it go away for you. To take your life as payment for Shane's." Parker looked up, a chill unfurling in his stomach. A voice trickling into his ears. If he wanted to get out of here, he had to be willing to make a sacrifice.

"I didn't give her what she wanted," Brett said, holding up his brass knuckles. "It was more of a gesture, anyway. She wants the truth. She wants her brother's killer to suffer."

"Maybe," Parker said, his heartbeat quickening. "I mean, she definitely does, but since we're all guilty, I bet she'd take any one of us."

"What do you mean?"

Brett was looking at him, gaze softened, and Parker told himself to stop. To shut up. There had to be another way. But just as he closed his mouth, the lights started flickering, and it seemed like a sign. A warning of flickering to come. Of fire. If someone didn't step forward soon, all five of them would die.

They'd burn alive.

Parker could already smell it. The air sizzled as the lights went out. In the darkness that followed, he pushed out the words, "She's desperate to know who killed her brother. And you're desperate to make up for—"

"I can't make up for it. I can't bring him back."

"You're right. But if you gave your life to save a house full of people, that would more than make up for it. Man . . ." Parker shook his head, as if impressed. "She really is brilliant, offering you that. But you could never take it. I mean, I'd never let you take it."

In the dark room, Brett sat very still, passing the brass knuckles from hand to hand. He looked like a child. Like a little boy who'd been abandoned by the person he needed most. That was how Parker had found him, all those years ago. He'd taken Brett under his wing, taken Brett into his *family*, because Brett had lost everything. His mother. His home. He and his father had to squeeze into a one-bedroom apartment, and Brett couldn't even afford to buy lunch at school. So Parker had done it for him. He'd taken him on weekend trips to the coast, and when Brett turned sixteen, Parker gave him the Jaguar he'd learned to drive in.

Over and over, Parker had saved him. Now he was the one who needed saving. Carefully, he placed his hands over Brett's, saying, "Don't even think about doing what she wants. Your suffering will end, eventually."

Brett inhaled, the metal clinking in his hands. "It won't," he said after a minute. "It gets worse every day. And if someone else dies because of what I did . . ." He pushed off the bed. "I can stop it."

"No." Parker darted after him, through the darkness. He reached out as Brett opened the door. But he couldn't stop him. Or rather, he *didn't* stop him. He felt a little scared, and a little sick, thinking about what he was doing, but underneath the panic, there was something else.

Relief.

He was going to escape. He was going to *survive*, and that

was what mattered. By now, Brett had reached the bottom of the stairs, and he pivoted left, heading for the patio doors. He didn't know they were locked. He didn't know about the line of gasoline either, but still, he was trying to save them. He really was courageous. Parker would make sure everyone knew what he'd done for them.

He followed Brett into the dining room, his eye catching a blur of white out on the patio. A pang shot through his stomach. Could he really do this? Could he really offer his best friend up to the slaughter?

"Wait," he called, as Brett wrestled with the patio doors. At the sound of Parker's voice, he turned. Their eyes met. Parker smiled softly, happy to see his oldest friend looking at him. "Don't—"

Brett pulled a chair from the table. Whipping around, he let it fly through the patio door on the left. Then he was climbing through the opening, shards of glass tearing at his skin. In one swift movement, he tossed the brass knuckles across the patio, toward the figure standing on the other side.

"It was me," he said, as Brianna bent to retrieve his offering. "I'm the reason your brother's dead."

31.

BRUTAL BALLET

Juniper's nightmare was coming true. Here she was again, immersed in icy water, and when she broke the surface, all she could see was that face. Moon-pale and porcelain, both cracked and smooth. That garish mouth. It might've been covered in actual blood; she'd never really know, and it didn't really matter.

What mattered was the hand.

Pale fingers sliced through the air. Pale fingers, glinting like metal. Was Brianna holding a knife? No, this was different. The metal clung to her fingers, like some kind of demented ornamentation. Nearby, Ruby and Gavin were splashing, their mouths making unintelligible sounds, but nothing settled and nothing separated. It was chaos. It was anarchy, and their circus tent was falling down.

Then, a twist in the narrative. A change in the story. The girl with the face of a doll swept right past them, stalking the boy by the patio doors. Brett. His deep purple suit was dusted with glittering shards, and he made no move to defend himself as Brianna took a swing.

The move was elegant, almost balletic, like a move Ruby would make in an ordinary kitchen on an ordinary day.

Something lovely and out of place, and eerily slowed down, until she made contact with Brett's stomach. Blood flew to his lips almost instantly.

The dance wasn't beautiful anymore. It was brutal. Brett's body jolted each time she hit him, but she didn't slow down. She sped up, her fists slamming into him so many times, it seemed impossible.

A betrayal of space and time.

And yet, Juniper thought, maybe it was her fault, for pausing on the balcony. Swaying with Ruby. Kissing Gavin on the lips. Maybe she'd been selfish, taking a moment with each of them, to let them know how much they mattered, not just to her, but to the universe. They needed to feel that now, so close to the end, and she was happy to be the one to show it to them. Juniper had always wanted to save everyone, and she'd always, *always* failed, but in that moment she'd felt successful.

Like the universe wanted her.

Now, watching blood blossom on Brett's white shirt, she slid through the water, believing she could save him, too. Her friends were screaming at her back, but she didn't stop. She didn't slow down. She'd made it halfway across the pool when Brett crumpled to the ground.

Brianna leaned over him, saying, "It would've been swift. It would've been sweet. But you chose to lie to me, darling, and now it will be slow. It will be agony."

Then, like a wraith who'd fulfilled her duty on earth, she backed away, into the shadows. Away from the pool. Away from the long, twisting pathway that led to the front of the house. She was practically begging the others to make a run for it. Now was their chance! No ropes stood in their way, and no fire could touch them. They were free, finally, but if they ran . . .

Brett would die.

"Go," he mumbled from his place on the ground. "It was my fault. It was *me*."

"Liar, liar, pants on . . . Well, let's see if the rhyme comes true, shall we?" Brianna plucked a long white taper from a bag on the ground. God, she must've had weapons stashed everywhere. Candles on the patio. Brass knuckles on her hands. At least the rope was accounted for, and Juniper couldn't even think of the gun in that moment. Ruby had sworn it wasn't loaded (it *wasn't*, was it?) and either way, a gun was meant for silencing people, and Brianna wanted them to talk.

No, she wanted Brett to talk. Why?

"Why not talk to Parker?" Juniper gestured to the head peering out of the shattered patio door. The golden head, framed in glass. "*He* got your brother wasted. Then your brother drove off in *his* car. Coincidence?"

"Parker will never confess to hurting my brother," Brianna said coolly, lighting her candle. She knelt on the patio stones, just outside the line of gasoline. If she tipped that candle down, Brett would go up in flames. Parker, too. "I lashed Ruby to a chair, and pushed her down the stairs, and still, he wouldn't admit to *making a video*. It wasn't until I slid a rope around Ruby's neck—"

"I am not the villain here!" Parker shouted, easing his body through jagged shards of glass. But he didn't try to tackle Brianna, or kneel beside Brett. He kept his distance from both of them. "All night, I've been trying to protect everyone, but I won't confess to something I didn't do!"

"Why not? Brett did." Brianna's gaze cut to the boy on the ground, her eyes finding his. "Your name is the Iron Stomach. You are secretly in love with the Human Torch. Your weapon is your fists because you love pounding things you're not supposed to. And your greatest secret is—"

"Stop," Brett whispered, his voice pleading.

"You will die to protect him."

Brett's eyelids fluttered closed. It seemed like a self-fulfilling prophecy, like everything Brianna had written was coming true. But Juniper had never believed in destiny, just as she didn't believe a chosen one would save them. In real life, you had to make your own destiny.

To choose to be the one.

Slowly, she inched toward the front of the pool. There was little chance of leaping out of the water, racing across the patio, and tackling Brianna to the ground, but if she could create a big enough splash, she wouldn't have to leave the safety of the pool. The water would slide across the patio, diluting the gasoline, and that candle would be rendered useless.

She just needed a distraction. Glancing behind her, she saw Ruby climbing the ladder at the far end of the pool, while Gavin treaded water, unwilling to abandon Juniper to the depths. Her cheeks flushed, and she tore her eyes from him, finding Ruby's in the darkness.

Help me, she implored silently, gaze flicking to the water, then the patio. *Distract Brianna, and I will save us.*

Ruby didn't acknowledge her. Instead she strode to the left side of the pool, where the doll of Shane Ferrick was bobbing on the water. "Of course Brett's protecting Parker," she said calmly, reaching for the doll. "If Parker handed his keys to Shane, when Shane was wasted out of his mind, then Brianna will kill him. And Brett will have to live with that for the rest of his life. He can't stomach the burden, after everything that happened last year." Ruby lifted the doll out of the water, laying him gently on the ground. Then her gaze shifted to Brett. "So give the burden to me."

"What?" Brett murmured, struggling to focus.

"You shouldn't have to tell Brianna what Parker did. The burden is too great." Ruby stepped toward him. "But if you tell *me* what happened, she'll let you go, and I'll have to decide whether to hand over Parker or take my chances with the flames."

"No." It was Juniper who said it, and it should've been a scream, a horrifying wail that ripped through the fabric of space and time. But it wasn't. It was less of a battle cry and more of a croak, something small and pathetic, as if a hand encircled her throat. In reality, a hand encircled her *arm*, as Gavin pulled her backwards, away from the edge of the pool. "Trust Ruby," he whispered. "She escaped Brianna once. She can do it agai—"

"No!" Juniper wrestled out of his grip, drawing Brianna's attention. That candle dipped closer to the ground. Juniper cringed. Her plan to soak the patio might have been thwarted, but she would not let Ruby step inside the circle of gasoline. "You can't risk your life for Parker. You *can't*."

Ruby looked at Juniper, and her face was calm. Peaceful. "I'm the only one who can. I'm the only one besides Brett who understands how to love Parker, and be crushed by him, at the same time." She swallowed, looking at each of them. "I know what you all think. That I must hate him by now, I'd be crazy not to hate him. But I'm perfectly sane. Shane told me I was, and I believed him. I believe him now."

"Ruby?"

Juniper watched her oldest friend, her best friend forever, glide over that line of gasoline. No hesitation. No fear. Kneeling beside Brett, Ruby brushed the sweat from his forehead. "You can trust me with this," she promised. "Parker took something from me that I deeply, desperately wanted and still . . ." She looked at her ex-boyfriend, standing dangerously close to the shards of glass. "I feel compelled to protect him. I feel compelled to get him help. If you tell me this secret, I won't take it lightly."

Now Brett was shaking, and a tear was sliding down his cheek. When he lifted his hand to Ruby's shoulder, Juniper wasn't sure whether he was going to pull her closer or push her away. It didn't matter in the end. Brett's hand swayed in the air, then fell back to the ground. Ruby leaned over, closing the gap between them. "I can save him," she said, cupping Brett's face with her hands. "I can save you both. But you have to tell me the truth."

And so, in a trembling whisper, Brett did.

32.

IRON STOMACH

Brett Carmichael felt sick. It had come upon him suddenly, somewhere between the third and the thirteenth punch, and soon, his stomach was roiling and his mouth was dry.

He stepped back. Away from the body, jangling in Parker's arms like a skeleton. Like Shane was already dead. Parker smiled, cocking his head to the side, and asked, "Getting tired?"

Brett wanted to say *yes*. He wanted to say *I'm done with this, and I'm going home*. He had the distinct impression that this was the farthest he'd ever fallen, his own personal rock bottom, and the thought brought his mother to mind. Had she hit rock bottom, when he'd slipped out of her hands and slammed into the balcony railing? Brett still had a scar on his stomach, from where the spire had opened his skin.

It had been impossible to get the blood out of his clothes.

Now, with three drops of blood on his crisp white shirt, he wondered whether he should bleach the thing or throw it out. Better to throw it in the fire and watch it burn. He'd dealt with enough blood in his life to know when something was a lost cause, when the time spent cleaning wasn't worth the result of wearing the clothes again.

He shrugged, trying to sound as casual as possible. "Just getting a little bored."

Parker let the body drop. One second Shane was dangling in his arms, and the next, he was a rock. Silent. Cold. Parker stepped back. Brushing his hands on his jeans, as if *he* were the one who'd gotten dirty, he looked to Brett, flashing a grin. "Want a drink?"

For the briefest of instants, Brett thought that Parker was offering him Shane's blood. As if, on top of kicking the guy's ass, they'd also drink from his veins. He knew, deep down, that it was a ridiculous thought, but what was more ridiculous? Feasting on Shane like a vampire or cheerfully going for a beer with blood spattering his shirt? Parker's mood was so light, so utterly unaffected by the sight of the boy on the ground, Brett found himself grasping for a supernatural explanation.

Then, as if reading Brett's thoughts, Parker shrugged off his jacket. "You look cold," he explained.

And he was right. Brett was cold. He shouldn't have been, considering the workout he'd put himself through, the jabbing and the bouncing from foot to foot. He should've been burning up. But now the sweat was cooling on his skin, and the wind was picking up.

He pulled the jacket on. It was warm, if a little snug, and it smelled like *him*. Like Parker's skin, salty with sweat. Like warm, golden honey and a hint of spice. Brett closed his eyes. Parker's hands were tugging on the jacket, zipping him in. It had been years since someone had zipped him into a jacket, and even though he knew, logically, that Parker was covering up the blood, it felt nice. To be cared for. Touched.

He opened his eyes to find Parker smiling. It wasn't the smile of a sadistic clown, or the empty grin of someone who doesn't know right from wrong. It was sweet. Understanding. Parker was the only person in the world who knew who Brett really was, under the sadness. He saw all the good and all the bad, and he accepted it without question.

No, he did more than accept it. He appreciated it. "You're a freaking superhero," Parker said, his arm swinging over Brett's shoulders. "We should get you a costume."

"Shut up."

"I'm serious! He'll never pull that shit again, I know it."

Brett swallowed, trying to buy the story that Parker was selling. But he didn't feel like a hero. He felt like a villain. He told himself that his stomach was turning *because* he was a good person, and good people felt bad about causing destruction, even if it was necessary. This feeling was exactly what separated him from a guy like Shane Ferrick, who could make his own little sex tape, send it to a bunch of his classmates, and then show up at a party like nothing had happened.

Shane was the messed-up one. Brett was just a person. A normal, healthy person with normal, healthy reactions to things. When someone bled, you *should* feel ill at the sight of it, and when they whimpered, your stomach should turn. And now, as Parker steered him toward the lighted kitchen, toward beer and pizza and holiday cheer, Brett let his gut guide him one more time.

"We can't leave him out here."

"Um. What?" Parker turned, his face twisted into a scowl, just like Brett knew it would be. "Why the hell not?"

"He'll freeze to death."

"And?"

"My DNA is all over him. If he dies, I'll go to prison for murder."

"Manslaughter, but yeah, okay. You're right. Let's get him off the ground."

"Really?" Brett was taken aback. He'd expected a fight. A dramatic standoff in the snow.

But Parker didn't fight. Parker didn't huff and Parker didn't puff. Instead he lifted Shane by the arms. Brett got him by the legs, and together they carried him toward the house. They'd just reached the patio doors when Parker stopped, a strange look in his eyes.

"What?" Brett peered into the kitchen. The hour was late, and half the partygoers had either gone home or slipped off to the bedrooms. The rest appeared too drunk to see two feet in front of themselves, dancing sloppily or scooping dip with their fingers. Nobody noticed the boys standing on the other side of the glass, waiting to slip inside.

Nobody noticed Shane.

"I was just thinking," Parker said, glancing across the body. Catching Brett's eye. "Dahlia's going to kill us if we get blood on her couch."

"Dahlia can deal with it."

"I know, I just . . ." Parker smiled slyly, and something unfurled in Brett's stomach. "I'd hate to get a reputation for ruining a party."

"Oh yeah. That would be terrible," Brett joked, playing along with the ruse. Parker *loved* having a reputation. For being wild. Unpredictable. But now, when he had the chance to present Shane to the partygoers, like a wicked Christmas present, he was shying away.

"Let's put him in my car."

Brett's heartbeat stuttered. He could envision Parker slipping back out here, in the dead of night, to mess with Shane while everyone was sleeping. He could envision him tying Shane up in ropes. Making a little video, an eye for an eye.

"Dude," Parker said, tugging on the boy they held between them. "What's your problem?"

Brett couldn't articulate it. He didn't want to, because the image of Parker tying Shane up had been so vivid. He could picture it perfectly, could picture the smile on Parker's lips, the absolute lack of tremble in his hands. The precision of his movements, both strong and graceful at the same time.

Brett shook himself, and the vision slipped away. A figment of his imagination. He stumbled a little, and then Parker was pulling him toward the driveway, keys already in hand.

"Wait. You can't—"

"He'll be safe in here," Parker explained, unlocking his car. He slid Shane into the driver's seat, then turned the key in the ignition. "See, I'll even make it cozy for him." With that, he flipped on the heat, aiming the nozzle down, so it wasn't blowing in Shane's face.

The flurry in Brett's chest started to settle. "Now what?" he asked.

"Now we grab that drink." Parker slapped him on the back. Then they were walking away from the car, away from the boy slumped over in the front seat. Again, they'd almost reached the house when Parker stopped. "Shit, I should text Ruby. Let her know it's safe to sleep, you know?"

Brett nodded, figuring he'd wait outside too. It was the polite thing to do. But Parker must've noticed the way Brett flinched every time the wind hit his knuckles, because he smiled, saying, "You go ahead. I'll just be a sec."

Brett's chest flooded with relief. He pulled open the patio doors. There was a fire blazing in the living room, and he could feel the heat of it as he stepped into the house. It wasn't until he'd trudged down the hall and locked himself in the bathroom that he thought to look outside. He hadn't even washed his hands yet. The water was running, slowly turning from cold to warm, when his gaze flicked to the window.

To the flash of gold.

Brett knew instantly who it was. Those movements were fluid and confident, that hair lit up by moonlight. Parker was striding back to his car. He reached for the driver's-side door, as if to pull it open, but it wouldn't budge. It was locked. Still, Parker yanked at the handle, trying to wrench the entire thing off the hinges, and Brett could see movement inside the car.

Shane Ferrick was awake. And he was not opening that door.

Parker spun around in the dark, trudging back to the yard. Brett thought he was giving up. He told himself that Parker had finally gotten bored, but it wasn't so. Parker was searching for a rock. He found one quickly, a big gnarly sucker, and then he was plodding back to the car.

What game was he playing?

Oh, that one. The one where Shane Ferrick, bludgeoned and bloodied and drunk out of his mind, would push on the gas just to get away from him. Backing up with a jolt, Shane went peeling out of the driveway and onto the road. Here one moment, gone the next. There was no way Brett could've stopped him.

There was no way Parker could've stopped him, not that he tried. The minute Shane disappeared, the rock dropped from Parker's hand, and he smiled. He flat-out grinned, so wicked and wide, Brett could see it from a distance. Could see it in the darkness. That smile was glowing. Then, and only then, did Parker pull the phone from his pocket and type out a message.

Brett forgot about the faucet. He forgot about the splintered knuckles, the cold outside, everything. He even forgot the most basic rule of the boys' friendship: never challenge Parker. Never call him out, and never call him guilty, because Parker Addison was a good boy. He was big, blond, and beautiful, and sure, he got into trouble sometimes, but he wasn't evil.

He'd never kill anyone.

He wouldn't, Brett told himself, over and over, as he raced through the house and out the patio doors. He made it as far as the bushes. That was when he ran right into Parker, slam, crash, clatter, and the two went tumbling to the ground. They'd barely bumped skulls, but the impact had sounded like tires screeching and glass shattering and . . .

Brett sat up, his throat dry and his hands shaking. He couldn't swallow. "What did you do?"

"I . . ." Parker's eyes were stretched in the darkness, more black than green. "I didn't . . ."

"Parker, what the hell did you do?"

"I was just messing with him! I thought he would piss his pants or something. I never thought—"

"I saw you, Park. After he left. *I saw you.*" Brett dropped his head into his hands. He knew he should push to his feet. Jog out to the road, in case Shane needed help. In case there was another car. But he couldn't bring himself to move, couldn't bring himself to do anything but rock back and forth like a trauma victim.

Funny, considering the trauma hadn't happened to him.

Still, he told himself that Shane might be okay. He'd probably crashed into the mailbox. Or maybe he'd made it down the street, to the oak that looped right up to the edge of the sidewalk, and he'd slammed into it. But Parker's car was sturdy, and the cops were already on the way. Brett could hear sirens. Yes, he thought, lifting his head, the police would come for Shane, and everything would be fine.

The sky *hadn't* brightened in the past few moments, and the air *didn't* smell of smoke.

"Hey, it's all right," Parker said, that honey-gold voice sticking to him now, making him heavy. Making him sweat. "No one will find out what you did."

"I don't care about that."

"You were never here," Parker said softly. "You never touched him."

"I . . ."

"Nobody saw you. Well, Gavin did, but he was wasted. Nobody'll believe him. You can still get out of here, take the back roads home. Okay? Burn that shirt, and my jacket."

Brett's gaze came into focus. There, kneeling in front of him, was Parker. Brett was splayed out in the bushes like a forgotten rag doll, but Parker was composed. Calm. He brushed the sweat from Brett's forehead, whispering, "We'll take care of each other, all right?"

More sirens. More smoke. Brett felt like he was choking on it, even though he knew it was impossible. The smoke was too far away. The car crash. The fire. Oh God, what had they done?

No, not they. Parker.

"You . . ." Brett pointed at his oldest friend. "You put him in the car."

"To keep him warm."

"You gave him the keys."

"I didn't give him anything, and I never told him to drive. Jesus, Brett, what do you think of me? I was pissed at the guy. I wasn't trying to kill him."

"But . . . I saw you smiling."

Parker jerked back, as if Brett had hit him. "You're starting to freak me out. I would never accuse you of trying to kill the guy, and you're the one who made him bleed. I saw *you*, and *you* were smiling. And I'm trying to protect you."

"Why?" Suddenly Brett needed to hear it. He needed to know that his existence hadn't been a mistake. A universal miscalculation, bound to happen with a population this large. Sooner or later, something slipped through the cracks. Some-one did, and that someone was Brett. Most days, he was sure of it. But when Parker looked at him . . .

He felt chosen. Wanted.

Parker reached for the collar of his jacket, as if to straighten it, but instead, his fingers curled around it, pulling Brett close. "If they find his blood on you, they're going to take you away from me."

"Yeah? So?"

"So, I want you here."

"You want me?" Brett asked, though he didn't mean it like that. He knew Parker wasn't into him. He'd always known. He'd accepted it. But now, with the sirens blaring and the night lit up by flames, Parker's head dipped down, until there was almost no space between them.

"I need you."

"You're lying."

"I'm not," Parker said, leaning so close, his lips brushed against Brett's neck. Just under his earlobe, in the spot that tickled. Brett shivered, but he didn't jerk back. He didn't move and he didn't say anything.

Parker spoke again. When he said the *L* in "Leave this min-ute," his tongue flicked against Brett's skin. "Take McKinley and then cut to the freeway," he added, still gripping the collar of Brett's jacket. Parker's jacket, fitting Brett so snugly. "I'll corroborate your story."

"Corroborate," Brett murmured, wanting desperately to stay in this moment. This bubble. This lie. He knew it was a lie, knew in his heart of hearts that Parker was manipulating him, but reality was a burning car and a boy with Brett's DNA all over him. Who wouldn't choose a lie?

"I'll protect you, and you'll protect me. Right?" Parker asked.

"You'll protect me," Brett repeated.

"And you'll protect me." Parker's head tilted up. Brett knew he should push him away, because this wasn't real, it wasn't real, it wasn't . . .

It felt real. Warm. Sweet. Parker pressed his lips to Brett's, chasing after him like he was starving. Like he'd been starving for a very, very long time, and Brett knew that feeling. He knew it better than anything.

"Please," Parker begged, tongue sliding into Brett's mouth. Breath hot. Body warm. "Please don't let them take me. Please protect me. Please save my life."

Brett hadn't thought of it like that, but now—well, now he couldn't really think of anything. His mind was a mess of buzzing bees. His body was electric, terrified one moment and then . . . this. Warmth, like the cold had never existed. Hunger that could actually be sated.

"Save my life," Parker said again, gripping him so desperately, it seemed like an impossibility. This was what Brett wanted, but he didn't want it like this. Parker was only doing it because he was scared. The second Brett realized it, he pulled back, and the distance gathered between them like darkness.

"I'm not going to turn you in." Brett paused, trying to catch his breath. He'd never thought his heart could beat so quickly. "I'll protect you, I promise. I'll keep your secret."

And for twelve long months, he had. He'd never spoken a word of it. Never written it down. He'd protected Parker, even after the two had drifted apart, because he'd honestly believed it was the right thing to do.

Until tonight.

Tonight, in a ragged whisper, he handed the secret to Ruby Valentine. He only told her the bones of the story. It was all he could manage. After he'd finished, his gaze traveled to Parker one last time, and Brett Carmichael closed his eyes.

33.

HUMAN TORCH

If Parker had been smart, he would've leapt into the pool. He would've hurled himself past the line of gasoline, bypassing Brianna entirely. He would've killed two birds with one stone. But Parker wasn't smart at this particular moment, and instead of bolting forward, he stumbled backwards.

Toward the house.

And Ruby followed him, a wolf stalking her prey, her brain hardly registering the burning candle in Brianna's hand. Truth be told, the house could've gone up in flames, and Ruby still would've followed him right then. She wanted vengeance more than she wanted life.

But luckily for Ruby (or maybe luck had nothing to do with it), no fires were lit as she neared the doors. Outside the line of gasoline, Brianna was kneeling on the patio, calmly watching the situation play out. It was funny, really, that in these final moments, Ruby was the storm, and Brianna was the eye in the center of it. Watching. Waiting.

She didn't know the truth yet. She hadn't heard Brett's muffled story, and she didn't know about the car keys. She didn't know about the text. Now, as Parker squeezed himself through the opening in the patio doors, Ruby kept her voice low, because *this* conversation was between her and Parker. "Shane texted me that night. Mere minutes before he died, a message came in. Can you guess what it said?"

Parker shook his head.

"That's all right, I remember it perfectly." Then Ruby recited the message she'd read over and over again, since the night of the fire. "Can't find my keys. Come get me?"

Below her, Brett gasped. His pallor was sickly and he couldn't seem to open his eyes. If someone didn't call an ambulance soon, he'd bleed out on the patio. Was it fitting, Ruby wondered, that he should go out seeing who Parker really was? Or should she feel sorry for him, now that he'd suffered his punishment, and do everything she could to keep him alive?

She didn't know anymore. Her reality had been distorted since the night of Dahlia's party, when the text had come in at three a.m. And Ruby, groggy from a night of tossing and turning, had climbed into her car and raced to meet Shane. But she'd never made it past the base of the hill, because that message found her too late.

Parker's message.

"You weren't just trying to kill him," she whispered, as shards of glass clawed at Parker's suit. Soon that pretty white shirt would be streaked in red. But unlike Brett, whose ragged breathing was giving her a sinking feeling in her stomach, Parker's pain did nothing to hinder Ruby's movements.

It fed her, and she feasted on it.

"You were trying to kill *me*. You texted me from Shane's phone, knowing I'd think it was from him. And I'd get into my car, groggy and disoriented, and drive up that narrow road while Shane was racing down."

She stepped up to the glass. By now, Parker had made his way through the jagged portal, and Ruby stared at him, like Alice peering through the looking glass. A drop of his blood was glistening on one of the shards, and she thought about using it to brighten up her lips.

But she couldn't. Not with Brett so close, his eyelids fluttering and his chest moving up and down. He may have been slipping in and out of consciousness, but he was alive, and for that, Ruby was thankful. This had never been about killing Brett. It had always been about catching Shane's killer, and so she knelt beside the boy on the ground.

"You ready to go home?"

Brett's eyes opened. He looked hot, and seconds earlier, he'd looked cold. Ruby felt the curious urge to protect him. She'd meant what she'd said, about understanding how it felt to love Parker and be crushed by him at the same time.

Now, finally, Brett could break free.

"Come on, sweetheart." She slid an arm beneath him. "Let's get you away from the house."

"Parker," he began, voice cracking.

"Don't worry," she said, too quietly for anyone else to hear. "I've got one more trick up my sleeve."

Brett smiled, fully trusting her in that moment. After all, she'd kept her promise to him. She'd taken the burden of Parker's death into her own hands and saved Brett in the process. Now, as she lifted him from the ground, he settled into her, as if certain she would save Parker from Brianna's wrath.

It was sweet, really. It gave Ruby a little boost of confidence. She practically danced toward the line of gasoline, where Gavin and Juniper were waiting, their limbs shivering and their hair dripping wet. "I can't carry you over the line," Ruby whispered in Brett's ear. "If I get too close to the gasoline, Brianna will think I'm trying to escape, and she'll light the fire. We'll both go up in flames."

Brett nodded, and Ruby shoved him toward his waiting classmates. *Bye-bye, Iron Stomach.* Brett lurched forward, and Ruby, jarred by the sudden shift in weight, stumbled backward, hopping on one foot. A potted plant broke her fall. It would've been funny, if anyone were in a laughing mood, but Juniper and Gavin were staggering under the weight of Brett's body, and Brianna had her eyes trained on Parker.

The timing was perfect. Ruby slid her hand into the potted plant, pulling out the object she'd hidden at the beginning of the night. She would *never* bring a loaded gun into a party with Parker Addison. He would find a way to turn it on her. Now, shaking away clumps of dirt, she pointed the revolver at Brianna.

"Go!" she shouted to her friends.

Chaos erupted behind her, just like she knew it would. Juniper was trying to reason with her, but Ruby was beyond reasoning with. In that moment, she was a tightrope walker, and her invisible wings had been shot full of holes. Eaten by moths. Nothing remained of their original beauty, like nothing had remained of Shane's beauty after Parker was finished with him.

"Please," Juniper pleaded at her back. "Please come with us."

Ruby shook her head. There was no "us" without Shane, like there was no "together" anymore. There was also no fear. Her greatest fear had come to fruition one year ago, on this very night in December, and unlike Shane, whose fear had compounded after he'd lost his mother, Ruby's fear had just . . . drifted away.

Like smoke from a body. Like a beautiful soul, rising above the trees and dancing into the darkness.

Ruby's fear had left her body, and she'd become hollow, unburdened. Then, when the invitation had arrived, she'd started to feel something again. Her skin had crackled. Her fingertips had buzzed. Now Ruby Valentine was a firecracker ready to pop, and here, finally, was the match.

"I'll meet you there," she told Juniper. "After I've saved Parker. After you've saved Brett. And we'll sit together in a bundle of blankets, and laugh about our death-defying escape, all right? Hot chocolate and blankets."

"Hot chocolate and blankets," Juniper repeated stubbornly and then she was backing away. Both she and Gavin were backing away, carrying Brett between them. Something tugged at Ruby's stomach. Longing. She swallowed it down. She had business to attend to, and besides, her friends were already fading into the blackness. Here one minute, gone the next.

Funny, how quickly a person could disappear.

Her gaze swept to the girl in the white lace dress. Ruby grinned. It was a Cheshire cat grin, a crescent moon slicing across her face. It was mischief and murder combined. "It was Parker. In the Mustang. With the car keys. But he didn't just get your brother onto the road. He texted *me*, trying to get me on that same narrow road." She paused, turning to her ex-boyfriend. "I suppose we should be happy no one else was on the road that night. What if Shane had plowed into a family of four? Would you have felt bad? Would you have even batted an eye?"

Of course, Shane hadn't plowed into a family of four. Halfway down the hill, he'd lost control of the car and had gone careening into the forest. According to the police report, the car had flipped several times before settling. And innocent little Ruby, clueless, stupid Ruby, had just reached the base of the hill when it happened. She made it just in time to see the fireworks.

The explosion.

"What do you say, Brianna?" she asked, finger sliding over the trigger. "Have I kept my part of the bargain? Siphoned the secret from Brett, and handed over your brother's killer? Am I free to go?"

Brianna stared at Ruby's revolver. Slowly, hesitantly, she waved Ruby across the patio. But once Ruby had passed the line of gasoline, she didn't race to safety, or plead for Parker's life.

Instead she held out a hand to Brianna. "Give me the candle."

"Ruby."

"You aren't a killer, and we both know it. Come on, baby doll, I did everything I promised. Now it's your turn."

Brianna swallowed. The candle was dripping wax, and ever so delicately, she slid it into Ruby's gloved hand.

Ruby exhaled in relief, turning to Parker. "Do me a favor, would you?" she asked. "Stay close when the fire starts. I want to see you transform into a dripping ball of wax. I want to see your big, clumsy fingers peel away to the bone. Would you do that for me, darling? Pretty Parker. My little Human Torch."

Parker jerked backwards, his mouth dropping open, but Ruby broke in before he could speak. "Oh, you're going to run? Well, don't waste time. That was my mistake, wasn't it? Taking my time getting out of bed. Searching for my warm winter gloves. Pushing the car out of the driveway, so my mother didn't wake up. What if I hadn't done all that? Could I have stopped him? Or would we have gone up in flames together, bonded to the death?"

"You . . . ?" Parker croaked, and Ruby couldn't help it. She envisioned a prince turning into a frog. She envisioned stomping on him, seeing his guts splayed out on her shoe. When he looked up, to the balcony, she said, "I suppose you could mimic our death-defying escape, but is there enough time? If I were a betting woman, I'd say you were a couple of minutes short. Like I was with Shane."

Parker swallowed, backing away from the glass when he should've been leaping through it. In Ruby's movie, he was the beautiful, big-eyed blond, and she was the killer. But she wouldn't be slashing anyone up tonight, oh no. She wouldn't be shooting anyone either.

Ruby knelt on the patio stones. Tipped the candle down, so gracefully, as the wind picked up. For a moment, she thought the flame was going to go out. It flickered. It sputtered. Then, kissing the line of gasoline, it snaked around the house.

Ruby leapt back. Something stirred inside of her, something like breath rushing into lungs. Something like life. As the flames rose, curling and tangling in the air, Ruby's limbs turned back into flesh, and her heart softened to red.

34.

INVISIBLE MAN

The monsters rose up, threatening to swallow Gavin whole. He couldn't stop running into them. That was the problem with lugging someone twice your size through impenetrable blackness. Every time he got a handle on his destination, some massive topiary beast clawed at his skin. By the time he and Juniper had carried Brett halfway across the yard, he thought his body was going to collapse.

But it didn't. He could see the tall, wrought-iron gate in the distance, and it strengthened his resolve. He told himself that he'd run into a million topiary monsters if that meant getting away from Brianna. His skin would be bloodied and his lungs would be pissed, but he'd make it to the end of his own movie, with Juniper at his side.

And so, Gavin ran. A Minotaur with horns made of branches tried to take away a chunk of his skin, but he simply veered around it, seeking the light at the end of the tunnel. The gate. Soon, it loomed over them. Gavin hoped that shorting out the power in the house hadn't shorted out the gate as well. Or if it had, he hoped he could open that sucker manually. Hell, he'd scale the damn thing if he had to. He'd do whatever was necessary, because Juniper was wheezing to his left, a body was hanging between them, and that body was growing cold.

They didn't have much time.

Carefully, they laid Brett on the ground. Juniper tended to him while Gavin tackled the gate. There was a little box to the right of it, and he flipped it open, fingers numb in the cold. For once, it seemed that fate was on his side. The big red button was clearly marked, and when Gavin pushed it, the gate started to open. It didn't even creak! No dust fell over his head, and no ghosts howled at his back. As he spun around to meet his companions, the smile fell from his face.

It wasn't the sight of Brett that scared him. It was Juniper, or rather, the tears sliding down her cheeks.

"What?" he demanded, sounding harsh and not even feeling sorry for it. They had not come this far to lose Brett now. They hadn't.

"He's freezing," Juniper said, placing her hands on Brett's cheeks. "I can hardly make out his breathing."

"No." Gavin dropped to his knees, refusing to see what Juniper saw. Sure, Brett's skin was pallid and his shirt was spattered with red, but that didn't mean he was dying. "No, you're not doing this."

"What?" Juniper looked up, her hair sparkling with ice. The water from the pool was freezing, right there on her head. She was turning into a snow princess. And Brett was turning into a corpse.

"Not you," Gavin said, his hands tightening to fists. He supposed he should feel sympathy in this moment. His chest should be swelling with forgiveness. But it wasn't. All he could feel was fury, hot, sharp, and invigorating, and before he could stop himself, he'd struck Brett across the face. "Get up."

"Gavin."

"No." He cut Juniper off before she got started. He didn't want to hear it. All he wanted to hear was Brett laughing or taunting him or doing literally anything but lying there like a stone. "Get up," he said again.

"He can't get up. Gavin, he isn't going to—"

"He isn't going to die like this! Are you kidding me? Like *this*?" He lashed out again. This time, Brett groaned a little, and Gavin's heart leapt. It was working, he knew it was. And because of this, he dug his heels in. "I will go to your funeral and tell everyone what you did to Shane. I'll tell them what you did to me. You should've fought for me, but you left me alone. You left me."

Gavin hit him again.

And again.

By the time Juniper got her arms around him, Brett's cheek was a stinging red, and still, Gavin struggled to break free. He fought and he fought, and he didn't even realize he was screaming until Brett started to cough. Softly at first, then violently, blotting out the wind that whipped around them.

Gavin lowered his forehead to Brett's. "About damn time," he whispered.

Brett inhaled sharply, his eyelids fluttering. He managed to say, "Didn't give me . . . much choice," before his eyes closed again. But it was all right. It was more than all right, because he was conscious, and on the other side of the gate, Gavin could see light. A car was coming up the hill. It inched along slowly, as if the driver was afraid of running into a tree and going up in a big, fiery burst, but still. A car was coming.

"Thank God." Juniper slid one of Brett's arms over her

shoulders. Gavin did the same, and together, they hoisted him off the ground. "Oh, thank God, Gavin. I thought he was going to die."

"He can't," Gavin said, feeling a little cavalier at the moment. Feeling giddy and dizzy and terribly light. "He isn't the disappearing act."

"No, that's Ruby."

A chill went up his back. "Kind of funny, isn't it, that she's been in front of our faces the entire night?"

"No, she hasn't. She got taken."

"For, like, ten minutes," Gavin said as they carried Brett through the gate. "And her punishment didn't fit with her name. How does being covered in bruises make her 'disappear'?"

"I don't know," Juniper admitted. "Maybe it had something to do with her dad."

"What does that mean?" Gavin asked, watching the light creep up the hill. He was starting to get a strange feeling in his chest.

"Her dad left her covered in bruises," Juniper explained. "Then he disappeared."

"Split town, you mean."

"Yeah, but she never says that. She always says 'my father disappeared.'"

"Right! Like she's a southern belle on a freaking plantation. It's like she can't help herself. Like it's—"

"Compulsive." Juniper's voice was breathy, and she'd turned away from the light. That light seemed like an illusion, like it'd never really reach the top of the hill. And even if it did, something much more interesting was happening inside Juniper's head.

"What?" Gavin asked, following her gaze back to the house.

"My name is the Disappearing Act," she said in a soft, ethereal voice. *"I am secretly in love with a corpse. My weapon is a revolver because I have a killer's instinct."*

"Juniper?"

"My greatest secret is . . ." Her breath hitched as she spoke the final line. *"I made an entire person disappear."*

"Yeah? So?" Gavin glanced at Brett. He was breathing. And now, pressed between them, he was warming up a little. Even better, the car was cresting the hill, and they were about to get out of there.

Two of them were. Gavin realized it as his eyes found Juniper's across the bloody expanse of Brett's chest. For God's sake, they'd been drowned, beaten, and almost consumed by fire. There was no reason to go back. But Juniper was going. Already, she was disentangling herself from Brett as the car pulled up to the side of the road. "Listen, I have to—"

"You cannot be serious. Honestly, I will drag you into that car. You saw me slap Brett silly."

A ghost of a smile, and then Juniper was walking backwards, into the darkness. "Call the police," she yelled, her voice wrapping around him. "By the time they get here, I'll know."

"Know what? Juniper! Know what?" It was pointless. She was gone, and the driver was climbing out of the car. It was a hunched, gray-haired woman, and now Gavin had the delightful task of trying to explain their situation. The blood on Brett's skin. The words written on his.

He stepped forward, taking a breath. But the words died in his throat, long before they'd made it to his lips, because something was happening on the other side of the estate.

First, a spark, rising in the night. The flicker drew Gavin's eye. In the span of a single breath, a glittering trail went snaking around the house.

Then the world exploded in light.

35.

BABY DOLL

Brianna Ferrick was taking off her costume. There was nothing left to do. A show was unfolding before her, and it was the greatest show on earth, but it wasn't tickling her quite like she'd expected. A human torch sounded fascinating in theory, but in real life . . . Well, reality was often disappointing.

And karma was a bitch.

Brianna's gaze cut across the darkness, settling on Ruby Valentine. Ruby was standing beneath the inferno, watching a person disappear. The flames hadn't reached him yet. When the fire had started, Parker Addison, in all his golden glory, had spun around three times and bolted to the stairs.

Then there was a pause. It wasn't quite like silence, what with the flames ravaging everything in their path, but it felt like silence, because the screaming hadn't started yet. That was what Brianna would remember, as the circus faded to black. The silence.

And then the noise.

There was a great clattering up above, like Santa's reindeer prancing about the roof. No. There was a *rattling*, like Marley's ghost dragging heavy chains. It was panic. It was prophecy coming true. It was Parker, banging on the inside of the balcony doors, trying to get outside.

But there was that rope. A rope had led to Ruby's downfall. A rope had lashed her to a chair. And now, wrapped around those balcony doors, a rope was doing the opposite.

Containing Parker and setting her free.

Ruby strode to the shadows, helping Brianna out of her dress. It was sweet. It was almost like they were sisters, and Brianna had wanted a sister, before she started losing the family members she had. Now she wanted a death-defying escape, and a story to guide her into it.

"Tell me again," she entreated, pulling on her jeans. "Tell me the story of the girl who turned into a doll."

Ruby seemed distracted. Her attention was split, half staring at the boy on the balcony (the boy still inside the doors), and half staring at the doll they'd hidden in the bushes. What she *wasn't* staring at was Brianna. It must've been hard for her, so close to the end.

"There's no time for that," Ruby said, gathering the white lace dress in her arms. Within seconds, she'd slid it back onto the life-size doll, where it had begun. "Are you ever going to take off the mask?"

"Eventually." Brianna flashed a big, creepy grin. She felt more comfortable this way. With the mask covering her face, she was protected from the world. Safe. "Please, tell me the story? I don't even hear sirens yet."

Ruby sighed, as if she were dealing with a petulant child. "Quickly, then. We have to get you on that flight. You never told me where you got the passport."

"Online." Brianna pulled the little blue booklet out of her bag. It was one of the only things she was taking with her. That, and the clothes on her back (a T-shirt and jeans, along with a sweatshirt that had belonged to her twin) and a big wad of cash, courtesy of Parker's trust fund.

"The world was on fire," Ruby said, her eyes glittering, like they always did when she told the story. "Inside the great, glimmering inferno was a car. Inside the car was a boy."

"Did he suffer?"

"He was tired after almost drowning. Tired after being hit. He would've just drifted to sleep, and his soul would've drifted into the sky, and there it remains, waiting for you. For me."

Brianna nodded, her eyelids fluttering. She understood being tired. It had been a long night. But she couldn't sleep, because she needed to hear the rest of the story, and then she needed to disappear.

"But?" she prompted, zipping her bag.

"But he wasn't the only one who changed that day. There was a girl climbing through the forest, her heart bleeding red. Skin so delicate, the slightest touch could make her gasp. As she watched the boy transform to a creature of ashes and bone, she transformed too, into an unfeeling doll. And she would remain that way until . . ." Ruby looked up, to the balcony. Finally, finally the rope had given way, but that gift was a curse. The *fire* had burned away the rope, which meant the fire had reached the doors. In order to escape, Parker would have to hurl himself through the wall of flame, and he wouldn't do it.

Parker was not brave. He would throw Brett to the wolves, drug Gavin's drink, and expose Ruby's most private moments, but he would not be exposed. Everything he did, he did behind closed doors, and now he would die behind them. When Parker bolted back into the house, the girls turned to each other.

Instantly, they forgot him.

"You have to get going," Ruby said, lifting the doll from the bushes and hurling it into the fire. It landed by the patio doors.

"It's a temporary illusion, but as long as the fire's raging, the police will suspect it's you. Who else could it be? And I'll spin a yarn about a struggle, where you knocked the revolver from my hand. Then, in a terrified frenzy, I shoved you backwards, and you stumbled toward the fire, and I ran off into the night."

A grin. Ruby was so comfortable when she was acting, wasn't she? She was so comfortable playing a part. But after the fire had died down, and the skeleton had been pulled from the wreckage, she'd have to face what she'd done.

"It's over, Ruby. It's time to come back."

"What do you mean?" Ruby's brow was furrowed, and there was a little wrinkle above her nose. In that moment, Brianna understood why her brother had fallen for this girl. It wasn't because she was beautiful, although of course he would've noticed. It was the life in her limbs. The color in her cheeks. Ruby was life embodied, a painting come alive, and when Brianna had found her at the funeral, wandering like a wraith emptied of a soul, she'd had to do something.

To bring her back to life.

She hadn't known, at the time. She'd had no idea what Ruby was planning. If she'd heard the story then, she would've said no. Girls couldn't turn into dolls, and a fiery inferno couldn't bring them back to life. But over time, over months of crawling into each other's windows, and curling into each other's arms, because it was the only way to feel close to him, Brianna had started to entertain the idea. It was horrifying but it was also . . . enticing.

The way a fire is enticing when it ravages through a forest, making it impossible to look away.

Ruby hadn't been able to look away. That night, watching the fire burn. Watching Shane disappear, a moon-pale face turning into a candle of wax. Dripping and contorting. Before she'd heard that, Brianna hadn't even been mad. She had known the futility of being angry at death, had known it was like screaming at a pebble in the road, and she'd honestly believed Shane's crash had been an accident.

Accidents happened all the time.

Once, when Brianna was five years old, she'd lost control of her bicycle and had gone careening into a bush of thorny roses. And Shane, trying to spare her the embarrassment of attending school adorned in slashes, had spun and spun in those very thorns until his skin matched her skin.

Until they were the same.

When they were seven, and Brianna had tried leaping from the roof with a parasol, Shane had limped beside her until her ankle was healed.

And when their mother had died in a bathtub, Shane had fought to keep Brianna from entering the room. He'd wrapped his arms around her, while she'd sobbed and struggled, until she was too tired to go in there and see the blood. He'd done everything in his power to make her feel happy, to make her feel loved, and then he was gone. Taken from the world. And the people who'd taken him were going to walk free?

No, Ruby had insisted. They needed to pay. They needed, at least, to confess to the terrible things they'd done, and explain why. *Why* had they found the most beautiful soul on the planet and stamped it out? Why had they taken the love of Ruby Valentine's life? And why, when the police rounded them up, had they lied through their teeth? Were they scared?

Or did they think he'd deserved to die?

Everyone at Fallen Oaks High thought Shane was a monster, and *that* was why he'd died. Because of the video. Because of the lie. But if the girls could prove his innocence, he would be remembered as the grinning, beautiful creature that he was.

"We did it," Brianna whispered, taking Ruby's hands. "We cleared my brother's name. We saved him, Ruby."

"We didn't." Ruby's voice cracked, the fire was crackling all around them, and for a moment, it seemed the world would crack open and swallow them whole. But it didn't, because only one of them was meant to leave.

And one, to stay.

In the final moments of the circus, Brianna took off the mask. Tossed it, away from the line of fire, into the darkness. Set Doll Face free and turned to meet its maker. Ruby Valentine, the girl with the rosy cheeks and perfect bow lips. Eerily pale eyes. "It was never really mine," Brianna said of the mask. "But you needed someone . . ."

Ruby had needed someone to play the villain, so she could be the hero. She'd needed someone behind the scenes. And so, after the porcelain mask had been made, Brianna had plucked it from Ruby's hands and slipped it on.

Funny, it had fit perfectly.

"And a star was born," she said, squeezing Ruby's hands. "And a star went out."

Ruby clutched her fingers tightly. "I thought I could do this, but I can't. I can't say goodbye."

"You can do anything you want. Don't you know that? You could set the world on fire, or you could save it."

"Bri . . ." But what else could Ruby say? The circus was falling down. The night was turning black, where it wasn't surrounded by flames. And Parker had gone quiet, the entire house seemed empty, but there was no way out of it.

There was no way out of this.

"I wanted the world to know who my brother was," Brianna said, as Ruby studied her face. "I wanted to bring you back. I knew what it would cost."

The stars glittered above their heads. Dark and light, black and white. Everywhere else, red. But Brianna knew that where she was going, she would see blue. In the bright twilight sky. In the rising waves of the ocean. Everywhere she looked, she would see him.

"You have to go," Ruby managed, her breath coming out in little gasps. "You have the key to the back gate?"

Brianna nodded. The back gate was covered in foliage, so hidden she'd hardly been able to find it. "I have it," she said, forcing a grin. She didn't say, *You could come, you know?* She didn't say, *I'm scared to go alone.* She knew that Ruby had to stay. Ruby had a life and a future here, and maybe she'd set the world on fire. Or maybe she'd save it. When Ruby's arms went around her neck, Brianna gripped her tightly, letting herself be held. Letting herself be loved, one last time. Then, pulling out of their embrace, she kissed Ruby's cheek and slipped into the darkness.

She disappeared.

36.

RING MASTER

By the time Juniper returned to the mansion, the fire was in full bloom. Maybe it was for the best, she told herself. As much as she hated the thought of greeting a smoking skeleton, it was better than watching her classmate burn alive and not being able to stop it. She'd heard Parker hollering as she'd raced across the lawn, had heard doors rattling, but that rattling had stopped.

The world had gone silent.

No, wait. Someone was murmuring, like a child playing alone in a closet. Soft whispers and gasps. Secrets shared, only with the wind. Juniper listened for a minute.

"I promised," Ruby said, kneeling on the far side of the pool, too close to the fire for Juniper's liking. "I promised to protect her, but she had to go."

Juniper stepped closer, her heart in her throat. Her hands were clamped firmly over her mouth, in case a strangled sound slipped out and warned Ruby of her approach. Who the hell was Ruby talking to?

Oh, there he was. Dressed in a black top hat and matching suit. The ringmaster of the circus, with ebony hair and startling blue eyes.

Shane Ferrick.

It wasn't him, not really. Shane had burned up in a fire, and this was only a sad imitation. A puppet instead of a real boy. A doll. But Ruby was talking to the life-size replica of Shane Ferrick like he was actually there, and it scared Juniper more than anything she'd seen that night. It *hurt* Juniper more than anything she'd seen that night, because she'd never really wanted to see Ruby as broken. Even when the cracks in her pretty porcelain friend became clear, over and over again. What was that old saying?

When someone shows you who they are, believe them.

Ruby had been showing Juniper the broken parts of herself for years, showing the chips and the cracks. The long, jagged scar over her heart. That scar had appeared the first time her father slid his fingernails into her arm, and had deepened the night he disappeared. That scar had become a chasm after the five of them took Shane Ferrick and reduced him to a pile of ash. When she thought of it like that, it almost made sense to see her childhood friend kneeling beside an inferno, talking to a doll.

That doll was the only boy who'd ever been kind to her.

Juniper crept toward her, feeling oddly intrusive. Ruby wasn't murmuring anymore; she was just kneeling there, running her fingers over Shane's face. Pale porcelain cheeks that would never turn back into flesh, no matter how many tears Ruby spilled onto them. This wasn't a fairy tale. This was real life, and in real life, puppets didn't turn into boys. Sleeping princesses didn't wake with a kiss. And all the king's horses and all the king's men couldn't put Ruby back together again.

"Hi," Juniper said, the hitch in her throat making her sound like a child. When Ruby glanced up, she looked like a child, and for a minute, they stared at each other, transported back to a time when happiness was a possibility. Love. Friendship. Then Juniper's eyes trailed to the body lying beside the patio doors, clad only in white, and the ugliness came crashing into her, filling her lungs with smoke. Stinging her eyes.

"How . . .?" she began, but she couldn't bring herself to say the rest. Maybe Brianna had trapped herself within the wall of flames. Maybe Parker had dragged her, kicking and screaming, against her will.

Or maybe Ruby had made her disappear.

She had to go, Ruby had said to the doll of Shane. She was still stroking his face. And Juniper, desperate to get her friend away from the fire, did what anyone would do in that moment.

She lifted the doll by the armpits and dragged him away from the house.

Ruby followed them into the darkness, jerking along like a puppet on strings. After that, it was only a matter of picking a place to sit, so Ruby could look at both of them. Once they'd made it halfway across the lawn, Juniper sat down beneath a towering unicorn, and Ruby sat beside her.

"I know," Ruby said softly, when Shane's hand was in hers. "I know it isn't him."

"Okay." Juniper's gaze flicked to the doll.

"I know you think I'm crazy, but—"

"I don't throw that word around. That's Parker's job."

"Not anymore." Ruby snorted, slapping a hand over her mouth. Juniper's heart sank. If Ruby could watch a person transform into ashes, and *laugh* at his memory like that, maybe everything she suspected was true. Or maybe Ruby was so tired of being followed around, threatened and manipulated, she couldn't help but feel elation at the thought of being free.

Yes, that had to be it, Juniper thought, making the same old excuses for her friend. She knew she was doing it, just as she knew, with sudden clarity, that she'd have clung to a doll too, if she'd witnessed Ruby's death.

Had Ruby witnessed Shane's death? No one had bothered to ask her, because it hadn't seemed as pressing as what *Parker* had witnessed, and what he'd done to get Shane into that car. But now, Juniper wondered about it. If Ruby had seen Shane's body go up in flames, it might explain the inappropriate reaction she was having now to Parker's demise. The longer she sat there, watching Ruby cling to a porcelain hand, the more reasons she came up with for why her friend was innocent.

She isn't innocent, Juniper thought, tearing her gaze from the sad little tea party in front of her. *She did something, even if she didn't do all this.*

That, really, was why Juniper had returned to the scene of the crime, instead of escaping with Gavin. Even if Ruby wasn't the Ringmaster, or Doll Face, she was something important. The Disappearing Act. And yet, all night she'd been right in front of their faces. Disappearing into thin air wasn't Ruby's trick. There was only one person Juniper could think of who had disappeared into thin air, and Ruby had never let them forget it. Ruby had never stopped talking about it, because she'd wanted someone to figure it out.

Now, taking Ruby's free hand in hers, Juniper looked into her eyes and searched for the person in there. Searched for the soul. There was a spark of something, a pale, flickering spark like the hope at the bottom of Pandora's box, made weaker by all the anguish and rage, but it was there.

Juniper saw it. And so, she pushed out the words, "Tell me

how you did it," and watched the light in Ruby's eyes flare. That was good. That meant she wanted to talk. But before she could open her mouth and tell a story of masks and deception, Juniper cut her off. "Tell me how you killed your father."

37.

DISAPPEARING ACT

Ruby was used to the yelling. She knew how to get out of the house in a pinch. Knew which windows creaked when you opened them, and which ones didn't. Two months into her sophomore year, her father had yanked her arm so hard, he'd dislocated her shoulder, and Ruby hadn't even cried. She'd never get used to the pain, but she'd learned little tricks to lessen it.

To kind of . . . drift away.

But when Mr. Valentine smiled, Ruby had no tricks. When he laughed, she just froze, staring at him. That was the part that people didn't understand. The brightness in him. The way his laughter could comfort you, and wrap around you like an embrace. Hold you close when you felt broken.

The evening before he disappeared, Ruby was sitting on the couch with her father, watching *The Maltese Falcon*. They were tossing popcorn between them, sometimes catching it in their mouths, sometimes losing it down a shirt or in a couch cushion. They were laughing. When he turned to her, his eyes twinkling with mischief, Ruby's breath faltered.

"What?"

A grin, slow and sly. "Guess what I got back today?" he asked, pulling a key ring out of his pocket.

"Really? It's ready?"

"Yep." He tossed the keys into her lap. He wasn't offering her the car. The family would never be able to afford something so extravagant. But after months of trying to fix the old, rattling clunker himself, Ruby's father had finally given in to the family's prompting and let a professional take a whack at things.

Now the car was up and running, just in time for Ruby's first driving lesson. "What are we sitting around for?" She leapt up from the couch. "These are prime driving hours. Up. Up!"

Her father laughed, spreading out on the couch. Giving no indication that he was going to hop up and play passenger to her frenetic driving. But now that the offer was on the table, there was no way Ruby was going to give up on her prodding. Wild horses would have to drag her away from the car. The authorities would have to show up at her house and cuff her to the radiator, because if they didn't, she was driving.

Tonight.

"Come on, come on! I did all my homework, and the dishes. Twice! I'll brush my teeth right now. I'll put the girls to bed, come on!"

Her father was chuckling, turning up the volume with the remote to block her out. But it was only a joke. She knew it was a joke, and if she pushed him, just the right amount, he'd give in.

"If you teach me to drive, I can take you to work in the morning. How cool would that be? You could stumble out of bed, and it'd save you the trouble of fully waking up, and—"

"Ruby. My darling. My firstborn. You are not driving your father to work. You have school."

"So what? I'll have plenty of time, and you're always saying that work is kicking your ass. This way, you can zone out while I—"

Uh-oh. Had she taken things too far? She didn't like the look on his face. That smile had slipped away like a mask falling off, and now he looked pensive, a little bit pained. But it wasn't like she'd said anything he hadn't muttered a million times before. Work was kicking his ass. Bills were kicking his ass too. So was life. It seemed like the only thing that made him happy was snuggling on this couch with various members of his family, getting lost in a movie. But Ruby didn't want to get lost. She wanted to find things, to slip off in the middle of the day with Juniper and go on an adventure. To drive Parker into the heart of the forest. Life was waiting out there, and all she needed were keys and a little parental supervision, until the state decided she could handle things on her own.

Falling dramatically to her knees, she clasped her hands together and begged. "Please, Daddy? Please. I'll love you forever. I'll bake you cakes. If you take me driving for ten minutes, I'll do the laundry and—"

"Fine. Fine!" He pushed off the couch, running a hand through his tousled ginger hair. "My God, girl. I don't know where you get all this energy."

Ruby shrugged, trying to keep from grinning. From gloating. From feeling like she'd won. This tug-of-war was their thing, and most of the time, it was a joyful dance that left them both giggling. It transformed them into better versions of themselves, the kind without burdens. Without sadness. She pulled him toward the door. There was still light in the sky, and if they hurried, they'd be racing down Old Forest Road in no time. That road was nearly abandoned. On nights like tonight, you could hit seventy without fear of collision, the wind whipping through your hair and the whole world smelling of the trees. And all the terror you carried, clutched to your chest like an infant that never stopped wailing . . . all the pain would soften to sweetness, and you could breathe again.

They'd come to the door. Ruby's heart was racing, maybe a little too fast, because maybe she caught sight of the lights in the driveway. Later, she couldn't be sure. The front door was framed in glass, but that glass was warped, making it hard to know for certain what waited on the other side. It wasn't until someone knocked on the door—pounded, actually, in that telltale way that officers did—that she realized what was happening.

She wasn't the only one. Before the door was opened, before the stranger announced himself in a booming voice, Ruby's father looked down at her, and that look was cut from glass. Fury twisted his features, bleeding into sorrow. And then, in the span of a couple of seconds, Ruby thought *she* must be the one wielding the glass, because her father looked injured.

She stepped back. She stepped back, because she was the teenager and he was the parent, and already, they were slipping their masks on before the strangers burst in. Already, they were rehearsing their lines, though they'd never performed this play before. Ruby sucked in a breath. She told herself, with absolute authority, that she would not cry.

Then came the hour of being sequestered in her bedroom, fending off impossible questions from a total stranger. A woman. It was a tactical move, a trick to make Ruby more comfortable, and maybe there was logic behind it. Maybe being trapped in her room with a strange, abrasive man would've made Ruby angrier. And Ruby was angry. Ruby was defensive.

And through her teeth, she lied.

She lied when the woman asked if her father had gripped her with bruising fingertips and dragged her from one room to the next. She lied about furniture stumbling into her path and stairs that came upon her too quickly. Over and over, she lied. Then, when the woman pulled out the dolly, the stupid, cliché dolly, Ruby shifted into the truth. When the woman asked her to point out any places on the doll where she'd been "touched," Ruby pointed to the heart. She said, "My father loves me." She said, "My parents are soul mates, and any love they feel for us is a reflection of that love."

The woman didn't have anything to say to that.

It only took an hour. An hour for her family to unravel. An hour for their palace of glass to shatter to the ground. After, Ruby found herself looking at the carpet, expecting to find shards in her feet. She could see glass glittering all around them, even though nothing tangible had broken. When *everything* is broken, do you even notice the individual parts? Or do you just keep looking around, trying to blink the glass from your eyes and failing miserably?

Everyone was blinking.

No, everyone was crying, except for Mr. Valentine, because five minutes after the officers left, he was gone. But he hadn't disappeared. All he'd done was visit one local tavern or another, doing the thing he'd promised her mother he'd never do again. All he'd done was ingest mass quantities of whiskey—his drink of choice from his wilder, off-the-wagon days—and return in the dead of night, when everyone was sleeping in the master bedroom. Everyone but Ruby. She was alone in her room, tossing in her bed. She'd even managed to slip into that half-asleep state, where darkness curled around the edges of her consciousness, the sandman desperately trying to get a grip on her.

He'd grab her, and she'd slip away.

Then, in the cold, quiet hours before dawn, Ruby looked up and saw him in the doorway. The sandman, she thought at first, blinking groggily. Her second thought was that it was a stranger. He looked like a stranger, bloodshot eyes staring down at her. He smelled like a stranger, because Ruby had been little when he'd chosen his love for his family over his love for oblivion, and she didn't remember the sour-sweet smell of it. The sharp sting in the air. She pushed to her elbows, ready to scream for help or call—God forbid—the police, but hey, at least they'd be doing their jobs this time. Catching an actual criminal and protecting the family.

Of course, all screams died in her throat.

Of course, she recognized who was standing in that doorway, and a cold chill unfurled inside her when she realized she'd wanted him to be a stranger. That would've been less frightening. Anything would've been less frightening than the sight of her father glaring down at her, a porcelain doll clutched in his hands.

Ruby sat up at that. That, more than anything, allowed her to slip into necessary denial, to tell herself this was all a dream. She had no porcelain babies anymore. All her dolls had been torched in a bonfire, and there was no way that she'd lost track of this red-haired, pale-skinned beauty, because it was the first one she'd ever been given.

The first one he'd ever given to her.

Then he stepped forward, the shadows slipping away from the doll, and Ruby understood. She thought she did. "You saved her," she murmured, speaking to him in the soft, coaxing voice she used when he was teetering on the edge. One wrong move, and her father would lurch toward her, and this time, he wouldn't be able to pull himself back.

She knew it.

And so, she spoke softly, ever so casually guiding her legs out of the blankets. Blankets could tangle up and trip you in an instant. Something so stupid would not be her downfall. And luckily for her, his blurry vision was making him slow to react, and slow to notice her movements.

His voice sounded blurry too, when he said, "I dug her out of the ashes. Your first baby. God, you loved her so much." For a minute, he curled in on himself, and she thought he might be crying. He'd done it before. If anything, crying signified the end of a fight, and Ruby hoped he was gripped by sadness now, rather than fury. But when he looked up, she saw the truth in his mangled expression, his lips twisted into a sneer.

"You broke my heart that day. I gave this to you, and you—" He broke off abruptly, the thought ending the way a road veers suddenly into a dead end. His movements were just as jerky. As soon as the word "you" left his mouth, he flung the doll in her direction. She didn't think he was actually trying to hit her, but she ducked to avoid the collision all the same. The doll slammed against her headboard, and that porcelain skull cracked.

Then he was lumbering forward. Maybe the doorway couldn't hold him up. Or maybe he meant to mimic the doll and hurl himself against her, his body too solid to crack. That was what she thought, before the worst of it happened—that nothing could hurt him. He was unbreakable, the exact opposite of porcelain, and he was also beyond reasoning with.

She needed to get out of there.

Ruby twisted to the side, her feet almost meeting the carpet, when he caught hold of her arm. That was okay, she thought, because grips could be twisted out of, and at least he hadn't taken hold of her leg. This was a game Ruby played, not often, but on occasion, when reality got too ugly for her mind to process.

At least he isn't pressing his weight against you, she would tell herself. *At least he isn't choking you for very long. At least you can still breathe.*

Except . . . she couldn't. This time, the game wasn't working, or maybe the universe was inverting itself to make the worst possible thing come true. Because he had staggered across the room, and he had loomed over the bed—really, it was like gravity had been suspended for a moment, and he was hovering over her at an impossible angle, and then . . .

Slam.

Then pain, as his arm gripped hers, yanking her back to the bed. Then pressure, as he leaned over her, taking her face in his hands. Sometimes it was the only way to get her to look at him, she told herself, but that was just another game she played. A lie, a subtle twisting of the truth, to put the blame on her. Ruby was no fool, and she'd never believed she deserved to be hurled into a wall. But if it all came about because of something *she'd* done, all she had to do was eliminate that behavior, and he'd never hurt her again.

Now the lies were tumbling over her, and she was suffocating beneath them. She was suffocating beneath him, too. His body was a weight against hers. His voice was a viper in her ear, hissing, "How could you do that to me? How could you call them?"

"I didn't! Daddy, I swear."

"You're lying," he told her, his hands slipping down to her throat. Spots loomed behind her eyes, but he didn't let go. As he whispered the words, "You know what happens to liars," she felt herself blink out of consciousness, so quickly.

Blink. Here. Blink. Gone.

When the room came back into focus, she was gasping, but he must've thought she was just scared of him. He didn't realize what was happening. Didn't realize he was choking the life from her, and there was no way to convince him of it.

"I thought I was going to die," Ruby confessed, sitting outside the Cherry Street Mansion, with Shane's fingers in hers. Porcelain fingers, like the porcelain doll her father had saved from the ashes. That doll had been kissed by the flames, and her red hair was blackened in places. Her skin was blackened too.

But this doll was safe. Ruby had saved him, the way she hadn't been able to save Shane. The way she hadn't been able to save her father. "I thought he was going to kill me by accident," she told Juniper, who was watching her from the side. Watching her fingers stumble over Shane's. Watching and worrying, and having no fucking idea how bad things had gotten inside of Ruby's head. How bad they'd been since the night her father wrapped his hands around her neck and forgot about things like lungs and breath.

"I thought he was going to stay there, hands gripping my throat, until my body went still and I breathed my last breath. Then he would jump up, surprised, because he hadn't meant to kill me. And I realized, as my elbow knocked into that hideous, burned doll, that I could do the same thing. Bash it over his head, and act surprised when he didn't get up. And then . . ."

"You blacked out again?"

Of course Juniper would think that, because that was what people always said in movies. *Sorry, Officer, I don't remember a thing*, they'd say, rocking back and forth like a child in a cradle. *The world went black, and when I opened my eyes, I had blood on my hands.*

But Ruby had been awake for all of it. She remembered the weight of the doll in her hand, and how she'd used all of her strength to slam it into him. She'd expected its skull to shatter on impact. But it hadn't. His skull, on the other hand, had made a whooshing sound, like something had caved in, and then he'd gone still.

He'd gone still, and she'd thought to herself, *You got what you wanted. You beat him at his own game. You should be proud.*

But she wasn't. Her hands were shaking and her guts were clenching and she was heaving sobs before she knew what had happened. As quickly as she'd been congratulating herself, she told herself stories about him waking up. He couldn't be dead. She couldn't even have done that, couldn't have stilled the life from a man twice her size, a man who'd never let her forget he was stronger than her. "You were supposed to be stronger," she said. She tried to, but strange sounds were coming out of her mouth, strangled sobs and hiccups accompanied by a trembling so deep, she thought she must be freezing to death.

She waited for the numbing frost.

But the frost didn't come, and her father didn't rise. Eventually, she bent down to feel for a pulse. That should've terrified her more than anything, because villains always came back to life to startle the hero. She would lean down, and he would leap up, his hands wrapping around her throat. But the funny thing was, Ruby wasn't terrified. Much like Shane, hoping his mother would wake up and scold him for tearing the bottom of her dress, Ruby *hoped* her father would spring to life, because then he wouldn't be dead.

She wouldn't have killed him.

Still, more silence, and after she'd felt for a pulse, she thought of calling Juniper. She thought of calling Parker. But she didn't even reach for her phone. Calling Juniper would only implicate her friend in the murder, and Parker would never look at her the same way. So, between the hiccups and the sobs, Ruby decided to do it all herself. The removal of the body. The burial in the woods. Pushing him over the windowsill took some work, but her first-story window was draped in shadow, and no one saw her dragging him to the car.

"I put a plastic bag over his head, to keep the car from getting bloody," Ruby explained, watching Juniper in the darkness. "I made him disappear, along with the doll. I wanted to make the car disappear too, but I wasn't clever enough to figure out how."

"You're clever," Juniper murmured. It seemed, at the moment, all she could manage. Carefully, she extracted her hand from Ruby's, but she was still looking into those cool blue eyes, the last eyes Parker had seen before he'd run into the house. "You could've called me. I would've helped."

"And you would've been ruined, like I am ruined," Ruby said. "I am gone, Juniper. Emptied. For a while, I thought Shane could fill me up, but he drifted away instead. And he took what was left of me."

"You went through something traumatic. Twice. And having to bury your own father, my God. Anyone would've cracked—"

"Cracked, like porcelain. Funny you should say that." Ruby pushed off the ground and strolled toward the patio. The revolver was sitting out in the open, but Ruby walked right past it, to the place where Brianna's mask had landed. Picked it up. Held it in front of her face. "Beautiful or terrifying? Come on, Junebug, you can tell me the truth. Who wore it best?"

"That isn't funny. You aren't Doll Face."

"You sure about that? It's certainly fitting. You'd have to be made of porcelain, to do what I have done. To see what I have seen. Walking in those woods, two different times, with two different bodies. Well, Shane wasn't *with* me, and I was too far away to pull him from the car. But I thought of climbing through the window, wrapping my arms around him one last time. Our souls could've escaped, together."

Juniper stepped forward, her mouth open and her eyes wide. "Ruby. You saw—"

"Too much, and not enough. I arrived too late. Parker's text reached me too late. I remember sitting on the edge of my bed, perched there, like a bird afraid of flying. Afraid of falling and crashing on the rocks. I *knew* Shane hadn't made that video. I knew it. But there was just enough doubt to keep me frozen for a moment. He'd brought the rope into my room, and the hair in the video looked like his. I used to think Parker was big, dumb, and beautiful, but only two of those things were true. Well, one, if you're speaking with a certain innuendo."

Ruby's lips curled, and then she shook herself, because Parker didn't exist anymore. He wasn't large or small. He'd reduced Shane Ferrick to a pile of ashes, and then he'd met the same terrible fate. Now Ruby had a choice to make.

There was a gun at her feet and a mask in her hand.

"Let's play a game," she said, tapping the gun with her foot. Lowering the mask. "I can tell you the thing you don't really want to know or I can shuffle off this mortal coil without saying anything. You'll have plausible deniability. Brianna will go down as the villain, and you'll be the hero. As for Parker, well, let's leave it up to the audience to decide."

"This isn't a movie. This is real. And he's . . ." Juniper looked up, to the flames devouring the second floor of the mansion. "He's dead."

"Very likely, yes."

"Did you kill him?"

"Technically, the fire did. Technically, Brianna lit the candle, and the three of you took off." Ruby shrugged, smiling at her gloved hands. "Who knows what happened after that?"

"I have a theory. After all, you are the Disappearing Act," Juniper said, oddly logical in that moment. But maybe, in times of immense distress, people's truest selves came out. Juniper had always been a student of the universe, logical and scientific.

Ruby was going to miss that about her.

Sweeping forward, she plucked an object from the patio stones. "And for my final trick, I'm going to make myself . . . disappear."

38.

UNDERWATER ACROBAT

Juniper was thirteen years old the first time she saw a revolver. Ruby had smuggled it out of the middle school drama department, and Juniper didn't know it was a prop. All she knew was that Ruby had wanted to play *Clue*, and when the culprit turned out to be Miss Scarlet, she'd pulled that revolver out of her purse. "I am caught," she said in a breathy voice, lifting the barrel to her temple.

Then, a deafening sound. What Juniper remembered next was kneeling on the ground beside her friend, tears rushing out of her like she'd never be able to stop crying. She'd imagined Ruby's death a dozen times before. She'd imagined it, and forcibly pushed it away, but to see it . . .

To feel it . . .

It had been too much.

Now, watching Ruby lift the very real gun to her temple, Juniper wished for childhood misunderstandings. "You told me it wasn't loaded."

"I told you what you wanted to hear," Ruby said, striding backward, until the length of the pool was between them. "I knew you'd believe I was innocent, because you always see me as the victim, no matter what I do. Never the villain."

"I know you." Juniper was calculating the distance between them. If she reached out, her fingertips would only brush the air. If she leapt forward, Ruby's finger would tighten on the trigger. "You aren't the villain."

"Who am I, then?" Ruby asked coolly.

"You're a killer," Juniper said, and Ruby's mouth dropped open. "You killed your father because he was going to kill you."

"Oh, let's not sugarcoat things, darling. I kill people, it's true. But let's not dress it up in tinsel and wrapping paper, all right?"

"Was he going to kill you? Was he going to squeeze the life out of you, intentionally or not?"

Ruby blinked, brow furrowing. "He . . ."

"What would've happened if you hadn't fought back? Would you still be here tonight?"

"No." She didn't think about it. She must not have, because the word fell from her mouth, as if it had been waiting to free itself.

Juniper pressed on, taking a single step. "And Parker? You said he texted you the night of Shane's death. Was he trying to bring you to the scene of the crime? Blame you for it somehow?"

"He was trying to get me into my car. He texted me from *Shane's* phone, hoping we'd meet on that narrow road and go up together in a big, fiery poof." A quick glance at the inferno. No lips twitching, this time. No laughter.

"He was trying to kill you," Juniper said, her guts clenching at the revelation. Really, she should've seen it before now. She'd known Parker better than anyone. She'd thought she had, but even she'd expected him to have a line he wouldn't cross. A point at which he would stop. "Do you think he would've stopped? If Shane hadn't . . . If things had gone differently, do you think he would've tried again?"

"Probably," Ruby said, tilting her head. Speaking casually of nightmares and death. But after a minute, she added, "But he didn't have to because—"

"Shane was gone. And you wouldn't even look at anyone else." A beat, as Juniper took her lip between her teeth. "But what if you had?"

Ruby's head snapped up. Her mouth was a perfect circle, and the barrel was pressed to her temple at a slant. Her grip was slipping, on the revolver and on reality—at least, the reality she'd painted herself into. She wanted to see herself as the villain because it was easier to deal with what she'd done. But there was another version of the events. A reality that Juniper was speeding toward, quicker than a bullet. "What if you had loved me?"

"What?"

"What if people were right? What if I was in love with you, and you decided to give me a chance. Would I still be alive?"

Ruby swallowed. Juniper could see it, as clear as if the sun was blazing, but of course, the sun had nothing to do with it. The sun wasn't even up. Still, the world was awash in golden rays, casting shadows across Ruby's face. Revealing her in an instant, then hiding her away. It was perfect. It was poetry. It was Ruby Valentine, still wearing a mask, even as the porcelain one dangled from her fingers.

And Juniper was going to shatter it. She was going to break it into a thousand pieces. "Do you think I'd be dead? How do you think Parker would've killed me, specifically?"

"I . . . I don't want to do this," Ruby pushed out in a rush, all air and no fire. She was tired, that much was clear. She tightened her grip on the gun.

"Please," Juniper started, but the word caught in her throat. Time was speeding up. Ruby's eyes were closing, the gun was too far away to knock to the stones, and Juniper couldn't get to it in time. She was the underwater acrobat, moving too slowly, through liquid. She needed everything to stop, the way it had on the balcony when their fingers had entwined. How had it begun? With love and laughter?

No. With a photograph.

Suddenly a room unfolded behind her eyes, a room that had seemed like an impossibility. Like someone had reached into her chest and read the contents of her heart. Only one person in the world could've known her like that, known her darkest fears and her deepest desires.

"It was you." She stepped closer, but only a little. Too close, and Ruby would panic. Too close, and that would be it. "You decorated my bedroom. You left me the tickets to Cuba. You're the only one who could've done it."

"I decorated all of them, except for mine," Ruby admitted, the inferno framing her in light. She looked as if she was on fire, that red hair blazing. That hair was like blood on a fingertip. Like fresh strawberries, plucked from the vine. She'd dyed it because of him. To embody his nickname for her.

All of this was because of him.

"You thought I tried to kill Shane," Juniper said, forcing the words past the lump in her throat. "First your father attacked you, after *I* called the cops on him. Then, one year later, you heard rumors about me trying to drown the love of your life. And you believed them."

"Until tonight."

"When I told you what really happened. And then . . ." Juniper gasped, her gaze drifting to the body by the doors. The girl in the *blackened* lace dress. "You asked Brianna to let me go. After you heard my story, you said it wasn't fair to keep me in the house. Did you mean that?"

"Yes."

Air rushed into Juniper's lungs. In spite of her unwavering voice, she'd been terrified of Ruby's reply. "And before that, when I wanted to run to the neighbor's house, you tried to stop me from leaving the living room. Why?"

"I was starting to doubt the rumors about you," Ruby confessed. "After you left the living room, I ran to the secret passageway, trying to cut Brianna off. She was always supposed to be there in between acts. That was the beauty of our plan! All we needed was a ladder to the balcony, and that secret passageway, and she could be anywhere she wanted at any time. Inside the house or—"

"Drowning me in the pool."

In a sharp, swift movement, Ruby's gaze cut across the patio, landing on Brianna's body. Then, a sob. Just a single sound, crawling out of the depths of her, before she slapped a hand over her mouth. She'd been clutching the mask, but now it slipped from her fingers and clattered to the stones.

Still, it didn't shatter.

"Is that why you killed her?" Juniper asked, her heart fluttering like the wings of a dragonfly. "Because she hurt me before she knew what really happened? Before she had proof?"

Ruby cocked her head to the side. It was eerie, and so entirely *Brianna*, Juniper almost turned and ran. She almost expected Ruby to point the gun at her. But that was the thing, wasn't it? All this time, Ruby could've used the gun against her, and she hadn't even tried. From that first terrible moment, when Ruby had picked up the revolver, Juniper had known exactly where the barrel would be pointing.

She'd never had a doubt.

Now Ruby looked up, the fire reflecting in her eyes. "This was never about killing Brianna. It was always about catching Shane's killer. And in the final moments of the circus, I pulled a wicked illusion and made her disappear. I saved her," she added, letting that flair fall away. Revealing herself, a broken, shivering girl, with an arm that wasn't used to holding a gun for this amount of time. Juniper laughed then, a single huff, because how ridiculous would it be, if all this went away, simply because Ruby's arm got tired?

"You didn't kill her." Juniper stepped closer, not to Ruby, but to Brianna. To the *doll*, disappearing in the flames. "You protected her, like you tried to protect me, once you realized the truth."

"And yet, I still plotted to hurt you. I still let it happen."

"Oh, and don't think I'm not going to get you back for it. Years from now, when you're performing on Broadway, I might just be waiting in the rafters, a bucket of blood in my hands."

"Really? A *Carrie* reference?" Ruby gestured to the fire with her free hand. "You know how that movie ends, right?"

"We watched it together."

"We watched everything together." Ruby frowned as tears slid down Juniper's cheeks, dropping to the snowy ground. "That's how I know what you're thinking. If you could get close to me, you could melt my icy heart with those tears."

"This isn't *The Snow Queen*," Juniper said, and it was work, just getting those words out. It was painful, like speaking through jagged shards in her throat. Shards of ice? No. But

Ruby's words were getting into her head. Fracturing her reality. She knew that tears couldn't melt Ruby's icy heart, but she started looking for something that would.

Then she saw it. Really, it was so obvious, staring her in the face. Flickering at her. Promising that no matter the fairy tale, something would always melt flesh. She turned toward the house, taking three long steps before Ruby called out, "What are you doing?"

"Isn't it obvious?" Juniper asked, eyeing the pool between them. Ruby couldn't get to her, like she couldn't get to Ruby. "I'm going with you."

"You . . . what?" Ruby's face crumpled. "No, you can't."

"Why not? You're going."

"Please." Anguish in Ruby's voice. "This isn't funny."

"No, it isn't funny. It sucks, doesn't it? To watch your oldest friend disappear? Even the possibility, flashing behind your eyes . . ." Juniper flinched, her eyes stinging from the smoke. "We've both lost so much, and still, you would take yourself away from me. For good."

Another step, and then she was really feeling the heat. Really feeling the parts of her that could burn and fuse together. The parts of her that could boil. She inhaled, trying to take a satisfying breath, but that only invited the smoke into her lungs. Then she was doubled over, staggering forward without even trying.

And Ruby was screaming, "Please! You can't do this to me. You can't make me watch it again."

Juniper paused, the heat singeing her hair, melting the sequins on her dress. "It won't be the same, if you don't love me. It won't feel the same."

"I . . ." Another sob, cut off quickly. Another slipping of the mask, quickly caught. That was what Juniper thought, until she heard Ruby's voice, distorted from crying. "I got into my father's car one night. Months after he disappeared, I drove over to your house and I stared at your window. But I couldn't bring myself to knock on the glass. I couldn't bring myself to climb inside, when all along, you were right. You were right about my father, and you were right about Parker. But you were wrong about Shane." She broke off, choking on sobs, like Juniper was choking on smoke. "We were wrong about him, Juniper, and he's gone. He's dead."

Then, a soft sound. Juniper turned in time to see Ruby's knees hitting the stones, and for a moment, her heart leapt. Springing to life at the last possible second. Feeling that cursed, foolish hope. But Ruby's hand, however trembling, still held the revolver. "I can't do this without him. I can't go back to being alone."

"You aren't alone. Don't you understand that? You promised to help me find my family, and you never even realized . . . my family is you. You are my soul, Ruby Valentine, and I will never give up on you."

Juniper walked into the wall of smoke. The flames reached out, grasping at her, and she could feel everything. Her skin unraveling. Her lungs tightening, as if shards of glass were sliding into them. She barely heard the sound of the gun over the fire.

She spun around.

When she saw her friend crumpled on the stones, her heart cracked open, but her mind was a mess of contradictions. Ruby was huddled there, head clutched in her hands, and yet . . . there was no blood to be found. Then Juniper was hurtling across the patio, a star streaking through the sky, a soul so entwined with another, they could find each other on the darkest of nights.

She fell to her knees, crushing Ruby against her. Ruby was warm. Warmer than she should've been, if the life were slipping out of her. Juniper's eyes darted this way and that, seeking the bullet. It wasn't until she looked down, and found the shattered remains of the porcelain mask, that she understood what Ruby had done.

39.

DOLL FACE

The world was on fire. Flames licked at the darkness, rising into the indigo sky. Inside the great, glimmering inferno was a house, paint peeling and chandeliers rattling from the ceilings.

Inside the house was a monster.

No, a beast.

No, a boy, Ruby thought, as Juniper led her away from the wreckage, into the garden of topiary creatures. Together, they traveled the long, twisting path to the gate. It swung open. Then the road was upon them, and a boy was racing toward them, his dark hair flying and his arms outstretched.

He hurled himself at Juniper, spinning her in a perfect, fairy-tale twirl. Both of them were laughing through their tears. Yes, Ruby thought, watching them spin around, they were laughter and love and light.

And she was darkness.

She was a vengeful goddess in a land of pyramids and sand, and here, blessedly, was the wind.

It whipped around her, and then she was dancing, if only for a moment. She was dancing with him. She could feel Shane's hands slipping into hers, could feel his eyes finding her in the darkness. Ruby's mask fell away, finally, and she let go of every illusion.

Let go of the doll. The goddess, too. Then she was herself. A girl with pale blue eyes and freckles on her nose. A long, jagged scar across her heart, and a chasm that kept her from happiness. From him. Now, as he spun her around, she could feel his hands slipping out of her grasp, his soul disentangling from hers.

"Goodbye," Ruby whispered, watching the smoke drift into the sky. She knew it wasn't him, knew his soul had drifted away last year, but she hadn't been able to speak the word then. She hadn't been able to think the word, and for a long time, she hadn't needed to. There'd been a party to plan, with a very exclusive guest list.

A killer to catch.

A match to strike.

Now the world was on fire, and Parker Addison was becoming a grain of sand. The wind rustled around her, tangling in her hair. One year ago, Shane had tangled his fingers into her hair and said, *We're going to stop being scared. Together.*

"And then?" Ruby waited for him to answer, but tonight there was no voice whispering in her ear. Or rather, the voice whispering wasn't *his*. Gavin and Juniper were murmuring beside her, and she picked up the words, "He's going to be all right. They took him to the hospital, but he was awake, and he was talking to . . ." Gavin paused, the smile slipping from his face. "Where's Parker? Did he—"

"We couldn't save him," Juniper broke in, gaze flicking to Ruby. "We couldn't save either of them."

Gavin inhaled sharply, clapping a hand over his mouth. "I didn't think she'd really do it. I didn't—" He broke off, narrowing his eyes. Now that he knew the worst of it, he was noticing other things. "What happened to you?" he asked Juniper, eyeing her singed hair and clothing.

Juniper's lips tugged into a smile. It was beautiful. It was the sunlight, after the longest night of the year. "The fire and I did a little dancing. But I thought we were doing the waltz, and it turned out to be more of a tango."

"But you're all right?" Gavin's fingers made a circle on her skin. The fire had barely touched her, but on her left shoulder, there was a welt.

Ruby believed it would heal. She had to believe it, because Juniper had danced with the flames for her. To save her life. To prove how it felt to watch the only person who *truly knows you* disappear into dust. Even Shane hadn't known the truth about Ruby's father, and now she'd never be able to tell him.

But Juniper knew everything, and still, she'd fought for Ruby. Still, she loved her. And Ruby needed to be loved. Maybe it was wrong, maybe she was supposed to love herself, the rest of the world be damned, but she couldn't stop waiting to be welcomed into the universe.

To be chosen.

Now, as Gavin leaned into Juniper, whispering about hot chocolate and blankets, Ruby stepped closer to them. "Do you think they have hot chocolate at the hospital? I just . . ." She swallowed, pushing out the words, "I don't want Brett to be alone."

Gavin studied her a minute, the tightness in his jaw softening. "They probably do, and it's probably terrible. But I bet if you asked very nicely, one of us might skip over to the coffee shop across the street and get you the good stuff."

"Skipping? Do you promise?" Ruby's lips curved up.

"I want marshmallows in mine," Juniper said.

"Oh my God." Gavin held out his arms, one for each of them. "So demanding."

"You offered." Juniper looped her arm through his. Then, before Ruby could take Gavin's arm, Juniper reached out, pulling Ruby to *her* side. "Stay close," she said.

Ruby nodded. She couldn't shake the feeling of not belonging with them, of not deserving to walk beside them. But she didn't fight it. She was too tired to fight, and besides, she'd meant what she said about Brett.

"Come on." She led them toward the police cars that were pulling up to the street. "They're going to want to talk to us anyway. We might as well ride with them."

Juniper sucked in a breath. "You, running toward the police. That's new."

"You know me, Junebug. I'm full of surprises."

Juniper started to laugh. It was sharp and sudden, taking over her body in an instant and leaving just as quickly. Her hand rose to her lips, as if she couldn't quite believe she'd just been laughing. Couldn't quite believe she was capable of it.

Gavin peered at both of them. "Something happened, didn't it? I missed something."

"You missed half the night," Ruby quipped, pulling them along, toward the flashing blue lights. Her stomach was tightening, and it wasn't because she had a complicated relationship with Fallen Oaks' finest. Deep down, in the core of her being, she knew she needed to come clean to Gavin about what she'd done. She needed to come clean to Brett. But tonight they would bring him offerings of hot chocolate and blankets, and make sure he knew that he wasn't alone.

None of them were.

The police welcomed them openly, eager to make sense of this night of fire and porcelain. They climbed into the car together, three little criminals ducking their heads. Three little liars, beautiful and terrifying in their capacity for love, their capacity for vengeance.

When the door closed, Ruby turned to the window. Juniper was squeezed into the middle seat, holding Gavin's hand, and Ruby didn't want them to know that she was crying. But she must've hitched in a breath too quickly, because Juniper turned, whispering, "Stay with me. Please?"

"I will. I am." Ruby's fingers laced through Juniper's, her gaze drifting out into the night. The dawn was coming, but the sky was still dark, the moon luminous above their heads. Blue and white. Sapphire and ivory, like the love of her life.

Someday Ruby's soul would dance into the darkness, and they would reunite. There would be eyes like eternal twilight and moon-pale skin. A mischievous smile. And maybe, if everything went exactly as planned, her broken heart would heal and her pain would soften to sweetness.

But first, there would be life.

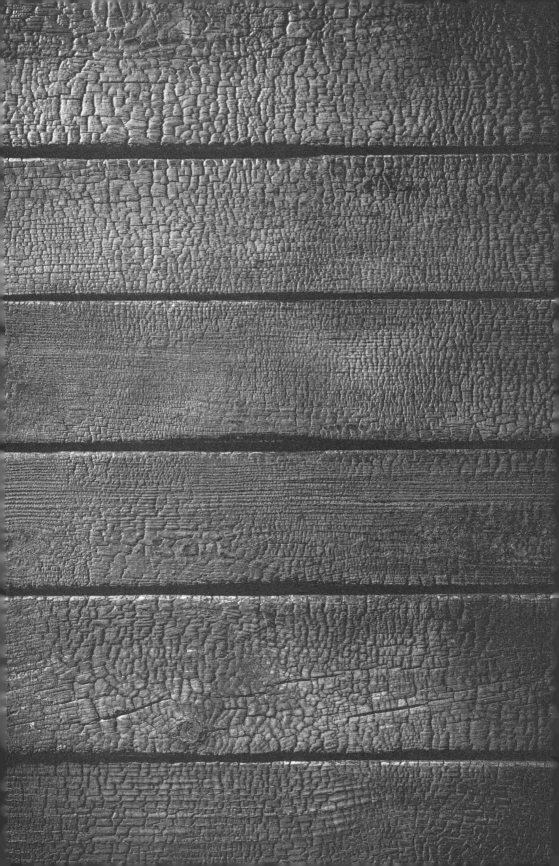

ACKNOWLEDGMENTS

Thank you to my unstoppable agent, Mandy Hubbard, for encouraging me, inspiring me, and being such a fierce advocate for my work. You are truly one of a kind.

Thank you to Ruta Rimas for your editing brilliance, your creativity, and your all-around awesomeness. This book is so much stronger because of you.

Thank you to Nicole Fiorica, Bridget Madsen, Valerie Shea, Dan Potash, Lisa Moraleda, Milena Giunco, and everyone at McElderry Books who helped put this book into the world. I could not have asked for a more talented, dedicated team.

Thank you to my early readers: AdriAnne Strickland, Jenn Kunrath, Alex Lidell, Dan Ward, and Mark O'Brien. You helped me more than I can possibly articulate, and I am eternally grateful to you.

Thank you to my family, the Pitchers and the Hauths, for your continued support and enthusiasm.

Thank you to Demitria Lunetta, Rachele Alpine, and all of The Lucky 13s. I am so lucky to be able to share this adventure with you.

Thank you to Chris Hauth for being an unending source of sweetness, humor, and insight.

And thank you to my readers for being the unique, wonderful people that you are.